THE BODYGUARD *Next* DOOR

New York Times & *USA Today* Bestselling Author

CYNTHIA EDEN

This book is a work of fiction. Any similarities to real people, places, or events are not intentional and are purely the result of coincidence. The characters, places, and events in this story are fictional.

Published by Hocus Pocus Publishing, Inc.

Copyright ©2022 by Cindy Roussos

All rights reserved. This publication may not be reproduced, distributed, or transmitted in any form without the express written consent of the author except for the use of small quotes or excerpts used in book reviews.

Copy-editing by: J. R. T. Editing

CHAPTER ONE

"I've been in some rough places," Pierce Jennings confessed as he tightened his grip on the couch and angled down the hallway. "Some of the worst hellholes on the planet. Places littered with gunfire and death. Places where ash filled the air, and every breath was laced with bitterness, but, until now, I have never, *never* had to deal the torture of being trapped in—"

The door to his left swung open, and a cheerful voice called out, "Pierce!" A sweet cream and honey scent filled the air. "Do you need some help?"

"The friend zone," he finished darkly.

Pierce was pretty sure his buddy Colt Easton choked out a laugh.

Forcing a smile, Pierce turned his attention to the little ray of sunshine who was currently giving him her dimpled smile. He tried—and failed—to ignore the hard kick in his gut. Every time that he looked at her, his whole body tightened. Hardened. *Wanted.*

Her dimples flashed at him. Fucking adorable. And sexy. Her blond hair—curling lightly with a mind of its own—trailed over her shoulders. Her heart-shaped face tilted up toward him. She had to angle herself up because the woman was *tiny* compared to him. All soft curves and delicate slopes. He clocked in close to six-foot-three, and he was all solid muscle thanks to what some had called his *too* rigorous workout routine.

"I can help carry the couch," Iris Stuart continued in that lush, made-for-a-bedroom voice of hers. A voice that stroked over his skin and made him have way, way too many fantasies.

"I got it," he growled back in a voice that Pierce knew sounded like a freaking bear's rumble. *Dammit.* "No worries." He *did* have the couch. He could carry it in his sleep. Did she not see the muscles he was deliberately flexing her way? Maybe he should flex a little more. But his t-shirt already strained around his biceps.

Another choked laugh came from Colt's direction. His asshole of a partner seemed to find the whole world to be utterly hilarious. Why, oh, *why* had Pierce thought confiding in Colt about his obsession with his new neighbor would be a good idea? Not like Colt would be offering him any life-altering advice.

"Well, if you're sure." Iris nibbled on an absolutely delectable lower lip. Her eyes—the darkest, warmest chocolate brown he'd ever seen—swept over him—and darted to his buddy. "Oh, hi." She took a quick step forward. "I'm Iris." The amber in the depths of her dark eyes gleamed, looking like a flash of battered gold.

"I have heard of you," came his partner's amused reply. "Name's Colt. It's a pleasure. Truly."

If it had been possible—if they had been close enough—Pierce would have kicked him.

"And let me just say," Colt continued in that faint Texas drawl of his, "you have completely exceeded my expectations." He acted as if he wasn't currently holding up one end of a couch. As if he had all the time in the world to fawn over Iris. "I love your tattoo," he added, as his gaze darted to her legs.

Oh, hell, no.

Iris currently wore a faded pair of old jean shorts, shorts with frayed edges and faint paint splatters on them. The shorts revealed the golden expanse of her legs, *and* the sexy-as-hell tattoo that drifted lovingly over the top of her right thigh.

"Do you have other tats?" Colt asked her curiously. "Because I've got—"

Pierce shoved the couch toward his partner. Hard. "Don't worry about any other tats that she has." *Keep your eyes off her legs.*

Colt turned his head toward him. Smiled innocently. "I was just thinking of getting a new one, and I figured she might be able to offer some inspiration."

Right. The hell he'd thought that. Pierce's eyes narrowed. "We need to move the couch inside. Now."

"Oh? Is it getting too heavy for you?" Colt asked, all fake sympathy. "Probably need more protein in your diet. Or maybe you should do more lifts."

Or I need a friend who isn't an asshole. "I can carry this thing on my own."

Behind them, the elevator dinged. Pierce and Iris were the only ones living on the second floor of the old, converted warehouse. For the elevator to ding...

Who is coming to visit her?

Automatically, his head turned as his gaze focused down the hallway. In the seven days that he'd been living in the building, no one had come to visit her place. He'd started to—rather optimistically—think that meant she wasn't involved with anyone.

But the man striding from the elevator immediately locked his eyes on Iris and a wide grin split his face. His expression warmed and—

And Pierce considered tossing the couch at him.

Nope. Can't do that. You're one of the good guys, remember? It was just that when he was around Iris, Pierce didn't feel quite so good.

"Iris Stuart?" The newcomer's smile broadened. "I'm Bentley. Bentley Prestang." He completely ignored the couch. And both Pierce and Colt. Instead, he closed in on Iris as he strode forward with his shoulders back, his chin up, and a gait rather like a rooster's. "I'm here for the modeling job."

Modeling job? Pierce knew she was an artist. He'd glimpsed some of her work when he'd poked his head inside her place to return the screwdriver she'd given him the other day. Not that he'd actually needed the screwdriver, not when he had six of his own, but borrowing hers had given him an excuse to talk to her. When he'd briefly gone in her place, canvases had been everywhere, and the work had been damn good. But this bozo...

"Let me just say," Bentley announced with a fierce nod of his bright, blond head, "I am completely comfortable doing nudes."

What. The. Fuck? Pierce dropped the couch.

"Ow! Sonofa—" Colt began.

Pierce had already whirled and was glowering at Bentley. "What the hell are you talking about?"

Iris grabbed Bentley's arm. Tugged him toward her place. She inclined her head toward her open door. "Bentley, why don't you go inside, and I'll discuss the position with you?"

The position? Red seemed to fill Pierce's vision. His head swiveled back toward her.

Her dimples winked again. "I should let you guys get back to moving furniture. If I can help, please shout at me."

Oh, he felt like shouting.

"Good luck with the rest of your move," she continued ever-so-sweetly. "Maybe I can bring some pizza by later and we can watch that movie you mentioned yesterday? I'll get extra pepperonis. I remember you said you like your pizzas that way."

Nudes. The dick offered to ditch his clothes for her. Pierce took a lumbering step toward her door. "My place," he gritted out. *I want you in my place now.*

"I'll be there. Eight sound good?"

Now sounded better, but he managed a jerky nod.

"Perfect." Her smile held mega wattage. "So glad you're in the building," Iris added with a dip of her head. "It's nice to have a good friend close by."

The door to her place closed with a soft click. He stared at the wood. In his mind, he saw *Bentley's* carefully styled blond hair. That too-white, capped-teeth grin. The jutting chest and rooster walk. Pierce's fist rose toward her door.

"*Ahem.*" Colt cleared his throat. "In case you missed it, I am holding one end of a couch by myself right now."

Pierce hadn't missed a thing. He never did. He'd been trained to be extra observant. "He's named after a freaking car."

"Yeah, but I'm named after a gun, so who am I to judge?"

Pierce wanted to slam his fist into the door. To, uh, *knock.* "Nude."

"I did hear that word mentioned, but she's an artist, so I'm sure she works with naked men—I mean, works with nudes all the time."

Not what Pierce wanted to hear. He slanted a glare at Colt. "I hate you right now."

"Nah, you hate *Bentley.*"

True.

"The friend zone," Colt mused. "Man, that is hell."

"Tell me about it."

***

Iris released a slow, soothing breath. Or at least, the breath was supposed to help soothe her. Only it didn't. As she stood in front of Pierce's door, a pizza box clutched in her hands, she felt anything but relaxed and soothed.

Her heart raced. Her knees did a little quiver, and her entire body just felt hypersensitive because—

The door swung open.

Hello. Because Pierce Jennings was right there. Every big, bold, delectable inch of him. He wore loose, gray jogging shorts and a black t-shirt that displayed his muscled perfection because it basically fit him like a second skin. He *filled* the doorway and just seeing him had every bit of moisture drying from her mouth. The man oozed sex appeal. Temptation of the ever most carnal kind, and she absolutely wanted to lick him all over.

Not going to happen. Not. At. All.

"Where's the dick?" he rumbled in his deep, make-her-body-quake voice.

And, automatically, her gaze jumped down to his—

"Bentley something, wasn't it? He finally gone?"

Her gaze flew right back up even as heat filled her cheeks. *Bentley.* He was the dick in question. The burn in her cheeks helped Iris to focus. "Oh, he's long gone. He won't work at all for what I need." The guy had been pushy as hell, and it had taken a serious effort to get him out of her place. He'd kept poking and prying. She lifted the pizza higher. "Got the extra pepperonis like you wanted."

His gaze—a truly gorgeous baby blue that she wanted to capture as a sky in one of her paintings—swept over her face. Swept over. Lingered. His jaw hardened.

Nervousness trembled through her. "Pierce?"

"You've got pizza." Another rumble. "And I've got wine. Come on inside." He stepped back, making room for her to cross the threshold.

She hurried inside, and when she did, her arm brushed against his chest. A surge hit her. Not electric. More like...pulsing. Throbbing. *Aching.* An awareness that she was very much going to ignore.

Pierce might look like walking temptation, but she knew how to resist. This was not her first ball game, not by a long shot. Just because he might have a stare hot enough to melt her panties, it did *not* mean that she would be jumping into his arms. Getting involved romantically would be far too dangerous.

For him.

Iris did a fast two-step away from him. "The couch looks great!" Her voice broke a wee bit. She might have put far too much enthusiasm into that announcement.

He took the pizza from her. His fingers tangled with hers.

More aching. More throbbing. Oh, jeez. She needed to get control. They were *friends.* She needed a friend. After far too much time being alone, of not letting anyone get close and having no one to trust, she desperately needed someone like Pierce.

Someone *good.*

Someone upstanding. All law-abiding. Someone who knew how to make the right choices even when things were hard.

She'd gotten background info on him. Her handler Franco had provided the intel to her before Pierce had set one foot in the place. Not like he was going to let some stranger just waltz into the building without doing a full check on the person. Pierce Jennings had come up clean. *Sparkling* clean. She knew nearly every single detail about him, and that was one of the many reasons why she felt comfortable being in his place with him.

He was a former Army Ranger. One who had a fistful of medals that he'd earned for bravery. He'd saved his team members. He'd risked himself over and over again. Then he'd come back home and gotten a job at Wilde, an elite protection and security firm. The man seemed hardwired to protect. He wanted to help people. And after spending most of her life with individuals who wanted to do just the opposite...

Such a nice change.

But who knew that being *good* could also mean being so hot?

"What happened to Bentley?" Low.

She let go of the pizza box. "He won't do at all. I thanked him for coming by, but he's not exactly what I need."

Pierce smiled at her. It was a slow, toe-curling smile that started with a tilt of his lips and ended with a sparkle in his eyes. "That's just terrible to hear."

If it was terrible, why was he smiling?

She trailed him into the kitchen. While he poured wine, she snagged plates for them, easily navigating around him and going unerringly to the right cabinet. After all, *she'd* helped him to unpack the plates, so she knew where they were stored.

They munched on pizza. She savored the wine. They made small talk. Even wound up on the couch together to watch an utterly awful old horror movie about clowns who came from outer space. Side note...she wound up loving that movie. And laughing as she flinched because she did enjoy her horror.

And just as the credits were rolling...

"So are you going to be in the market for another model?" Pierce asked, voice casual.

"Uh, yes. I just have to find the right look." Her wine glass was empty. She toyed with the stem even as she darted a glance at the clock. She'd need to leave soon.

"What look do you want?"

"Honestly?"

"Um."

"I'm going for more of a Greek-god-type thing. Muscles and strength. Power. Bentley was just too..." She didn't want to say pretty-boy. "Runway ready." That was better. He'd been handsome in a high-fashion manner, while she wanted savage strength and barely contained passion.

"I see." A murmur. "Figured that out when he stripped, did you?"

Her hold tightened on the glass. "Things didn't progress that far. I knew as soon as I saw him in person that it wasn't going to work."

"Good to fucking know." He looked away.

She frowned. His words had been growled so she hadn't quite made them out clearly, but it had sounded like—

Pierce glanced back at her. "I've got a great idea." His smile came again.

Her stomach quivered. The quiver was not from the wine. "I should go." She jumped to her feet.

"I can model for you."

Her feet became rooted to the spot. "Excuse me?"

"I'm right next door. Talk about convenient. And I still have a week before I start my next case at Wilde. That means my schedule is pretty flexible. I can be your model."

The sudden visual she had...Pierce, standing in her studio, all the wonderful, perfect morning light falling on him as he posed before her...totally nude. *Oh, my.* Her knees wanted to dip.

"Such a bad idea," she mumbled.

His brows shot together, and he raked a hand through his thick, dark hair. "Why do you say that?" He rose to stand next to her. *Towered* over her. "Am I not savage enough for you?"

Breathe. In and out. That was what she did. Then she shoved a smile onto her face. "You really want to stand naked in front of me for hours and hours—"

"Absolutely."

"While I—wait, what?"

He shrugged. "I'm good at standing still. Not moving at all. When you're in some of the most dangerous spots on earth, you have to move with care—or often, not move at all. You have to wait out the enemy if you want to succeed."

"I...um, I need to go." Now. Fast. "The movie was fun. The wine was great. Top-notch. Truly. And you are—" *Hot.* No, no. Wrong thing to say. Maybe she'd had too much wine. Time to go. She made a beeline for the door.

"Are you afraid of me?"

His question stopped her cold. Her hand hung in the air. She'd been reaching for the doorknob when he asked his question. "What?" Iris glanced back over her shoulder. "Why would you think that?"

"Because a lot of people are afraid of me. I'm a big guy. I make certain people..." He stalked toward her. "Nervous."

Nervous wasn't the right word. She didn't feel nervous. Iris felt edgy. As if she might jump out of her skin. And hot. She felt really hot. It *was* hot in there, though, wasn't it? Maybe she should tell Pierce to get his air conditioning checked.

He stopped just inches from her. "Do I make you nervous, Iris?"

She turned to fully face him. Sucked in a breath. Then lost it on a laugh. "Oh, goodness, no. But that is adorable." Her hand lifted and patted his cheek in a friendly gesture. His stubble tickled her palm. "You're the hero. The *nice guy.*" She dropped her hand because that wasn't a tickle that she felt. It was something more.

Awareness.

Desire.

"Nice?" he bit out.

Her head bobbed. "You're the kind of man who makes a woman feel safe. You don't scare me. I've seen plenty of scary guys in my time."

A furrow appeared between his brows. "What—"

"And I've developed a radar for them. You don't set off the radar. I'm not the least bit afraid of you." If she'd been afraid, she wouldn't want him the way she did. Her hand pushed to her side. Her fingers pressed to her shorts. "I'm glad you're in the building. It's nice to have someone here with me." She tried a smile. "How great is it that we get along so well already? Talk about being fast friends."

"It's just awesome." A muscle jerked along his jaw. "Awesome," he repeated. "I love being your friend."

Her breath caught. That was awfully sweet of him to say. Her hand reached for his, an impulsive gesture. His fingers were rough and strong and about twice the size of hers. She still squeezed them gently. "Thank you. That's the kindest thing anyone has said to me in a very long time." Far longer than he would suspect.

The furrow between his brows deepened. "Iris?"

"I need to go. I plan to be up by dawn so I can go down to the park and sketch the sunrise." She let go of his hand. "Thanks for a lovely night, Pierce."

"Anytime, Iris." His gaze held hers. "Anytime."

***

A knock sounded at her door. Iris glanced up, frowning. She'd snagged a book from her shelf and been in the process of heading for the couch. She always liked to curl up and read before bed.

A lick of excitement filled her as she hurried for the door. Pierce was the only other tenant on the floor—actually, the only other tenant in the whole building—so she knew her late night visitor had to be him.

Had he forgotten to tell her something? Or did he need to borrow something else? A smile was on her face as she swung open the door. "Do you need the screwdriver again—" The words died in her throat.

Just...died.

Because Pierce wasn't on the other side of her door. A man in a tailored, black suit waited. A man with midnight black hair and cold, gray eyes.

She immediately tried to slam the door.

His foot pushed across the threshold, stopping her. "Iris..." A sigh of her name. "Is that any way to greet an old friend?"

He wasn't a friend. Never had been. "Move the foot and get the hell out of here."

He didn't move his foot. "We've been looking for you. Wasn't very nice of you to hide."

She should never have opened the door without looking through her peephole. She'd gotten complacent. *Sloppy.* "Move your foot."

"I'm here to offer you a job, Iris. My boss will pay you well—"

"*Get the hell away from me!*" She hadn't meant to yell. Had she?

But...now the nearby door was squeaking open. Pierce's door. A jerk of her head showed him standing in his open doorway, still wearing those jogging shorts but now minus a shirt. He was big, muscled, and looking very, very dangerous as he locked his gaze on the man who stood so close to her.

"Iris?" Pierce called. "There a problem?"

Yes, a huge, terrible, back-from-the-past nightmare. "No," she hastened to say. "He's at the wrong door. And he was just leaving."

But the man before her didn't leave. Constantine Leos leaned toward her and lowered his voice as he told her, "If you don't contact me to take the job, there *will* be trouble."

Oh, God.

He took her book from her. Tucked a card inside the pages before slamming it closed. "Call the number. It's my direct line."

She yanked her book back from him. "No. I don't do that stuff any longer." She'd never *chosen* to be in that world. Her chin lifted. "Whatever your boss wants, the answer is *no*. So be a good errand boy, and tell him what I said, will you?" Her words were barely above a whisper.

His features tightened. "Don't piss me off."

Don't come to my door.

"Iris?" Pierce's voice held a definite edge. And his voice was louder. Because he'd marched closer. "You need me?"

Constantine tossed her one more glare, then he spun and stalked for the stairwell. The stairwell, *not* the elevator.

"You said he was at the wrong door. How the hell did that guy get in the building?" Pierce wanted to know as he eliminated the distance between them. "He should have needed to type in the security code downstairs."

Yes, he should have. But a man like Constantine would be able to get past *most* security setups. "We'll have to check on that tomorrow. Call the building manager."

His gaze held curiosity as it assessed her, then Pierce nodded. "I'll just make sure our unwanted visitor gets his ass out of the building *and* that the system is functioning properly once he's gone." He started to follow Constantine—

"No!" She grabbed his arm.

Pierce frowned at her. "What's wrong?"

You don't have a weapon. You're just wearing jogging shorts. Constantine could have a gun hidden on his body. Constantine habitually fought dirty. Iris did not want Pierce anywhere near the guy. "He's already in the stairwell. Gone. I don't think we need to worry about him again."

Lie, lie, lie. All she would be doing for the rest of the night was worrying.

He tugged free of her hold. "I'm just going to make sure."

"Pierce—"

But just like that, he was gone.

This is not good. She grabbed for her phone and dialed her handler. *Answer, answer, answer—*

His voicemail picked up.

"Franco," her voice sounded breathless to her own ears, "we have a problem."

***

The stranger had almost slipped away. Pierce bounded onto the sidewalk and surged after him. His fingers closed around the guy's shoulder, and Pierce swung him around.

The man came up in a battle-ready pose.

Interesting.

"Who the hell are you?" Pierce demanded.

The fellow just laughed. "Didn't Iris tell you?"

No, she hadn't told him jack, and Pierce had a very, very bad feeling knotting his gut.

"I was at the wrong door," the stranger murmured. "Surely you picked up that part?"

Wrong door, my ass. He let go of the other man's shoulder. "How did you get in the building?"

"The main entrance was open. I just walked right in."

Pierce blinked. "Do I look like the type of man who believes bullshit?"

The gaze on him sharpened. "You look like the type of man who is smart enough to heed a good warning." A long pause. "So consider yourself warned. Don't go playing white knight. The pay for the gig is shit, and you'll just wind up bloody in the end."

Pierce angled his head to the right. Squinted his eyes as he stared at the fool who was *threatening* him, and laughed.

It was obviously not the reaction the jerk had expected. "What the hell?"

"Indeed. What the hell?" Pierce let a shark's smile curve his lips. "You have me confused with someone else. Obviously. Someone who minds blood. See, I don't mind it. Not even a little. I don't mind getting my knuckles absolutely fucking bloody when I fight. Because I fight hard, and I fight very, very well when I'm protecting something—or someone. So how about *I* give you a warning?" He paused a beat. "Stay away from Iris." Because he'd seen the fear in her eyes when she'd looked at this creep. He hadn't liked that fear. Not at all. "If you come around her again, let's just say that our next interaction won't be so pleasant."

"Am I supposed to be scared?"

"I don't know, are you supposed to be smart? Because if you are, then you might want to step back and think...how bad will you feel when a wannabe knight kicks your ass?"

The guy yanked away from him. Stomped down the road. With his eyes narrowed and his hands fisted, Pierce watched him leave. When he was sure the SOB was gone, only then did Pierce turn back to the building. After he went inside, Pierce made damn sure the building was secure. And he stalked back up the stairs to Iris.

Sweetheart, what in the hell was that about?

His Iris had secrets. It was a good thing that he excelled when it came to *uncovering* secrets. Truth be told, uncovering secrets was his favorite hobby.

CHAPTER TWO

Iris gripped the knife in her hand. She stared at the canvas before her. The lines. The colors. The dips and weaves that the brush had painstakingly taken to make the creation before her come to life. Hours and hours of time spent on the task. Working without pause because she'd felt compelled to see if she still *could* make this art. And she had made it. It was just as good as the paintings she'd made back in another life...

But I am not the same person any longer.

The compulsions came to her, and she could not deny them. Even as she hated what she could do...

The tip of the knife pressed to the canvas. A tear slid down her cheek. Pierce thought she was a good person. *Pierce* was a good person. He wouldn't like her, not if he knew the things that she'd done before. Not if he knew about her past.

The knife sliced into the canvas. She yanked the blade down.

Swallowing, Iris slashed again. There was no need for Pierce to ever know about her past. No need for anyone else to know. She was a different person now. Totally and completely different.

She slashed with the knife once more.

Constantine had been at her door. He'd been right there, and now—

Now someone was pounding on her door again. Loud, angry raps on the wood. Whirling toward the sound, she tightened her hold on the knife. Her heart pounded too quickly as her bare feet flew over the floor. This time—*this time,* she looked through the peephole.

Pierce stood on the other side of her door. She yanked the door open.

His hands pressed along the doorframe. He leaned forward. Blinked. Reassessed. "Iris..." A low growl. "Is that a bloody knife in your hand?"

The knife fell from her fingers. It hit the floor with a clatter. She looked at it, and he was right. Blood did seem to coat the blade of the knife. Dark red. Terrifying. But it wasn't blood...

He bent. Curled his fingers around the handle of the knife. Rose slowly.

"Paint," she gasped out. "It's just paint." The paint hadn't been fully dry when she'd started slicing the canvas. "I was, um, getting rid of a piece that didn't work." Her tongue swiped over her lower lip, and she took a half-step back. A little rock onto her heel. "Sorry. I should have left the knife in my studio." She opened her hand. Held it palm out toward him. "I'll just get rid of that."

He stared at her open palm. Then at the blade. "Paint."

"Um. Yes. Paint." She pushed onto her toes and peered around him. Tried to, anyway, but the man was massive. "Is he gone?" Low. Hushed.

A curt nod. "And he'd better not be back."

She could certainly second that sentiment.

Instead of giving her the knife, Pierce stepped over the threshold and into her home. He headed for her kitchen.

"Oh, sure," Iris announced as she shut the door. *And* locked it. "Come on in. Make yourself at home."

Water was running in the kitchen. Apparently, he already *had* made himself at home. She raced to catch up with him and found him rinsing the paint off her knife. The water was red as it trickled down her drain.

"Friends don't lie to each other," he said. Was it her imagination, or were his broad shoulders extra stiff? "I'm sure that's like, step one, in all good friendships," Pierce continued somewhat gruffly. He turned off the water. Put the knife to the side. Rolled back his shoulders and faced her. "Wouldn't you agree?"

She rocked back onto her heel. That little half-step. "What lie?"

His lips kicked up into a faint smile. One that never reached his eyes. "You didn't like him. *He* scared you."

"Any late night, uninvited visitor would make me nervous."

"*He* made you nervous."

Hadn't she just said as much?

Pierce's arms crossed over his chest. "Guessing he's one of those scary guys you mentioned before? The kind who set off your radar?"

Yes, indeed, Constantine was. "I thought it was you," she confessed. "I didn't even check the peephole. Just swung the door right open." What an amateur move. "I won't make that mistake again, and I'll definitely check with the building manager about security." Maybe they needed some additional security measures.

His lips tightened. "Anything else you want to tell me?"

Nope. Not a thing. But he was staring at her expectantly. "Like...what?"

"Like who he really was? How he knew you? *Why* he scared you?"

She swallowed the big lump in her throat. "It is so late." Iris faked a yawn.

He didn't yawn back. Just stared.

"I have to get up early tomorrow. Remember that, um, whole sketching the sunrise thing I told you about? I'm preparing for a show soon, and I need some more pieces." She backed away, thinking he'd follow.

Grudgingly, he did.

She moseyed for the front door. "Sorry to interrupt your night-time routine. Hopefully, there will be no more unwanted visitors."

He stopped right beside her. "You're not going to tell me who he was."

"I—"

"And no BS about him being at the wrong door. We both know he was at the right door. But you didn't want to talk to him."

She'd be happy never seeing his face again. "He's no one. Distant history. Someone in my rearview mirror."

"An ex?"

"Dear God, *no.*" A vehement denial. "Constantine and I were never involved that way." She shuddered at the thought.

Some of the tension seemed to leave his body. "If this Constantine comes around again, if he bothers you in any way, you come to me."

"That is so nice." It was. Made her feel all warm and glowy. And like she wasn't alone in the big, dark, and scary universe. "But then, you are a nice guy, and I super appreciate—"

His eyes squeezed closed. "Don't."

"Don't...what?"

His nostrils flared as his eyes opened. "Don't be grateful. You don't owe me a damn bit of gratitude."

Iris tucked a lock of hair behind her ear. "I feel like I do," she mumbled. He didn't get that most people hadn't done *nice* things for her. They hadn't helped out of the goodness of their hearts. Mostly because the people who used to be in her world? They just hadn't really understood goodness. Her mind scrambled for inspiration. *Got it.* "Maybe I can cook dinner tomorrow? My way of saying thanks for rushing to the rescue?" She was actually a passable cook. A new hobby she'd started in the last six months. She hadn't wanted to venture out to the unfamiliar Atlanta restaurants. She'd wanted to stay, all safe and secure, in her home.

And then Constantine just had to show up.

"Dinner." He inclined his head slowly. "I'd like that."

Relief had her shoulders sagging. She didn't like to *owe* anyone. Dinner would make them even. "Then it's a date."

His gaze sharpened.

"Not a date-date." Jeez, now she sounded crazy. "Just you know, us. It's a dinner that involves us." *Of course, he knows that.*

"Right. Us." A muscle tensed along his jaw. "Two friends getting together."

She hurried the remaining steps for the door. Time to see him out because she had some evidence—in the form of a slashed painting—that she needed to go cover up. "See you tomorrow night."

Pierce took his time heading for the door. Sort of a slow, ambling stride. His gaze swept over her. "You can trust me, you know."

She didn't know that, but she was starting to suspect it could be the case.

"If you ever need help," he continued in his truly toe-curling voice, "you can count on me."

Iris forced her toes to uncurl. "I'll remember that."

"Good." He stood in front of her. Seemed to lean over her. Around her.

She could feel the heat from his body, and Iris had to fight the urge to rub up against him. She wasn't a freaking cat. What was her deal? "Good night," Iris forced herself to say. "Sweet dreams."

"Oh, they'll be anything but sweet. I'm pretty sure of that." He turned toward the door. "Lock it after me."

Like she had to be told.

As soon as he was gone, she shut and bolted the door. Set the alarm. Then shoved a chair underneath the doorknob, just in case. With a past like hers, you could never be too careful.

And that's why I should always check the damn peephole.

***

The call came in the middle of the night. He wasn't sleeping, so he answered on the second ring.

"I spoke to her."

His body instantly tensed. "And...?"

"Approached her tonight, said everything just like you wanted."

He shoved upright in bed. *"And?"*

"Um, is there someone else you might want to use?"

His feet swung over the side of the mattress and hit the floor. "No, there isn't anyone fucking else. Iris is the best. I want *her*."

A cough. "About that..."

He began to stalk across the penthouse. "Constantine, don't feed me your BS. Get to the point."

"I don't think Iris is interested in a *working* relationship with you, boss." A sigh. "She said no, all right? She refused to take the job."

And he...laughed. "God, that is precious." So very Iris.

Silence came from the other end of the line. "You expected her to refuse?"

"It was a possibility." A probability. "But I thought it would be interesting to see what happened if I tried to approach her in a fairly normal fashion." So much for that shit. "Now we move to option two."

"Option...two?"

Why the hell was Constantine being so hesitant? The man had been known to play dirty as hell. One of the reasons he'd recently brought Constantine onto his team. Maybe the change was because of Iris. Stories said she had a way of working herself under a person's skin. "Option two," he returned flatly. "She *doesn't* get to refuse. You find her at the next opportunity, and you bring her to me."

"Hold up. You want me to kidnap her?"

"What the fuck is your problem tonight, Constantine?" He rubbed the back of his neck with his left hand. "Bring Iris to me. That's what I want you to do. Get her. Bring her to me. I'll make sure she understands this is a job she *has* to take."

"But, she's not gonna come willingly—"

"That's your problem. Not mine." He paused a beat. "If you can't handle this—if you can't collect one woman who is all of five feet two inches tall—then maybe we need to rethink your position in my employ."

"I'll get her."

"That's what I thought you'd say." But he would still make plans to have two of his trusted men accompany Constantine for his next meeting with Iris.

***

Iris moaned his name. Arched up against him and raked her nails down his back.

Pierce couldn't look away from her. Black silk surrounded her, framed her, as she undulated beneath him. Her lips were parted and full, and his head dipped toward her because he just had to taste—

The blaring of the alarm shattered his dream.

His eyes jerked open, and he glared at the ceiling.

Sweet dreams, my ass. His hands slammed over and stopped the shrieking alarm. A quick glare toward the window showed him that the sun wasn't even up yet. And, normally, his ass wouldn't be up at this time, either, not on his off day.

I can almost feel her nails on my skin.

He kicked off the covers. Ignored his giant dick.

Iris had said she would be going to the park to catch the sunrise. Maybe it was stalkerish, but he intended to be at that park, too. *Not* because he was obsessed with her or anything—though, yeah, he'd examine that possibility later—but because after last night and that creepy visitor of hers, Pierce just wanted to keep an extra eye on Iris.

After all, a good *friend* watched your back.

And a good lover fucked you like crazy.

Something told him Iris would be an incredibly good lover.

***

She loved a good sunrise. One where the colors streaked across the sky in every shade of red and gold imaginable. Her pencil flew over the sketchpad as she tried to catch all the nuances of the clouds and the birds and even the skyscrapers in the distance. She loved the way the light trickled and played. Loved the beauty that she would never be able to truly replicate because that was just a skill beyond—

"Still a creature of habit, I see." Constantine's low voice came from behind her.

Her shoulders stiffened. She'd been sitting on the ground. A blanket rested beneath her, while her sketchpad lay cradled in her lap. Her fingers automatically tightened around the pencil as she glanced back over her shoulder. In the soft, morning light, she could easily see Constantine as he stepped from the cover of nearby trees. "Are you following me?"

"No, I'm predicting you. You used to like sunrises. This was the closest park to your building. Thought I might just take a stroll...and, well, I found you out here, all alone."

There had been an emphasis on *all alone* that she didn't like.

She particularly didn't like it when two men—guys she'd never seen before—stepped from the cover of the trees to flank him. The men wore matching, tough and angry expressions, and the bad feeling that had been quivering in her gut suddenly got a whole lot worse.

Iris jumped to her feet. The sketchpad fell and hit the blanket, but she didn't let go of her pencil. "What's happening here?"

"Option two," Constantine told her grimly.

She had zero idea what that crap meant. But she *did* see the two goons closing in on her. One—a guy with a shaved, bald head and a wolf tattoo on his neck—even smiled at her. It wasn't a friendly smile.

Then again, this wasn't a friendly visit.

"You should have just taken the job offer." Constantine sighed. He waved his hand toward her. "You still can, you know. Just say yes and we can all walk away from this park together."

"No," Iris replied deliberately.

"Don't worry," the bald guy groused. "She won't have a chance to scream."

Constantine's head whipped toward him. "What?"

What? A mental echo from Iris.

A shrug lifted the hulking creep's rounded shoulders. "But it's not like there's anyone around to hear her scream but us."

What. The. Hell? Instead of asking that burning question, she opened her mouth and let loose the most powerful scream that she possessed. It sliced through the air like a—

A heavy, sweaty hand clapped over her mouth. "Don't do that," the man with the wolf tattoo snarled.

Her heart nearly slammed out of her chest as the other goon rushed to grab her. Her body twisted as she kicked out at them—and she drove her pencil into the hand of the bastard with his fat fingers over her mouth.

Swearing, he let her go.

And her powerful scream hit the air once more. She screamed—and ran.

CHAPTER THREE

Her scream echoed in his ears and iced Pierce's blood. His legs pistoned as he shoved through the trees and burst into the clearing.

Pierce knew the sight before him would probably haunt him forever. Two hulking bastards—big and rough—had Iris in their fierce grip. One SOB held her legs. The other asshole had his arms wrapped around her upper body. She fought them, twisting and heaving, but they just held her tighter.

Oh, the hell, *no*. A guttural roar broke from him, and the two men whipped their heads toward him. So did Iris. Her wide, frightened gaze met his.

And she—

She smiled.

"You are in so much trouble," she told the men.

Yes, they fucking *were*.

"That is my new best friend," she added quickly, "and he is going to kick your—"

The men started running—while still carrying her. And she kept fighting. But they each outweighed her by well over one hundred pounds. Those bastards—putting their hands on her...

So he put his hands on *them*.

Pierce lunged forward and grabbed the SOB who held her legs. He locked am arm around the jerk's throat and hauled him back. The guy choked and sputtered but had to let Iris go. Pierce whirled the asshole to face him, then drove his fist straight into the prick's face as hard as he could. Pierce felt bones crush and saw blood pour from her attacker's nose. But he wasn't done. He needed this one out of commission. So he hit hard and brutally, and soon the piece of shit was on the ground.

"Pierce!"

His head whipped up. Iris was on her feet, but the other bastard still had his arms locked around her. She head-butted him but didn't do much damage.

Pierce stalked toward them. "I'll count to three, and if you haven't let her go by *three,* you'll be choking on your own blood."

Both Iris and the hulking attacker froze. Then their heads whipped toward him.

The man holding her—bald, totally shaved head, with a shitty wolf tattoo on his neck—dropped his gaze to his fallen partner, then snapped it back up at Pierce.

"One," Pierce said deliberately.

Iris strained against her captor's hold. She also kicked back and landed a damn good blow to his shin.

"Two."

Her attacker swore and shook her—

Fuck three.

Pierce drove his fist into her attacker's side. The guy let her go, and Iris scampered away. The fool reached for her, but Pierce grabbed his hand—vaguely noticing that blood gushed from it—and he twisted hard, knowing he would be breaking some of those fingers.

That will teach you to ever put your hands on her again. You don't fucking shake a woman. You don't try to abduct her. You don't hurt her.

The creep's other hand plowed toward Pierce's face, but he easily dodged the blow, and then Pierce concentrated his attack on the fellow's body. Did a rib or two break? Maybe. Pierce pounded until his prey was down—a groaning, sorry pile on the grass.

His breath heaved in and out, and Pierce's hands clenched as he stared down at the fallen man, almost daring him to attack again. But the guy wasn't getting up. Not anytime soon.

Slowly, Pierce's head rose. He looked for Iris. She stood a few feet away, her eyes huge in her face and fucking *fingerprints*—red impressions of fat fingers—circled her bare arms. He growled.

She lifted up her phone. "Calling for help."

Right. She should do that. Get these bozos tossed in jail. "Cops," he growled. Speech was rather hard because bloodlust and fury rode him so hard. He wanted to destroy these men. They'd tried to take her? Kidnap her?

And what the hell would have happened if I hadn't been here? She just never would have come home to him and then—

"Feds," she fired back quickly even as she lifted the phone to her ear. "I'm calling the Feds. They can take care of these goons."

Feds? Dazed, still reeling from the fury that burned his blood, Pierce said, "Beat cops will be fine. They can lock up these assholes."

But Iris shook her head. "Don't worry. I have a contact number. The agent will be here in no time."

The blood that had been burning in his body suddenly chilled. Iris had a personal contact at the FBI? He cast an assessing gaze over the two prone men on the ground. Just what in the hell was happening?

"Where did the third one go?" she blurted.

Third one?

"Dammit, he got away, didn't he?"

Slowly, Pierce closed in on her. With every step he took, her eyes seemed to widen. Her grip tightened on the phone until her knuckles were white.

"Can't help but notice," he rasped, "you seem awfully calm for someone who was nearly abducted just moments ago."

"I—" Then she blinked.

He could hear a man's voice coming from her phone. The Fed?

Iris cleared her throat. "Agent Robertson? It's Iris. I-I have a problem."

***

Meatloaf didn't seem like the best present to give a man who had quite literally saved your life. A guy who had swooped in and single-handedly defeated the bad guys who were hell-bent on taking you away.

Meatloaf just seemed...not enough.

Iris nibbled on her lower lip. She had mashed potatoes, too, but they still didn't scream, *Thank you! You are a lifesaver.*

She wasn't used to people swooping in to save her. She'd been thrown to the wolves more times than she could count, so this whole saving-the-day business left her floundering.

Maybe when he knocks on the door, I should just throw my arms around him and—

Nope. Iris stopped the thought. As tempting as it might be, she couldn't give in to that fantasy. Not with the trouble heading her way. Her contact at the FBI had gotten the authorities on the scene immediately. He hadn't been there, not personally, but he'd called in some cops he knew to arrest the would-be kidnappers. Of course, they'd clammed up—once they'd regained consciousness—and were refusing to say anything about why they'd tried to take her.

She just hoped they didn't get out on bail anytime soon. If they did, Iris had a sinking feeling they would just be coming after her again.

A knock pounded against her door. She jumped because her home had been so very still and silent, then hurried across the room. A quick glance through the peephole—not like she'd make that mistake twice—revealed Pierce's chiseled features. For a moment, she savored him, distorted view that it was, then she swung open the door. "Right on time! You are—"

"Not in the mood for bullshit."

Her bright smile faltered. "Oh. I was, um, planning to serve meatloaf. Not bullshit."

A muscle flexed along his jaw as he pushed inside. He did not laugh at her joke.

Automatically, Iris had to back up. The man was just *big*.

He kicked the door closed. Stopped. Swung back around and flipped the lock. *Then* he faced her again. "Your FBI buddy had me removed from the scene."

Oh, yes. About that... "He was just making sure you were safe. That's what all the authorities wanted, to make sure you were—"

"Again, not in the mood for bullshit."

She wet her lips.

"I *am* in the mood to know what in the hell is happening with you." His nostrils flared. "And dinner smells fantastic."

Heat stained her cheeks. "Thanks." She ducked her head.

"Fucking fuck, but you are so damn adorable sometimes. Even when I'm about to lose my mind, you are—"

Her head shot up. Her eyes widened.

"I want to kiss you," Pierce told her flatly.

Her head shook in automatic denial.

His chin notched up. "No? Fine. Got it." His hands lifted, palms up, before his body. "Won't talk about it—"

She missed whatever he said next because she was lunging toward him. Throwing her arms around him just like in her recent fantasy. She hadn't been shaking her head to say *no*. She'd been doing it because she was so stunned. She'd shaken her head because she couldn't believe what he was saying.

*Bad idea. Ever so bad, but...*She grabbed tight to his shoulders, shoved up on her bare toes, and hauled him toward her. Her mouth pressed to his in a fast, hard, closed-mouth kiss. Not the most graceful or sexy thing she'd ever done in her life. One of those definite heat-of-the-moment situations that she'd read about in books, but in real-life felt super awkward now that her mouth was crushed to his and—

"Guessing you want to kiss me, too," he murmured against her lips. "So how about I help out the situation and give you a little boost?"

A boost?

His hands closed around her waist, and he lifted her up. Her lips parted in shocked surprise. He used that moment to dip his tongue into her mouth, and Iris just melted. No other word for it. Heat flooded through her, and the whole tense, awkward moment vanished as she softened against him.

Her legs curled around his hips. Her mouth opened even more for him as his tongue teased her. His cock shoved against her core. No missing that thing. Not with it being designed along his usual giant proportions. But his mouth was oh, so careful on hers. Kissing her with a sensual skill that made her want to moan.

Fine, she *was* moaning, and arching against him and thinking that no one had ever made her feel this good with just a kiss.

Then the knocking started again.

Who in the hell is interrupting this perfect moment?

Pierce stiffened against her. His head slowly lifted. His eyes—a darker blue than before—locked on her.

She panted. Swallowed. Tried to act nonchalant. Hard to do while her legs were still wrapped around his waist and her eager hips still rocked against him.

Down, girl. Literally, like, she needed to get down. Her legs unhooked. Before she could bound down ungracefully, he lowered her gently until her feet touched the floor.

"Expecting someone else?" His voice rumbled. Deep and dark and hot.

"You're the only one I invited." Her knees were unsteady. *Everything* felt unsteady. "That was—"

"Not a mistake."

"I was going to say hot. But, sure, yes, let's say it wasn't a mistake."

If possible, his blue gaze darkened even more. "Iris—"

The pounding came again.

Swearing, Pierce whirled for the door. He put his eye to the peephole. "Who is that?"

She couldn't see, so she had no idea.

He tossed a frown back at her. "Dark red hair. Cheap suit. And I'm pretty sure he's packing a gun. I can see the bulge beneath his coat."

Her heart sank. "Let me look." But she already knew. And yep, a quick glance confirmed for her that FBI Special Agent Bryce Robertson waited impatiently beyond her door. Talk about some poor timing.

"Who is he?"

She exhaled slowly. She needed to get rid of that panting. "He's my FBI contact." One who had not said he'd be paying a house call.

"He knows the security code for the building."

Yes. "He's...been here a few times before."

Bryce pounded again. She had to open the door. "Maybe we should take a raincheck on dinner." Because Bryce wasn't going to just disappear. "Or I could make you a to-go plate. That way, you can enjoy everything while it's warm."

Pierce's blue eyes narrowed. "I'm not going anywhere."

He had to go. She couldn't talk freely with Bryce if Pierce was there. She didn't want him knowing the truth about her. She...

Liked the way things were with them.

I like him.

"Iris!" Bryce shouted. "I know you're in there! I saw your car outside. Either let me in or I'll be dragging you down to the station!"

He would not *dare*.

"I don't like his tone," Pierce muttered.

What?

Before she could say anything, he'd flipped the lock and wrenched the door open. "Don't scream at her," Pierce snapped flatly. "And you're not dragging her *anywhere*."

Bryce's mouth gaped open, only to be hurriedly shut. His gaze swept over Pierce, no doubt sizing him up, before darting to Iris as she peered at the agent.

A long sigh escaped Bryce. "Making new friends, are we?" He stepped forward, obviously intending to come into her place.

But Pierce moved to block his path. "I didn't hear her give you an invitation."

"I do not have the time or patience for this crap." Bryce shook his head. "Iris, tell the boy toy to hit the road. We need to talk. Got a code 'You're Screwed' that we have to handle." He sniffed. "And is that your meatloaf I smell? I hope so because I am freaking starving." Bryce surged forward.

He surged straight into Pierce's hand. A hand that pushed back against the middle of Bryce's chest. "You weren't invited for dinner. *I* was."

Bryce looked down at the hand. Then back up at Pierce. And, finally, over to Iris. "Is he going to be a problem?"

"Damn straight, I am," Pierce responded without missing a beat. "Iris was nearly *abducted* today. Yet she's acting all calm and collected like it's the most normal shit in the world."

Oh, no, she wasn't. She was barely holding herself together. Cooking had soothed her a little bit, but, truth be told, she'd been shaking for most of the afternoon. She hadn't left her home even once—thus the meatloaf. Originally, she'd intended to hit the market and get all kinds of awesome items. Maybe lobster. A super fancy bottle of wine but...

But she'd been afraid.

She was *still* afraid.

"Who the hell are you?" Pierce blasted as his hand remained pressed to Bryce's chest.

"Bryce Robertson," came the curt reply. "FBI Special Agent Bryce Robertson." A pause, probably just so he could let that title sink in. Bryce did enjoy being dramatic. "And you are?"

"Pierce Jennings." A pause. "Next door neighbor. Taker of no shit. All-around ass-kicker and dangerous-situation handler. And I'm also the guy who is feeling really hyper protective of Iris right now. So how about you don't push me, Special Agent?"

Bryce seemed to reassess. "Fine." A nod. His green eyes swung to Iris. "Do I get to come in and speak freely with the boyfriend present? Put all the cards on the table? It's your call. Always has been."

Damn. She couldn't do this. There was no way she could just spill her painful past in front of Pierce. *He won't look at me the same way.* She liked the way he looked at her. "I'll get Pierce a plate ready to go. Give me just a second." And she spun away. Practically ran for the kitchen. Her fingers were shaking as she threw the food onto a plate. Some mashed potatoes plopped on the floor. *Plop.*

"You don't need to be scared."

She stiffened.

Pierce's voice had come from right behind her.

"You ran in here as if you were terrified of me."

No, she'd run as if she'd been terrified of what would happen when he learned the truth about her. She wrapped up the plate. Kept her spine straight. "There are things you don't know about me." Iris turned to face him.

He nodded. "Sure. We just met, after all. Only been in each other's lives for a week."

Had it really just been a week?

"I get that you don't tell someone all your secrets in one fast rush."

No, you didn't. Sometimes, you didn't tell your secrets at all. Especially when you were trying to protect other people. That morning, Pierce had come to her rescue. He'd saved *her*. Tonight, it was her turn to save him. The best way to do that?

Get him to leave. He didn't need to be involved in the mess that surrounded her. "I'm sorry our dinner has to be canceled." She rocked back a little.

His eyes narrowed.

"Maybe we can catch up tomorrow?" Iris added.

"Sure thing." Growled. He took the plate from her. Their fingers brushed.

She sucked in a breath.

"I'll be close if you need me." Low, for her ears alone.

Iris managed a quick nod. She also managed to walk him out, even though her knees wanted to knock together. With every step, she could feel Bryce's watchful gaze on her. At the door, she hesitated. What should she say to Pierce?

"I'll see you soon," Pierce promised her gruffly. Then he just strode away. Didn't even look back once.

Craning her head, she watched him until he vanished into his home.

"Don't look desperate."

At those soft and chiding words, she whirled around. Glared at Bryce. "Excuse me?"

He was munching on meatloaf. "The guy is obviously into you. Don't go looking all needy and desperate. Keep the air of mystery." He shoveled more meatloaf into his mouth. "It's good that you kicked him out. No sense in your hero getting in over his head. You just met the man. Not like you want him winding up dead."

Winding up dead. No, that was not the outcome she wanted for Pierce. Iris took the time to secure the door before walking—with as much grace as she could manage—toward Bryce. Then she snatched the plate from him. "That was not for you."

His jaw dropped. "But I'm hungry!"

"And do not ever call me desperate!" She sniffed. "You have no idea what I'm like."

"Oh, I've got a few ideas..." His gaze lingered on the food.

She pushed the plate down on the table. "And another thing—Pierce is certainly not dying." Her hands flew to her hips. "We are not going to let that happen."

His head tilted. "If you want him to keep breathing, then maybe you shouldn't invite him into your world—or your bed—when you've got danger dodging your steps. Not like being close to you is ever a safe place to be."

His words hurt. Mostly because they were the truth. "I thought I was safe."

"There is no safety, not for you. You were warned they'd look for you. That plenty of people would have you on their radar. When you have a skill set like yours, it's often in high demand." His gaze swept around her apartment. Lingered on a few of her canvases. "Been up to your old tricks?"

"I don't know what you're talking about." The canvases in that area were of local scenes. Buildings. People.

A whistle. "Come on, Iris. If I walk down the hall and go into your studio, what will I see?"

"Awesome, amazing works of art." Brittle. "What else?"

"Oh, I don't know." He scratched his chin. "Maybe some truly world-class forgeries?"

He was such an ass.

"The kind of forgeries that people would kill to get their greedy hands on...because those forgeries can be traded—by the right people—for the real deal. And by traded, I mean swapped. Used as tools so the masterpieces can be stolen."

"I didn't really need a breakdown, Bryce, but thanks so much. I know how things work in that world, remember?"

He stopped scratching his chin. "Then you get why you were targeted in the park this morning."

"I *got* it when Constantine Leos showed up at my door and offered me a job! Then *he* was in the park, mumbling something about option two, and the next thing I knew, those goons were grabbing me, Constantine had vanished, and if it hadn't been for Pierce, I would have been kidnapped!" Okay, her voice had risen. A lot. That happened when your day had truly been hell. She surged forward and jabbed him in the chest with her index finger. "I was out of the game! They shouldn't have found me!"

He winced. "You're poking kind of hard there, Iris."

"Your U.S. Marshal buddy told me that I would be safe here! That I would have a whole new life. That no one would know about what my past was like. I thought I was starting fresh. Then *you* showed up. Now, weeks later, Constantine is sniffing at my door!" She poked again. Hard.

His muscles tensed beneath her touch. "You're not suggesting I led him here?"

"I can't even get my handler to call me back. Franco has ghosted me!" So at this point, hell, she didn't even know what she was suggesting. Things were just *off*. Terrifyingly off.

"I didn't lead anyone to you," he fired back. "I was transferred, dammit! Once I got to Atlanta, I just checked in as a courtesy so that you would know you had a friendly face in town. Someone who could help in an emergency. How the hell was I supposed to know you had some kind of street fighter next door who would gladly kick the shit out of your enemies for you? When did he move in, anyway?"

"Last week." It had been at least three months since she'd last seen Bryce.

"Last week? And he's already coming by for dinner? Someone moves fast."

"It's not like that! We are friends." Except for the kiss. A kiss that had blown the whole friendship idea to hell and back. "For the record, he's not a street fighter. Pierce is a former Army

Ranger. And, second, *shouldn't* you know? I would have wagered that as soon as you got his name from your buddies at the police station, you would start a full search on him."

His eyelids flickered.

"You *did,*" she accused.

"Well, yes. But only because I thought it was one hell of a coincidence. He moved in, got close to you, then bam...your past is creeping back? And wasn't it super convenient that he just happened to be at the park this morning?"

"It wasn't convenient, it was more like a miracle. He saved me!" Pierce wasn't the villain. "Franco already did a check on him before Pierce moved in the building. He cleared Pierce. Said that Pierce was a decorated veteran."

Bryce didn't look either reassured or impressed. "Why was he there, Iris? So very early in the morning. In the exact same place you were. Doesn't that seem a little suspicious to you?"

Her finger stopped poking him. A chill swept over her body. "I didn't ask why he was there." In all the confusion, she'd just been grateful that he *had* been there.

"And that is why I am here tonight. Because you don't always think logically. I know you. You get ruled by emotion."

"Don't be a prick."

"It's an artist thing. Your head is in the clouds. You don't see danger when it's right in front of you—"

He was pushing her buttons. Every single one of them. "My head might be up in the clouds," *occasionally,* "but you keep on like this and my fist will be up your—"

"Okay! Jeez. I get it. The day was tense." He sidled around her. Sniffed the mashed potatoes. "Just don't go trusting the man just because you think he has nice eyes or some lovesick crap like that. You can't trust anyone in this town but me. You should know that."

"I *don't* trust you." How could she? "It's because of you and your FBI buddies that I lost my brother."

"About dear old Remy..."

Her stomach twisted.

"Guessing it's been a while since you've seen him."

There was no *guessing* involved. She turned to mirror his movements. "You know it has been."

"How would you like to change that situation?"

The twist got harder.

"How would you like..." Bryce studied her with a hooded gaze. "To make it so that your brother is a free man? No longer hunted by authorities. Given a whole, brand new, clean slate."

Her heartbeat doubled. "That's not possible."

"Anything is possible." His lips pursed. "But nothing is *free*. That's how it works. You just have to pay the right price, and amazing things can happen in this world."

"Are you trying to get me to bribe you?" Seriously? He was a Fed. "I don't have any money." She barely made enough to cover her rent.

A wince. "It's not a bribe. That would be illegal. And all the necessary pieces are not even in motion yet, but they are coming."

A frustrated huff of air escaped her. "Get to the point!"

"You don't have money. You have skills. You can trade those skills for your brother's freedom." He offered her an encouraging nod. "If you can do a certain job for the FBI, then we can talk about helping Remy."

"I don't like where this is going." At all.

"You don't like the idea of giving your brother a second chance? That's cold. Didn't expect it from you. Thought you'd jump at the opportunity to help him." He surged away and headed for her front door. "Oh, well. Time to go. I need to get dinner since *someone* wouldn't share."

She grabbed his arm. "Who were those men working for?"

"I told you earlier, they clammed up."

Her grip tightened. "But you suspect someone. That's why you're here. You...you want me to take the job with him?" With Constantine's boss? With the man who'd tried to have her *kidnapped?*

He turned toward her. All innocence. "Did I say that?"

"Do *not* make me start screaming at you." If he would just explain things in a normal, full manner, this conversation would be so much more helpful. And clear.

"There are more logistics to work out. But...you taking a new job, you reporting every single thing about that job back to me...let's just say that *could* be in your future."

She snatched her hand from him. "You—you can't be serious!"

"Sure, I can be. I'm a Fed. We're a serious group. Think about it, why don't you? I'll be back soon." He left her while she stared after him, stunned.

He could not be serious. He...

He was asking her to go back to the life she'd left behind. A life of lies and treachery. A life of danger and death.

And, most unbelievable of all, she was thinking about doing it...

Because I might be able to get my brother back. Her brother Remy—the only family that she had left. A brother that she hadn't seen in years. Not since the Feds had hauled her away, not since the terrible day she'd found her father, covered in blood.

***

Bryce Robertson exhaled as he stared at the door he'd just closed. He'd been sketchy on the details with Iris for a reason. There was one whole hell of a lot that he *had* to keep from her. When it came to secrets, he'd been holding them back from Iris for years. As for this nightmare of a case, yes, there was plenty she didn't know. Couldn't know. But she still had to take the job.

Iris wouldn't have a choice. Neither would he. He had orders to follow.

He turned from her door. Began to head back to the elevator. And wasn't even a little surprised when he heard the creak of nearby hinges. A quick glance showed him the big bruiser had just come out of his place. Pierce Jennings.

Sure, he knew the man's full name. He knew more about Pierce than Iris realized.

Pierce didn't smile. Didn't look curious or friendly or anything like that—he just glared.

Bryce sighed. *I knew he'd be a problem.* "Have a good night," he called cheerfully. "Real pleasure meeting you." And he kept heading toward the elevator.

Pierce followed him. More like, stalked him.

I do not have time for this crap.

Bryce slid into the elevator. He turned for the door. Pressed the button. Hoped the doors would close quickly—

They didn't. Mostly because Pierce had thrown up an arm to halt their progress.

Bryce kept his smile in place. "May I help you with something?"

"Is she in trouble?"

You have no idea. "Could you move your arm? I have places to be."

"Who wanted to take her?"

Bryce let his gaze sweep over the other man. "I don't see a badge." He double-checked. "Maybe I'm missing it?"

"Who wanted her?"

"You're not a Fed. You're not a cop. You're a bodyguard, a highly paid one, I'll grant you that, but still just a bodyguard. So why don't you run along and leave the real investigative work to the professionals, hmmm?"

And…Pierce smiled.

Oh, shit.

That grin was evil, and Bryce realized he needed to do a whole lot more digging on this guy. A *whole* lot more. "Uh, well, wait—"

"I am a bodyguard. So I'll do my job—and I'll keep a very careful watch on Iris's body. Don't you worry about that."

Nope. That wasn't the plan. Iris needed to—

Pierce stepped back. "I'll get started with that right away."

The doors were closing. Hell. Bryce's fingers flew forward. "No, wait—"

The elevator doors shut.

CHAPTER FOUR

Fury still burned inside of Pierce. He didn't like that FBI prick. Not even a little bit. He marched back to his place, pausing only briefly at Iris's door. Yes, he *had* said he'd go and watch her body, and as tempting as the prospect was...

This isn't a good time for me to be near her. Because he was far too close to the edge. He needed to get control back. Needed to get intel. Needed to get a sense of what the hell was happening and who he was dealing with.

Once inside his home, Pierce locked his door and reached for his phone. Wilde had amazing resources, and he intended to tap every single one of those outlets. When it came to tech and research, the Wilde crew was top notch. His call was answered on the second ring. After identifying himself, he said, "I need background. Everything that you can find for me on a woman named Iris Stuart." He rattled off her address. "I need this info yesterday."

"She a new client?"

"Potentially."

"I don't see anything about this case in my files. Has this check been approved?"

"Eric will back me up." Of that, he had no doubt. He and Eric Wilde—the owner of the company—went way back. When Eric learned about what had happened to Iris, he'd be all in for her protection. "Dig into her life." Yes, fine, he was prying. He was a nosey bastard by design. "Look for red flags. Danger signs. She was nearly abducted today, and I want to know why." He also wanted a deep dive performed on the federal agent. Agent Asshole had not inspired a ton of confidence in him. "Also, see what you can find on—"

A light rap at his door. Tentative. Nervous.

He took a couple of quick, quiet steps toward the front door. A glance through the peephole showed Iris. She looked absolutely delectable but uncertain. "Federal Agent Bryce Robertson," he bit out.

"Wait!" The female voice notched up as she pushed, "You want me to dig into a Fed's life? I am absolutely going to have to speak with Eric first before—"

"Do whatever you have to do. I just want the info." Yesterday.

Through the peephole, he saw Iris take a step back. She turned, as if to leave.

Oh, no, sweetheart. You came to me. You don't get to run now. "Got to go. I'll check in with you tomorrow." He slammed down the phone and wrenched open the door. "Iris."

She spun toward him. "I, um, thought you might be sleeping."

Not likely.

Her hands twisted in front of her. "Sorry about tonight."

"You don't need to apologize for a damn thing."

She nibbled on her lower lip. Sucked it in between her teeth.

Aw, fuck.

Then she let the lip go. "You're a bodyguard."

People kept bringing that up.

"I have heard about Wilde. Seen stories about them on the news. The firm has a great reputation."

Where was she going with this? "You want to come inside?"

She peeked inside, then back at him. "It's late. This probably wasn't a good idea."

"Come inside." Not a question. He had the feeling that if he let her go, he would be making a terrible mistake. It was all he could do not to put his hands on her, curl his fingers around her slender shoulders, and pull her into his home.

"How does one go about hiring a bodyguard?" Iris blurted. "You know...should one be in the market for that sort of thing."

His eyes narrowed. "You need a bodyguard."

"Me? No." She rocked back half a step. "Well, you know. Potentially. I did have that incident today, so I was curious."

Oh, yes, the incident. As if he could ever forget it. "Iris?" With a mighty effort, he kept his tone mild. Mildish.

"Yes?"

"Get in my place. *Now.*"

Her nose scrunched. "Bossy."

"Want me to carry you in?" He would be delighted to do so.

She walked by. Sniffed.

He slammed the door behind her. Secured it. Then shoved his shoulders back against the wood. "Talk."

"Did you eat the meatloaf?"

"Nice try, but that's not what I want you talking about."

Her hands fluttered in the air. All delicate and butterfly-ish and nervous-like. "How much are your fees?"

Honestly? They were a fucking lot at Wilde. "Negotiable," he answered, voice clipped.

"How negotiable?"

"We'll get to that later." One step at a time. "First, I want to know what kind of trouble you're in."

Her hands twisted in front of her even as her chin dipped down. "You won't like me."

"What? Couldn't quite hear you." He pushed away from the door and closed in on her. He *thought* that he'd heard her words, but he must have been wrong.

"Do you have to take a case, even if you find something about the client objectionable? Is that perhaps a bodyguard rule?"

There wasn't a damn thing objectionable about her. She was pure perfection as far as he was concerned. "Personal feelings don't matter on the job. The client's safety is the only priority." Truth.

Her chin nearly touched her shirt.

His hand reached out, slid under her chin, and tipped back her head. "Iris?"

Her eyes were so very dark and deep. Shadowed by secrets. "Is there a contract I should sign?" she whispered. "Something that swears you to secrecy? I mean, confidentiality?"

"I will keep your secrets." Contract or no contract. "But, yes, there is something you can sign, if that makes you feel better. We can go to Wilde tomorrow and take care of business." His thumb slid over her chin in a light caress, and he *had* to say, "There are lots of qualified agents at Wilde. You can talk to—"

"I want *you*."

Heat flooded through him even as he yanked savagely back on the leash of his control. She hadn't meant that she wanted him physically. Iris had meant that she wanted him for the job. Obviously.

But try telling that to his overeager dick.

"You were quite incredible today," Iris continued quietly. "I've never seen anyone fight like that."

He kept his hold light on her chin. "You mean you never saw anyone that vicious." He knew what he was. Long before he'd joined the Army, he'd been fighting in the streets. Not like he had some enchanted freaking backstory. He'd grown up poor and on streets that had been hell. He'd fought for everything he ever had. Then he'd joined the Army and fought for Uncle Sam. Been trained to be even more brutal.

But he could be careful. He knew how to handle delicate things. Iris was very, very delicate. Especially compared to him.

"I didn't call you vicious." Low and husky. Her tongue darted over her lower lip. "I thought you were tough."

He wanted her mouth. When he'd had her in his arms before, desire had ignited. He wouldn't be forgetting her sweet taste anytime soon. Pierce even found himself leaning toward her.

No. Stop.

Because she'd come to his door out of fear. Not desire. Only a bastard would take advantage of her emotions.

I have been known to be a real bastard on plenty of occasions.

But, maybe this one time, he could be something else. Maybe. He let her go. Stepped back. "I can have a contract waiting for you at Wilde first thing tomorrow. We can drive to the office, get the paperwork signed, and you will have yourself an official bodyguard for however long you want me."

Her head bobbed in a quick, eager nod. "That would be very good."

"But..." He had to warn her, "I'll need answers at that point."

"A-answers?"

"Yeah. Like I'll want to know a few pesky details. Details about just *why* you want protection. About who is after you. And why the hell the FBI is involved."

Iris swallowed. "Right. Those details."

"Um." She did not look to be in the sharing mood. Maybe once she had the contract signed, things would change. Or maybe not. So he decided to push. "I'd also like to know just what you think I might find objectionable about you."

Her arms wrapped around her stomach. "Have you ever broken the law?"

"Have you?" An automatic response.

She flinched.

*Well, well...*He'd take that flinch as an affirmative.

"I should go." Her gaze jumped to the door, then back to him. "We'll talk more after the contract is signed. Much better plan." But she didn't move.

Neither did he. He was actually blocking her path and trying to figure out what the hell he could say to—

"I should go," she repeated. "But they know where I live."

They.

"Constantine Leos was at the park today. He was the third man there. He—he was the one at my door last night. And I'm really afraid he might come back while I sleep."

The hell he would. "You're staying here."

Her eyes flared. "You—is that okay?"

More than okay. He insisted on it. "Hell, yes. You're staying here." If she tried to leave, he'd just be carrying her back. Or he'd be bunking on the floor at her place. If Iris thought those jokers might make another run at her while she slept and was vulnerable, he *would* be close. Every moment.

"I can take the couch." She darted a quick glance at his new couch. "Plenty of room for me. And I promise, I won't be any trouble."

Oh, baby, you have been trouble from the word go.

She winced. "Correction, I won't be *much* trouble. I get that having your neighbor pop over with all this drama is probably not what you expected when you moved into the building." She huffed out a breath. "Know what? I'm probably worrying too much. I'll be okay at my place. I'll set my alarm. I'll lock my doors. I'll be fine." A fast step forward. "I'll see you tomorrow." Another step.

A step that had her nearly brushing against his body. Her honey and cream scent teased his nose, and he inhaled deeply to draw her in. "You're not going anywhere."

Her head tilted back. Those chocolate eyes of hers met his.

I won't let you get away.

"Pierce?"

"You will sleep in my bed." Oh, the images those words conjured. If only. *Soon.* For now... "I'll take the damn couch."

"No. I'll be fine. I'll be—"

"The contract might not be signed yet, but I consider myself to already be on the clock." He didn't, but whatever. He thought that line might sway her. "You need to be able to sleep peacefully. If you go back to your place, you'll be nervous. Jumping at every creak and rustle."

"How do you know that?"

"Because it's what other clients have done. I know fear when I see it." He hated to see it in her eyes. "You're safe with me." A promise. "In order to get to you, your enemies will have to walk through me."

"I'm smaller than you."

His gaze swept from the top of her head down to her sneaker-clad feet. Then back up. "I have noticed that."

A delightful red filled her cheeks. "I meant that I would fit on the couch better than you. There is no need for you to give up your bed."

He thought about offering to share the bed with her. Ever so tempting. Unfortunately, they weren't quite to that point yet, but a man could dream. "I've slept in plenty of spots that were a hell of a lot less comfortable than the couch. Don't worry about me."

"You are so nice."

Friend zone, dead ahead. "Yeah...about that..." A long exhale. "No."

She blinked. "No?"

A most definite *no*. "I'm a bastard. I'm dangerous. Devious. Possessive." Oh, he had lots of bad traits. Probably best not to hit the whole highlight reel just yet. "But when you've got trouble tracking you, I am just the right kind of guy you need at your side. Not a *nice* guy. Nice guys don't get shit done. I do. Count on it."

"That's...good to know?" The words were a definite question.

"It's fantastic to know. So don't make the mistake of thinking I am *nice*."

"Duly noted. You're dangerous. Devious."

Damn straight. He pointed to the right. "Bedroom is in there. Make yourself comfortable."

"I should go back to my place. Get some essentials."

Sure. "I'll escort you."

"I—"

"Bodyguard, remember? That means I will be keeping the best possible watch on your body. From here on out, I'll be your shadow. So you'd better get used to me sticking close."

***

I will be keeping the best possible watch on your body.

He hadn't meant those words in a sexual way.

Iris shifted on the bed. His bed. His massive bed with black silk sheets and the most cushiony mattress ever. Pierce had helped her pack up for the night, then he'd escorted her back to his place. He'd made sure she was settled before shutting the bedroom door.

He hadn't pushed for more info. Iris suspected he was saving the push for tomorrow, for right *after* she signed the contract with Wilde. She'd been desperate when she knocked on his door. With what the Feds wanted her to do...

I'm terrified.

And the only safe place to turn?

Pierce.

So now she was in his bed. He was on the couch, and she was unable to sleep because she kept thinking not about her attack, but about him. About the kiss they'd shared. And about the fact that they hadn't talked about the kiss at all. Not even a casual mention of the most intense kiss she'd ever experienced.

Priorities. She should have them. The goons after her were priority one, but thinking about

Pierce was a whole lot less scary. Thinking about Pierce made her feel good. Thinking about him—

The door hinges creaked. She stopped breathing. Her body just froze as—

His head poked inside the doorway. She'd left on his bedside lamp because she liked a little light, and Iris could easily see him. The tension swept from her body even as a gasp spilled from her lips.

"You're still awake?" Pierce asked. He'd obviously heard her gasp.

She tugged the cover a little higher. "Y-yes."

"I was just checking on you." He opened the door wider. "You need anything?"

It would be so very wrong to say...*You.* "Nope. Nothing. Not a thing. I'm great."

He took a step inside.

Her breath caught in her throat.

"It's okay to be scared," he told her, voice all low and soothing. And there he went, being nice again. She didn't buy the devious line he'd tried to sell her. She'd met plenty of devious people in her time—hell, when it came to deviousness, her family pretty much held a controlling share in the empire. She knew someone good when she saw him, and Pierce was *good*. That was why she was so drawn to him.

"You had a terrible experience today," he added somewhat roughly. "It never should have happened, and I'm just—fuck, I'm glad I was there."

Right. Yes. There. And about being *there*...Iris slowly sat up. She wore a tank top and a pair of cotton pajama pants so it wasn't like she was flashing him, but she still tugged the cover with her, as if it was some sort of shield. "Why were you there?"

"Excuse me?"

"Why were you in the park this morning?"

Tension seemed to snake through the bedroom.

"I could say..." His voice came slowly. Deeper than before. "That I was just out for an early morning run. There are lots of jogging paths in that particular park."

Yes, there were.

"But I'd be lying if I gave you that story."

She fisted the cover.

"I was in the park because I knew you'd be there."

Bryce's words rushed through her mind. *Why was he there, Iris? So very early in the morning. Doesn't that seem a little suspicious to you?* "Because of me?" A whisper.

"I was worried about you. After the scene last night, with that jerk at your door, I thought it might be a good idea to keep an eye on you."

Some of the tension slipped from her. "So you aren't some crazy stalker or something? You were just doing random bodyguard duty on a new friend?"

"Sure."

What kind of response was *sure?* Iris needed more than that. "Could you just very specifically tell me that I don't have anything to fear from you, that you don't intend to lie and betray me, and that you are not working for anyone who may want to use me for nefarious purposes?"

He took another step toward the bed. "Nefarious? That's an interesting word. Means wicked...criminal."

Yes, she knew exactly what it meant.

"I won't be doing anything criminal. But are you sure you don't want me doing wicked things with you?"

Her heart thudded hard in her chest.

His hands were loose at his sides. He looked extra big and dangerous in the weak light cast from the lamp. He didn't have on his shirt, and she could make out the expanse of muscles on his chest. The line of abs that stretched for days. The twelve pack. Not a six there, no way. All fierce strength. Hard male. *Wicked*.

"I'm not working for anyone." A pause. "Except for you, and we both know that's a recent development."

Very recent.

"You can count on the fact that I will never betray you, I will never hurt you, and I will never do anything to cause you so much as a moment of fear."

Her breath whispered out. "Thank you."

He leaned forward, opened his mouth as if he'd say more, then seemed to catch himself. His head jerked in a hard nod. "I'll go back to the couch."

Stay. Her lips clamped together. She was not quite in control of herself. "Thank you for being so nice to me."

He turned away. "You don't need to thank me."

"When someone saves your life, I'm pretty sure it's customary to do so. Super polite and all that."

His back stiffened.

"Thanks for being my friend," Iris added a little weakly, mostly because she didn't want him to leave. She felt better when Pierce was close.

But at her words, his head turned. His stare locked on her. His expression had hardened. Shifted into more savage lines. "I'm not just going to be your friend."

Of course, he'd be her bodyguard, too, once she signed the contract—

"The kiss mattered, Iris."

The kiss. The one that had made her whole body ache and yearn. The one that had led to her legs being wrapped tightly around him and her rubbing herself against him as frantically as she could.

"We will be talking about it again," he promised.

Then he walked out. The door closed softly behind him.

"Yes," she agreed. "We will."

CHAPTER FIVE

The Wilde office building was impressive. Correction, make that super impressive. Huge and gleaming and filled with people running around like bees. And Pierce? He had an office on the top floor. An office with a magnificent view and fancy furniture, and she'd sort of thought that he spent his days working as a bodyguard but this whole scene made her think that maybe he was actually...in charge of things? That he might hold some seriously imposing title at the company?

She peeked out the window. Her fingers automatically twitched because Iris sure wished that she had a pencil and sketchbook with her. The view should be captured. It seemed a crime not to share it with everyone.

Crime. Right. That would be the reason she was currently in the building.

"Okay," Pierce announced as he strolled back into the office. "Got the paperwork. You sign it, and you officially have me. Twenty-four, seven, at your beck and call."

She whirled around. "Who are you?"

He held the contract in one hand. An eyebrow quirked. "Your neighbor? Pierce Jennings? That ringing some bells?"

Her hand waved toward the luxury around her. "This isn't the office of some junior bodyguard."

A smile pulled at his lips. "I never said I was junior anything."

She hurried toward him. "Are you in charge?"

His head moved in a slow, negative shake. "Nope. That would be my buddy, Eric Wilde." Pierce glanced over his shoulder. "Honestly, I figure he'll be making his way inside pretty soon. He's gonna want to talk with you."

She'd actually crossed paths with Eric Wilde once or twice before. Most people in the town knew of him. "Why?" Surely, it wasn't standard practice for him to talk with all clients.

"Because you're a VIP."

No, she was not. "What is happening here?" Everything felt out of control. Including her.

Sighing, he marched around the desk, removed a pen from a drawer, and then put the contract flat on top of the desk. He lifted the pen toward her. "Why don't we go ahead and sign, hmmm?"

Not so fast. "Why do you live in my building if you are some big deal here? I'm sure you get paid bags of money."

"Bags?" His lips twitched. A gleam appeared in his blue eyes. "Not quite. And I like the building. That's why I'm there. I also like Eric Wilde, and that's why I'm working for him here. As for the office...yes, technically, I am a VP at the company."

"Then you *shouldn't* be taking some lowly bodyguard job with me." This was all wrong. As a

VP, he probably didn't even go out into the field. She'd misread everything. "I should get someone else..." No, correction. She *had* to get someone else. No way could she afford to pay some VP. His rates had to be astronomical. "You are way beyond my budget."

He kept offering her the pen. "Told you already, the fee is negotiable."

Iris inched toward him. "If you're a VP, you can't just drop all of your responsibilities and shadow me." They probably needed him close for big meetings.

"You don't quite get how Wilde works. Even VPs are expected to do field work. We *want* to do the work. It keeps us fresh and focused. I have a partner, you met Colt the other night. He'll have my back, both for things here in the office and for your case. There is nothing for you to worry about."

There was plenty for her to worry about. She hadn't given him any specifics about her case yet, and when he learned just what she was facing...

He wiggled the pen. "Come sign the contract, Iris."

She took another inching step toward him.

The phone on the desk rang. Sighing, he reached forward, tapped a button on it, and said, "I'm in a meeting right now—"

"*Federal agents are here,*" a hushed voice said. The voice was hushed, but Pierce had the speaker on, so Iris could easily make out the words. "*Coming up the elevator now. They want your client.*"

Her heart sank.

"They won't get her." A flat response from Pierce. He hit the button again. Only this time, the call ended, and silence filled the room. Pierce kept his right hand around the pen. Wiggled it once more. "Sign it before they arrive."

She shook her head. "No, I can't drag you into this mess—"

His head cocked. "Want me to forge the signature for you?"

Forge. Ice poured through her veins, and she had to blink quickly. "That's what got me into this mess." Another hard shake of her head. Her hair flew around her shoulders. "No. No. I-I'll do what they want. I'm sure they will give me backup." God, she hoped so. "Everything will be okay." Iris spun away from him.

"I am your backup. And when you sign this contract, we will have a legally binding agreement. That agreement will tie us together, no matter what happens when the Feds arrive. I'm not going to let them take you away. Whatever is going on—whatever is scaring you, trust me, I can handle it."

She wanted to trust him. She was tired of being afraid and shouldering everything on her own.

"Sign it..." Pierce said, voice low.

Her head turned back toward him.

"Sign it, then you can tell me all your deepest, darkest secrets, and I will carry them to my grave if that is what you want."

Her feet took her to him, as if drawn helplessly. Iris stopped when their bodies nearly brushed. "I don't want you in a grave. That is my major stipulation. You don't get hurt."

"I tend to be the one who does the hurting, or did you miss that at the park?"

His skills at the park were the whole reason she'd come up with her desperate plan in the first place.

He took her hand. His slightly callused fingertips slid over her skin as he curled her fingers around the pen. "Better hurry. Your Fed buddies will be arriving any moment."

"They aren't my buddies." She leaned over the desk. Signed her name on the line. "They are—"

The door flew open with a *whoosh* of dramatic sound. She jerked up and partially turned, even as Pierce's arm wrapped around her stomach, and he pulled her back against the hard strength of his body.

FBI Agent Bryce Robertson stood in the doorway, his cheeks flushed a red to match his hair. Another man—with dark hair and glinting eyes—glowered behind him. And a stylishly dressed woman with cheetah-colored glasses shoved her hands against their backs. "I tried to keep them out!" she announced. "Don't worry. I'm going to get Eric. No Feds are gonna push us around!"

Bryce strode forward. He held out his hand to Iris. "We need to go. Now."

"Go where?" Iris asked. But she knew. The job. He wanted to feed her to the wolves.

Before Bryce could answer, Pierce's hold tightened even more around her. "Yeah..." He drawled. "That's just not going to happen. Iris is not going anywhere without me."

"Who the hell is he?" The low question came from the man nudging closer to Bryce. The man wearing the same starchy-looking type of suit. Bryce's partner. Travis Clark. They'd both been relocated to Atlanta together.

"He's the neighbor," Bryce fired back. "No one for us to worry about." His gaze remained on her. "Iris. We are leaving, now."

Pierce very gently—but firmly—repositioned Iris so that she was behind him. How did he do that repositioning? He picked her up. Put her down behind him. Then placed the wall of his body between her and the Feds. "So, point one, I am someone for you to worry about. You should worry very much about me. Smart people do. And, point two, I have a signed contract that says Iris goes *nowhere* without me."

"What are you talking about?" Bryce demanded.

"I'm her bodyguard. That means I go where she goes. I stand between her and any threat. Iris isn't coming with you. So you might as well turn around in your shitty suits and get the hell out of my office."

***

"You just couldn't take my advice, could you?" Bryce Robertson demanded an hour later.

Pierce sent him a cool smile. "I like to make my own choices. A little personality quirk I possess." The Feds hadn't cleared out. They also hadn't taken Iris. Because they couldn't. *I will not give her up*. And legally, they seemed to have no excuse to take her. At least, not one they'd shared...yet.

Pierce's patience was about to run out. He was skating way too close to the empty line on the tank.

"Yes, well, you've made one hell of a bad choice today, buddy." Bryce began to pace. He and his partner—a guy who'd identified himself as Special Agent Travis Clark—kept exchanging nervous glances. They should be nervous. Pierce was not in the mood for their shit.

What he did want? Answers. Every single one of them.

"It would have been so much easier if you'd just come with us, Iris," Bryce grumbled. "But no, I go to your place this morning. You're gone, and I have to track you down."

"So sorry to inconvenience you." Iris didn't sound the least bit sorry.

Pierce's shoulder brushed against hers. He wasn't moving away from her. He wanted the agents to know that he would be standing at her side no matter what.

Bryce paused in his pacing and pointed toward Pierce. "What the hell do you think he'll be able to do?"

Watch and see, asshole.

"Well," came Iris's cool reply, "he was able to save me the other day in the park, so I'm rather hoping he can continue with that trend."

Bryce snorted. "You don't think he's out of his league? Have you even told him what he's up against?"

"Hard for me to do when I don't know exactly myself." Again, she was cool. Surprising, because Pierce didn't think of her as a particularly cold person. She was fire and emotion. Energy brimming to the surface. "You wouldn't tell me who hired those men who came after me."

"That's because they didn't talk," Bryce fired back. "They clammed up and haven't admitted jack."

"But you suspect someone," Pierce cut in to say. "Obviously. So why not share?"

Again, Bryce and his partner exchanged an uneasy glance. Bryce shuffled a little closer to Iris. "You sure you want him knowing all this? I told you before, you can't trust anyone—"

Pierce took Iris's small hand in his. Threaded his fingers with hers. "She can trust me. I've got a signed contract that says my first and only loyalty is to her. I will protect her, I will keep her secrets, and I will stand between her and any danger that comes." The danger he saw at that particular moment? It was the Feds. The Feds who'd just been stalling and wasting his time.

"They want to use me," Iris confessed.

Bryce looked briefly uncomfortable. "You'll get something from the deal. I told you that."

Pierce didn't let go of Iris. "What's the deal? And, please, do go into detail. Lots of detail. Be very specific."

The faint lines near Bryce's mouth bracketed. "They want Iris's talent."

Her talent. "Her art?"

"Her specialty is Impressionism. She can do a Monet so well that you would swear you were looking at an original." Admiration filled Bryce's tone. "Hell, I once brought in four experts who couldn't tell the difference between hers and his—so I am not just bullshitting you. She's the real damn deal. Best in the world, in fact, when it comes to replicating his work. There is no comparison for anyone else."

Pierce's head swung toward her. "You're a forger?"

She flinched. "No."

"She *was* a forger," Bryce qualified. "A very high priced, very good—"

"No!" Louder. Harder. She yanked her fingers from Pierce's grasp. "I wasn't. I was practicing. Experiencing art. I didn't know why he wanted the paintings. I didn't know what he did with them. If I had known, I would *not* have made them. I was a kid, for God's sake. Only seventeen when I realized the truth."

"That's why you stayed out of prison," Travis pointed out, his voice gravelly. "Because you were a minor."

"I stayed out of prison because I didn't do anything wrong!" A sharp retort from Iris. "I didn't know what was going to happen with the paintings I created! I didn't know what he intended to do!"

Bryce's face twisted. "Still saying that, are you?"

"I *trusted* my father. That was my mistake." Her gaze darkened with pain. "Not like it's a mistake I will ever repeat since he died during the course of *your* investigation."

What in the fuck? Pierce wished he'd been able to get hold of her file before this meeting. But the Wilde team hadn't finished their research. There were so many things he needed to know. Iris remained too much of a mystery to him.

"Your father was taken out by his employer. An unforeseen and tragic event." Bryce straightened. The lines near his mouth deepened. "You know I have always been very, very sorry about what happened to him."

She swiped a hand over her cheek. God, was she crying? Pierce stiffened.

"So am I," Iris returned. Pain cracked in her voice. "Because I trusted *you* when you said everything would be okay. You were a Fed. You were supposed to help. Instead, I walked in and found my dad covered in blood. My brother had vanished, and I was left with *no one*."

Her pain beat at him. Pierce glared at the two Feds. He held them responsible for this shit. All he wanted to do was pull Iris into his arms and take away all her pain.

"So you can see, Agent Robertson," Iris continued grimly as she swiped at her cheek again, "why when you came to me last night and said you were the *only one* I could trust—"

Oh, he'd said that, had he? Prick.

"You can see why I didn't jump at the opportunity you presented to me. Trusting you didn't work out so well for me before, and I wasn't going to enter any deal with you blindly ever again. I needed someone who would have my back. Someone I actually *could* trust." Her tear-filled eyes—eyes that could break a man's heart—met Pierce's. "I needed you."

And she had him.

He reached onto his desk. Snagged a tissue. Very gently patted it over her cheek. Her hand flew up and caught his. Her fingers curled around his wrist.

"I'm not a criminal," Iris told him.

His brow furrowed.

Her eyes searched his. "Don't hate me, don't—"

His head shook. "Sweetheart..." The endearment slipped from him. "Do I look like I give a damn about what you've done?"

Her breath caught. Hope flickered in the darkness of her gaze. The amber flecks burned. "You...you don't care?"

Bryce swore. "Of course, this jerk doesn't care. He probably doesn't care about anything or anyone—"

"Wrong." A growl from Pierce. The FBI agent kept pushing his buttons. But he didn't waste energy glaring at Bryce. Instead, he kept his focus where it mattered. On Iris. "I care about you," he told her simply. The words were true. He did care about her. Iris had become very important to him, very quickly. Where she was concerned, he was all the fuck in.

Her breath shuddered out. "Thank you."

He caught another tear drop with his tissue. Carefully wiped it away. "Don't do it again."

Her lashes fluttered. "The art? I—"

"She's gonna have to do it," Travis cut in to say, sounding both pompous and pissy at the same time. "She's part of the plan. We need her or it won't work."

"Not talking about the art." Pierce's gaze still stayed where it mattered—on her. "Don't cry, Iris. I don't like it when you hurt."

Her lips parted. He wanted to kiss her, but they had an annoying audience watching their every move. If he had his way, Pierce would get Iris far away from those guys. He'd get her someplace safe. And he'd keep her there.

But, first, apparently, there was some unfinished business from her past that needed handling. Good thing he excelled at ending unfinished business.

"You don't even know her," Bryce groused. "And you're going to jump in and play hero? Seriously?"

Her tears had stopped.

"Yes." No hesitation. "Seriously." It was what he did—or rather, what he would do, for her. Slowly, his gaze pulled from her, and he gazed at Bryce because that guy had to be the senior FBI agent. He was, after all, the one doing the most talking. "How about you speed things along, tell us your plan, and we'll see if Iris and I are going to be participating?"

Bryce jerked his head in a nod. "Fine."

He'd rather thought it would be *fine*.

"This is what needs to happen. Iris will reach out to Constantine. He gave her his number when he visited before. She'll tell him she changed her mind, that she will take the job." He sniffed. "You can name some crazy amount of money, Iris, say that you need it so that you can go back to living that high-class life you used to love, and you can act like the money is why you changed your mind."

"I want to know who Constantine is working for first." Iris's voice was low but determined.

Bryce began to pace again. "Once you're pulled into the game, we'll make sure you're wired for your interactions. We want to catch this whole ring. Get enough evidence to lock them all away."

"I want to know," she repeated, "who Constantine is working for *first*."

His gaze swept toward her.

"I thought Constantine had gotten out of the business," Iris added. "He was on the edges when my father died. Not a major player at all. Everything blew up, and I assumed he ran as fast and far as everyone else."

Bryce's head tipped toward her. "You assume that because he used to be close with your brother, Remy."

Pierce made a mental note to conduct a deep dive on her brother's background, ASAP. This missing brother was apparently a very important piece of the puzzle that was Iris.

"Yes." A hiss from her. "And I can't help but wonder..." Her words trailed away.

Bryce and Travis shared a long look.

"Is the brother involved or not?" Pierce snapped into the lingering silence. "Dammit, I told you I wanted a fast retelling. I don't want you two keeping secrets. That's not going to work." At all. "Either you deal straight with us, or you don't deal with us at all."

Iris's gaze flickered to him.

He rolled one shoulder. "I have a tendency to hate unnecessary bullshit."

"I will remember that," she promised him.

Bryce cleared his throat. "Her brother—he *is* part of the deal." A cough. "As I indicated to Iris previously, if she cooperates, if she is able to secure the evidence we need, then the FBI is willing to enter into an…arrangement with her brother."

He didn't like where this was going. "What sort of arrangement?"

"They'll wipe away his crimes," Iris answered. "That's *my* arrangement. If they want me helping, then they'll agree that Remy can stop being a wanted man."

A jerk of Bryce's chin. "Yes, provided that in the course of this investigation we don't discover that Remy *is* in fact, the man pulling the strings."

So the Feds might be sending Iris in to bring down her own brother. How wonderful. "You don't know for sure who you're after." What a cluster. They didn't have a target, but they were pushing Iris straight into danger.

"The men in custody won't talk." From Travis. "They're too scared. But we've been after someone for a while who has been executing a global art theft ring. Taking masterpieces and leaving flawless substitutes. We're talking about millions and millions. We want this ring stopped, and Iris is the in that we need in order to achieve our goal."

All eyes turned to her.

Her lips twisted in a sad smile. "Lucky me."

CHAPTER SIX

Normally, she had terrible luck. After all, her life had turned out to be a lie. Her father had been a criminal all along. Not some devoted family man. And she'd been the one to find him as he bled out and struggled to speak.

Definitely *not* what she'd call a charmed life.

Then there had been the whole witness protection drama. Iris had been ripped away from everything she'd ever known and loved. She'd been ordered to switch locations—and identities—multiple times over the years. Atlanta had been her most recent relocation. It had just started to feel like home and then...

Pierce. He'd moved in right next door. And maybe, just maybe, he might be the luckiest thing that had ever happened to her. The luckiest and the best.

"Don't do it," Pierce ordered her. They were back in her home. The Feds had finally left them. Pierce had gathered with some other Wilde agents for a fierce and fast briefing—one that she hadn't been allowed to witness. Then he'd grabbed a manila file, shoved it into his briefcase, and they'd rushed back to their building. The drive home had been quiet. Tense. In fact, these were the first words he'd said to her...

Don't do it.

"Excuse me?" Iris turned back toward him. She had Constantine's card in her hand. She'd just been about to make the call.

"Don't." He stalked toward her. Reached for her hand. Took the card. "You don't have to do this. Screw the FBI agents. There is no reason to put yourself in danger for them. You don't owe them anything."

He was wrong. There was a very big reason to put herself at risk. "I want my brother back."

"Your brother could be the one behind this mess. The FBI agents could know that and be deceiving you. This whole thing could be a trap."

She shook her head. "No. Remy wouldn't do this."

"Baby..."

Her shoulders stiffened. It was the second time he'd used an endearment with her. First, he'd called her sweetheart. Now baby. Was that a casual thing for him? It wasn't casual for her. Nothing about this situation—or Pierce—was casual for her. "He wouldn't. Remy saw what that world did to our family. There is no way that he'd go all dark side and now be the evil mastermind running things."

His head tilted to the right. "I get that you believe that."

Good. Because she did. With all of her being. Her brother wouldn't become some evil international thief.

He wouldn't be like our dad.

"But people can change," Pierce warned her. "Everyone has a bad side. Some people are just better at hiding that side than others."

"I don't believe that." Yes, her father had hidden secrets, and when she'd learned the truth, she'd been gutted. But, not everyone would do that. She couldn't believe that. Wouldn't.

"You don't believe that people can hide their true selves? Oh, trust me, it can be done."

"No, I get that it can be done." She certainly understood that far too well. "I'm just saying it's a minority of the population. Not everyone is like that." Her left hand rose and pressed to his chest. "You don't have a bad side."

He stiffened. She actually felt the tensing of his muscles beneath her touch before he glanced down at her hand. "You're wrong." Rasping. "I have one of the baddest sides you can ever imagine. Just doesn't come out often." He swallowed. "Only when absolutely necessary."

"Are you talking about what you did in the park? Because that wasn't a bad side. That was you saving my life." More badass than anything else.

"When that side of me comes out, you'll know it."

A little shiver skated over her. She should probably stop touching him.

Iris didn't move her hand. "Do you think less of me?"

"What the hell kind of question is that?"

A fair one. "Other people did. I was a seventeen-year-old girl who suddenly had every friend in her life cutting her dead. My boyfriend wouldn't even talk to me—"

"Dumbass."

Yes, true assessment. Grady had been a dumbass. But he hadn't been the only one to cut her out. "Neighbors turned away. My father was dead. My mother had passed away when I was much, much younger. And my brother had just vanished. At first, I thought...maybe someone would help. Maybe someone would take me in." But... "There was no one." She slowly pulled her hand back. "I'm sure it was for the best." Iris cleared her throat. "I had to go into witness protection anyway, so it was better to leave without any ties holding me back—"

"There's someone now," he told her roughly. "And I don't plan to go anywhere."

Do not throw your arms around him. Do not. But she wanted to, so very badly. Again, Iris had the thought that maybe, finally, she'd gotten lucky. "Thank you."

"You don't need to thank me." His eyes were on her mouth. "I haven't done anything...yet."

"You took the job." Her heart suddenly pounded way too fast. Her body leaned a little bit too close to him. "That's something."

"You shouldn't make the phone call."

She'd been angling up toward his mouth. His words hit her like a surge of icy water. *The case.* Iris shook her head. "I'm doing this. If you want to back out, if I need to find another bodyguard—"

"We just covered that I'm not the type to leave. If you want to make contact with this Constantine, fine, we will. But I'll set the ground rules."

Her eyes narrowed. "I'm not sure that's how this relationship works." Wasn't the bodyguard supposed to follow the orders of the client?

"No?" His brows lifted. "You've had lots of relationships with bodyguards, then?"

"This is my first one."

"Um, thought so. We'll cover the ground rules, and then *I'll* make the call."

"You're rather bossy, aren't you?" Not the first time she'd noticed this tendency.

"Sorry. I'll work on that."

"Do that." Her arms crossed over her chest.

"Our goal is the same." He towered over her. "To keep you alive. To keep you safe. To keep you from getting so much as a bruise on your silken skin."

He thought her skin was silken? "Okay..."

"You have to follow my orders. Even if you don't understand why I'm giving an order. I have experience, I know danger, and I know the steps we have to take to ensure your protection. The ground rules are...you follow my lead. You stick with me. You don't allow yourself to be separated from me under any circumstances. I can't protect you if I'm not close."

Now she felt her brow scrunch. "How are we going to manage that? There are probably going to be some instances when they want you away from me. Actually, how are we even going to keep you—"

"Sweetheart, I have a plan."

"You did it again," Iris had to point out. "Do you know that you've used an endearment with me three times so far?"

He smiled at her. His baby blues twinkled. "Been counting, have you?"

"No." She took a half-step back.

His grin stretched. What did he find amusing about this situation?

"Yes," she decided to confess. "I counted. But only because you shouldn't be doing it. We are not in a-a relationship and—"

"We'll pretend to be. So do keep that in mind. It's showtime."

We'll pretend to be.

He peered at the card he still held in his hand. Then pulled out his phone. He dialed quickly and put the phone to his ear. His eyes stayed on her, but his smile had vanished. After a beat he said, "Constantine?"

Her chest tightened.

She heard the rumble of Constantine's voice.

Pierce smirked in response. "Who am I? I'm Iris's fucking boyfriend. That's who I am. I'm the man who left your piece-of-shit buddies moaning on the ground in the park. You come at Iris again, and I'm the man who will kill you."

She was pretty sure her eyes were about to pop out of her head. With a monumental effort, Iris clamped her open mouth shut.

Pierce wasn't done. "You don't mess with her, understand me? You don't even look sideways at her." A snarl.

Constantine said something in response. She couldn't make out the words.

Then Pierce snapped, "What? You think you have business to conduct with her? The hell you do. Any business you have will go through *me*.

And because of the shit that went down in the park, Iris's fees just doubled."

She *could* hear the sudden curses that exploded from Constantine.

"Did I stutter?" Pierce wanted to know. "Do you have a poor connection? Just in case, I will repeat...*doubled*. Try anything else, and they will triple."

Silence.

Maybe Constantine was afraid to say anything. Iris realized she was holding her breath.

"And here's the big deal *breaker*," Pierce continued grimly. "She will do the job, but *only* if I am with her. After the BS you pulled, there is no way I'm letting her out of my sight. So either accept the terms of the deal or you and your boss can screw off."

Pierce hung up. Rolled back his shoulders as if shaking off tension. Then said, "I think that went well, don't you?"

CHAPTER SEVEN

No, things had not gone well. They had gone horribly. And...fast. They'd also gone fast. Because an hour later, Iris was in the back of a mysterious limo with Pierce at her side. The car had appeared at her doorstep, and she'd gotten a text from Constantine telling her to get into the vehicle.

Pierce had gotten in first.

They hadn't taken any bags. She sure hoped this wasn't some long trip. But Iris was certain that Pierce *had* come packing—she'd noticed the slight bulge under his jacket. *A gun.*

He lounged against the seat of the limo as if he didn't have a care in the world. Meanwhile, she kept twisting her hands together in a vain attempt to hide the shaking of her fingers.

"Relax," his voice rumbled toward her. "This is what we wanted."

Not exactly. She'd never *wanted* a life of crime. She'd tried very hard to put it all behind her. Iris shook her head. Her lips parted. "I—"

He pulled her toward him. His mouth took hers.

What is happening?

His tongue dipped past her lips. A sensual tasting that made her forget about her shaking fingers. He kissed her slowly, leisurely, seductively. As if they had all the time in the world. As if they weren't being delivered straight to the bad guys.

It took her a moment to kiss him back. Mostly because she was so stunned, but then Iris thought...what the hell? She enjoyed his mouth. And being turned on was a whole lot better than being terrified.

He tasted good. He felt *good*. His arms wrapped around her and pulled her against his body, and oh, damn, but he was heavenly. Hot and fierce and strong. Maybe heavenly was the wrong way to describe him. Because he sure felt like the best sin she'd ever—

His mouth slipped from hers. Kissed a scorching path toward her ear. "Be careful what you say," he whispered, and his breath blew lightly over her lobe, making her shiver. "I'm sure someone is listening."

She jolted. Her hands came up and pushed between them. Hard.

His head lifted as he frowned at her.

Had he just kissed her as some kind of cover? Red covered her vision. She sucked in a deep breath, but, dammit, she still tasted him. Her hands flew out, wrapped around his shoulders, and she hauled Pierce back toward her.

Surprise flashed on his handsome face.

Her mouth went to his ear. She could play the whisper game, too. "Don't ever kiss me like that unless you mean it." Because she wasn't into games. Her reaction to him had been real. Iris pulled back. Put some needed distance between them. Her hands twisted in front of her once more as she tried to settle against the plush leather seat.

His hand reached for hers. Twined with her fingers. He closed in once more, caging her with his body, and, sure enough, his mouth went right back to her ear. Even before the soft stream of his breath teased the shell of her ear, Iris had goose bumps.

"Be sure of this," he told her in a low voice for her alone, "when I kiss you, I always mean it."

She swallowed. Twice. That was certainly good information to possess.

Before she could respond, the car slowed.

Pierce swore. "Remember, you don't leave my side."

Right. Because she wanted to run away from the fierce bodyguard with super deadly skills. That was her masterplan.

The door swung open. The limo driver stood to the side. "You're supposed to go inside. The main door will be open for you."

Pierce exited first. He kept a strong grip on her hand and pulled her behind him. When she climbed out of the limo and got a look at the house waiting...

A soundless whistle escaped her. *This wasn't a house. It was a freaking castle.* Massive, made with deep, charcoal gray bricks. Stunning white columns surrounded the entranceway. Gas lamps flickered on either side of the gleaming, wooden doors. Heavy stone steps led up to the entranceway. The limo had parked right near those steps, pausing in the middle of the horseshoe drive. Iris counted thirteen windows on the front of the home's exterior. One massive window rested over the entrance doors, then there were six on each front-facing side of the house. Double chimneys poked from the top of the home, easily visible thanks to the light from the setting sun. She turned, scanning the property. Heavy, lush woods. No sign of any other homes. They hadn't traveled that far, so she suspected, based on the size of the house and the land...that they were in Buckhead? Yes, they must be in one of the lavish Buckhead subdivisions.

"You're supposed to go in," the limo driver prompted.

Who would be waiting inside?

Iris squared her shoulders. Lifted her chin. Pierce was at her side as they walked toward the waiting entrance. Sure enough, the doors were unlocked. They stepped inside.

Twenty-foot ceiling. Had to be. Marble floors. A glittering, antique chandelier that hung overhead.

"Hello?" Pierce called out. His voice seemed to echo.

The house had a still, almost empty feeling about it. She could see furniture to the right, in what looked like a study. And to the left, in the room that waited there, she saw the heavy, curving body of a billiard table.

An engine growled. She heard the crunch of tires.

"Limo's leaving," Pierce noted casually.

"How are we supposed to get back home?" She spun for the door.

"Oh, that's easy," Constantine announced.

Her head whipped to the right. He stood near the billiard table.

He smiled at her. "You're not."

Damn. She'd been very afraid he would say something like that. Good thing she'd brought her bodyguard. Her bodyguard who was—

Storming toward Constantine with his hands clenched into fists.

"Um, Pierce," Iris began.

"You were fucking there!" Pierce snarled.

Constantine tensed. "Want to call off the guard dog?"

Not particularly, she did not.

"You were *there* while they tried to kidnap her. She's got damn bruises on her arms from them!"

She did? Iris frowned and pulled up the sleeve of her blouse. Huh. There were faint, brownish smudges on her skin. How had he even noticed—

"So it's only fair that you get some bruises, too."

Her head whipped up just as Pierce drove his fist toward Constantine's face. She had to give Constantine credit, though, because his hand flew up and his forearm blocked the blow. A block that had to be pretty jarring because Pierce had obviously put some power behind his punch.

Still, Constantine started to smile—

Until Pierce drove his left hand into Constantine's side. She heard the *whoosh* of air leaving Constantine's mouth right before he doubled over.

"Sonofa—" Constantine began.

Pierce pulled back his fist for another blow.

"Stop!" Iris screamed as she surged forward.

And, somewhat surprisingly, Pierce did. He froze at her scream. That freezing gave her time to reach him, to lock her hands around his arm, and to pull him back.

Constantine kept groaning. "Bastard...I think I taste blood."

"Do you believe I care?" Pierce laughed.

She dragged him a little closer. He came easily. "If you beat him up, we can't get paid." That was the cover, wasn't it? That they were doing this for the money? Iris sucked in a breath and put on what she hoped was a sultry smile. Truth be told, she'd never actually tried one of those before, but she determinedly beamed up at Pierce. "And, darling, if we don't get paid, then how are you and I going to get down to the Cayman Islands where I spend my days modeling the smallest bikinis in the world for you?"

His face went slack with what looked like shock even as a blaze burned in his blue eyes. His hands flew up and locked around her hips.

"Oh, jeez," Constantine muttered. "Now I'm gonna be sick."

She turned her head to look at him. Glared. "Do you want me to let him beat the hell out of you?" Sweet. Coy. "Because I *saw* you at the park. You just watched while they grabbed me."

He straightened. Groaned again. Touched his side. "Bruised rib, at the least. Might be broken." He sniffed. "I did *not* stand there. I was reacting, only not as fast as lover boy. And just so we are all clear, I don't ever give orders for anyone to put hands on a woman."

Her experience would say otherwise.

"The boss went behind my back. He gave those bozos orders, not me. My plan was to *talk* with you. To make you see reason. When I realized they were grabbing you, I knew I had to stop them."

"Odd," Iris returned as she felt Pierce's hold tighten on her waist. "I don't remember that part of the scene."

Constantine pointed at Pierce. "That's because your guard dog came in roaring like some kind of freaking berserker or something and started knocking people out like he was in a televised wrestling match. Figured he had things under control, and it was time for me to make my exit."

Iris wasn't sure she believed him. Mostly because why should she? "Who's your boss?"

A tired shake of Constantine's head. "That's not how this works."

Pierce finally let her go. But Iris swore she could still feel the heat of his fingers on her skin. "You're not the man with the money," Pierce said flatly. "So I don't really see why we should listen to anything you say." He took a step forward.

Constantine tensed. "Not the face, okay? I like my face."

"He's not going to hit you." *Again.* Iris huffed. "Dang it, just cut to the chase, will you? We're not here to waste time."

"No, right. You're here for a job. Because you want to get paid." His gaze sharpened. "Would Remy approve?"

Now she lunged toward him. But Pierce locked his arms around her waist and lifted her up against him. Her feet dangled in the air.

"Love," Pierce breathed into her ear, "if I don't get to attack, then neither do you. Fair is fair."

Technically, he'd gotten a hit in. He *had* been able to attack. Maybe she deserved a shot at one hit, too.

"When you were a kid," Constantine reminisced, "you seemed so different from your old man. Guess time changes a person, huh?"

She stiffened. Stopped fighting. Pain and rage twisted inside of her.

Pierce immediately let her go. "Change of plans. We'll both hit—"

"Dammit! Would you two calm down?" Constantine jerked at his collar. "Look, the job isn't yours yet, Iris. This is a test run. You don't learn more about the boss until you pass the test run. So how about we all put our personal feelings aside before this scene turns ugly?"

Just what did that mean, "turns ugly"? Was he threatening them? It sure seemed like it to her.

Then she had a flash of her father. The blood that had covered him. At first, she'd thought it was paint. That he'd spilled paint while he was working...

But he never used that shade. He worked in soft pastels. Teases of light and—

"You have twenty-four hours," Constantine continued doggedly as he kept pulling at his collar. "You will find all the supplies that you need in the studio upstairs. The room was picked deliberately. I am sure you will love the play of light in there."

"What in the hell are you talking about?" Pierce growled.

But Iris knew. "I have to paint." This was almost insulting. "Do you seriously think I don't have the skills to do the job? If it's a Monet, I'll nail it."

"You've been out for a while. You spend your time sketching morning sunrises these days."

Oh, he had not—

"My employer wants to make sure you can still get the job done."

"I assure you, I can."

Interest flashed on his face. "Does this mean you've been keeping up your practice with the classics? Now why would you be doing that? Why would you still be working on duplicating the masterpieces if you'd gone all legitimate?"

Iris flushed. "I don't have to explain anything about myself to you."

"Um. Maybe. Maybe not." He turned away. Strolled back into the billiard room. She and Pierce followed him, their steps quick and—

Gun.

Constantine had a gun in one hand, and it was aimed right at her chest.

CHAPTER EIGHT

"Relax," Constantine ordered even as Pierce tensed.

"That's gonna be impossible," Pierce snarled back as he put his body in front of Iris's. "Because you just pulled a gun on *my* Iris. Bad mistake. A fatal one, I'd say."

"Relax," Constantine repeated. "No one is getting shot."

"Then put the fucking weapon down."

"I will, *after* you let Iris run a scanner over your body. Then you run it over hers."

"What?"

Constantine's features tightened in a grimace. "Settle down, will you, big guy? Don't want you punching my ribs again. I need to make sure that nothing funny happened before you arrived, like say...that the two of you put on listening devices or shit like that. That Iris decided to enter into some deal with the Feds and she's wired."

Iris laughed. A laugh that held a definite nervous edge. "Why would we do something like that?"

"Iris." Her name was a sigh. "You rushed away with the Feds when you were seventeen. You went into witness protection. My boss has been searching and searching for you. A search that lasted for a very long time. The first time I call on you, you slam the door in my face. Now, so soon after that awesome encounter, you're suddenly all-in for his job? Do you think I am an idiot?"

"Yes," Pierce retorted instantly. "You're an idiot because you pulled a gun on her. I won't forget that dumbass move."

"All right, superhero. I've been warned."

"Excellent," Pierce retorted as he prepared to—

"Do *not* lunge at me!" Constantine ordered. "I get that you probably know some awesome Ranger fighting techniques that make you think you can get the gun before I fire, but let's not risk it, shall we? I'd hate for a stray bullet to hit Iris. Any injury would be completely unnecessary." His jaw hardened. "Iris, pick up the scanner that's on the billiard table. Run it over your guy so I can be sure he's clear. Then he can do the same for you. After that, we'll talk specifics about the job."

"Don't move, Iris," Pierce bit off the words. His eyes narrowed on his prey. "How the hell do you know I was a Ranger?"

"I know lots of things. My boss doesn't just trade in art. He manages secrets. I know plenty about you. Now if we could just move things along? Ahem, Iris? You're up."

Her fingers pressed to Pierce's back. "Let's just do this so he can lower the gun."

I can take that gun from him.

But, dammit, he didn't want any risks sent her way. And a stray bullet? The idea of it hitting her skin—that just wasn't something that could happen. Pierce moved with her toward the table, making sure he shielded her as much as possible. She picked up the scanner.

"Everywhere, Iris," Constantine directed. "Be thorough."

Pierce turned to face her. He could see the fear in her eyes, but her shoulders were straight and her chin up. The scanner trembled in her grasp, and he eyed it curiously. Interesting bit of tech. Probably government tech.

Red flag number twenty-nine.

She ran it over him.

"Yes, so, it might be awkward as hell, but I said *everywhere*," Constantine announced. "Scan it over his dick and his ass."

"Seriously?" Pierce swiveled his head toward the jerk.

Constantine's gaze held suspicion. "I don't like that jacket he's wearing. Take it off."

"So it's a strip show now, huh?" Pierce taunted.

"Drop the jacket."

Snarling, he did.

"*Get his gun, Iris!*" A roar from Constantine. "Bring it to me, *now*."

Fuck. This scene was a mess. "I'll take it out. Relax. Don't get twitchy." He removed the gun. Put it on the billiard table. "You come and get it if you want it."

Constantine did. Slowly. Not lowering his weapon at all. He snatched up Pierce's gun and tucked it into the back of his jeans.

"Just so you know." Pierce heard the lethal edge in his own voice. "I could have taken *your* weapon a dozen times. I'm playing nicely now. Later, I won't be."

Constantine sniffed.

Iris finished scanning Pierce. "Is this thing supposed to beep if there's a listening device or something? Because there were no beeps. That should prove to you that he's clear."

"Scan her now," Constantine directed without answering her question.

Pierce took the scanner from her. Eyed it with mild curiosity. He hadn't seen this exact type of equipment before. Was it even doing what Constantine said? The whole thing felt like freaking theater to him.

"Scan her."

"Dude, you are pissing me off." But he did. Quickly, efficiently. He wanted this BS over with because Iris was afraid. He scanned her body. Her legs. Her stomach.

"Everywhere," Constantine blasted. "Just hurry and do it."

Once more, his head turned toward the asshole holding the gun on them. "I don't like you. I will not forget anything about this day."

Constantine swallowed.

"Just do it," Iris whispered.

Pierce's gaze jerked from Constantine and swept over her. Iris shifted her stance a little, parting her legs.

Fucking bastard. Pierce could see the racing pulse at the base of Iris's neck. She was trying to act calm, but he could feel her terror.

"It's okay, baby," he promised her. "I've got you." Quickly, coolly, he did the job. A swipe of the device along her body. There were no tell-tale beeps. No sounds at all. "Happy now?" Pierce growled before he tossed the device onto the billiard table.

"No, but at least we've cleared step one."

What other steps were there? Pierce fisted his hands on his hips. "Lower the gun. That's my step two."

"Okay, but, before you go charging at me, I would like to point out one very important fact."

Oh, he'd charge, all right.

Constantine dangled the gun before him. "It wasn't loaded."

What. The. Hell?

"I actually *like* Iris. Sort of view her as a younger sister. So shooting her isn't on my agenda. I just needed your cooperation."

This guy was a serious prick. Pierce lunged forward—

But, once again, Iris wrapped her hands around his arm. He didn't want to lurch her with him, so he stilled.

"Take a breath, Pierce." Her sweet scent surrounded him. "I get that there is nothing good about this scene, but we need to hear what else he has to say."

His head turned toward her. "Fine." *For you.* But he wouldn't be forgetting the payback that Constantine had coming his way.

"Everybody cool? In control?" Constantine prompted.

Iris and Pierce both glared at him.

"Wonderful." He put his gun down on a nearby table. "Here are the rules for the next twenty-four hours. Rule one, you don't leave. You can go anywhere in the house that you want, you can even wander on the grounds, but you try to leave the property before the twenty-four hours are up, and you will be escorted back by the *many* guards who are being paid to watch the perimeter."

Pierce hadn't seen any guards when they came in, but if the guards were good, they *would* have stayed hidden.

"Rule two, you don't call any authorities. No cops. No U.S. Marshals who might have developed a soft spot for you and thus became wrapped around your little finger..." Constantine's eyebrows beetled. "Be careful, man," he warned Pierce, "that shit happens. You blink, and a guy is falling all over himself to help her out of danger. Happens over and over again."

"I get the picture," Pierce muttered.

"Thought you might. Seeing as how *you* are the current guy pulling that shit. Ahem. Rule three..."

"Get the hell on with it," Pierce urged.

"She paints." His stare shifted to Iris. "She paints her beautiful, artistic heart out and creates a work of art so good that no one will be able to tell it from the original."

Iris didn't speak.

So Pierce did. "In twenty-four hours? Isn't that kind of like expecting a miracle?"

"No, it's like expecting Iris."

"Paint has to dry," Iris murmured. "I have no idea what I will even be painting. It could be something that will have to dry in stages and require multiple layers. By only giving me twenty-four hours, you are setting me up for failure."

Worry flashed on Constantine's face. "God, I certainly hope not. Because if you don't pass this test, I have the feeling that my boss is not going to be very pleased. I'm not quite sure what orders he gave to the goons—I mean, guards outside—but judging from past experience, I'm thinking nobody here will like what happens if you don't create something stunning."

Her breath shuddered out. "No pressure."

Could she do it? Pierce wasn't sure *anyone* could. And, sure, he'd eyed some of her canvases that had been in her den. They'd looked gorgeous to him, but he knew jack and shit about art. The colors had just worked, and he'd thought they were pretty. *I have no idea how to spot a masterpiece.*

"Use blow dryers or something to help the paint dry," Constantine said. "Make it happen."

"It's not always that simple. It depends on the medium I'm using. It depends on about fifteen factors that I am not even going to begin discussing with you." Another shudder of breath from Iris. "What am I supposed to paint?"

"You'll see it when you go upstairs." Constantine lifted his hand. Pressed a button on his watch. "The countdown starts now." A nod. He grabbed his discarded gun—the unloaded one—and marched back into the foyer.

Iris trailed after him. "Where are you going?"

He paused. Looked back. "You and the boyfriend will be inside alone." His gaze darted to the right, up near the chandelier. "But just because you're alone, it doesn't mean you aren't being watched. Try to keep that in mind and make things PG, would you?"

Pierce had already noticed several security cameras strategically placed in the house.

"Step one was making sure you didn't come bugged. Step two was going over the game plan. Step three is leaving you to take care of business."

The jackass seemed to like his rules and his precious steps.

Constantine offered Iris an encouraging smile. "I've got faith in you."

"Wonderful." Sarcasm dripped from her voice. "Then I am sure everything will work out just perfectly."

His smile faltered.

"Is the house stocked with food?" Iris wanted to know. "What about toiletries? Necessities? I *need* things—"

"You'll find everything you need in the house. Even extra clothes. I tried to remember the types of food that you liked before, but since you're not seventeen anymore, I also added some wine for you. Thought that might take the edge off."

Pierce didn't like the way that Constantine's gaze lingered on Iris. He also didn't like the personal references the guy kept dropping.

"Have some faith in me," Constantine added. "Not like I'll let you down. You'll find everything in the house that you need."

With that, he left. The door closed softly behind him.

Iris stood under the chandelier, her pose uncertain. "This is not what I expected."

Sure as hell wasn't what he'd planned for, either. "We should go upstairs. See what's waiting in the studio for you." *Give me a chance to explore and find out where all the cameras are located.* The house felt like a giant goldfish bowl to him. And he didn't like people peering at him.

A curved staircase waited to the right. A gleaming, dark cherry banister disappeared upstairs. The tops of the steps were stained in the same dark cherry as the banister. Iris started up the stairs, and he followed right behind her.

"Someone has too much money," Iris noted. "This whole giant place and no one else is here?"

He knew the Feds had been tailing them. They would have the location. They'd know exactly where he and Iris were. But Pierce didn't expect the Feds to rush the scene. They were waiting and hoping that the elusive art theft mastermind would take the bait that Iris offered.

At the top of the stairs, Iris paused, just a moment. "The best light would come in during the morning, to the right." She turned. Headed to the right. The door there was already open. When they slipped inside, he saw the carefully stocked paint—looked like every color imaginable. Tubes and tubes. Oils. Acrylics. Who the hell knew what else? Lots of brushes. Canvases of all sizes and shapes.

"Overkill much," he muttered.

Iris ignored all the supplies. She went straight to the easel that had been setup in the middle of the room. A heavy white cloth covered the easel—and the painting that perched on it. Pierce saw her square her shoulders before she lifted her right hand and tugged on the cloth. It slowly slithered away from the image...

Frowning, he inched closer. A framed print. A woman in the foreground, looking to be wearing an old-fashioned, white dress. Blue skies dotted with white clouds surrounded her, while a green field waited at her feet. In the distance, Pierce could make out another figure.

"Woman with a Parasol," Iris whispered. "Good choice."

He slanted her a glance and found her drinking in the image. "So you're familiar with it?" Pierce was feeling his way along. Probably not the time to admit he knew nothing about art. He didn't want her thinking he was in over his head.

But it wasn't like art history lessons had been handed out on the streets where he grew up.

He figured she could handle the artistic part of the equation.

He'd handle the protection.

A nod. "You could say that." Her hand lifted. Traced the curve of the woman's back. "Also known as *Madame Monet and Her Son*. Painted back in 1875. An oil on canvas work. It really showed Monet's skills when it came to figure work. If you look closely, you can tell he focused just as much on the features of his subjects as he did on the world that existed around them. He painted it while outdoors, and I'm happy to say experts think he created this piece with a session that lasted probably for several hours." Another nod. More brisk. "So I can definitely have mine done in twenty-four hours. No sweat."

"Monet," he repeated. "As in...Claude Monet?" Yeah, even with his limited art knowledge, he knew the name. She'd mentioned Monet before, but it was just fully sinking in that replicating Monet—*that* was her specialty. The Monet.

She nodded.

Fucking Monet. "They're going to steal a Monet?" No wonder the Feds were freaking the hell out.

She removed the print. Set it down nearby. Eyed the array of blank canvases. Picked one and settled it in place on the easel. "Why bother stealing something small when you can go for big game?"

Shit. Shit. "And you can do this?"

Her hands were still wrapped around the edges of the canvas. Her head turned toward him.

"You can create a Monet so good that people who know this shit won't be able to tell the difference between your work and his?"

A little frown appeared between her brows. "Not shit. Exceptional art."

Right. Yes. Got it.

"And, yes. I can. Actually, this piece is one I've done before. Many times."

Many?

"I could do it in my sleep."

Well, damn. "Call me impressed."

"Because I'm a great forger? That's hardly something to be impressed by." She let go of the painting. "For all we know, they could be planning to steal *this* painting. We don't want them ditching us so soon, so I'll be sure to leave a big, giant signature on it. Maybe make a few other small, deliberate changes, too. They'll be able to see the image, they'll know what I can do, and then, hopefully, we'll get that meeting with the mystery boss." She headed for the tubes of paint. "This is going to take a while. You don't have to stay."

"You're going to paint it—now?" Didn't she want to wait for good lighting or something? Morning light? Hadn't Constantine been rambling about that very thing?

"I can do it in my sleep."

"When you say that, it doesn't make it seem easier. It just makes you seem—"

Her shoulders stiffened. Iris spun back toward him. "Like a thief? A cheat? A forger?"

No. He closed in on her. Curled his hands around her shoulders. "Exceptional."

Her dark eyes widened. "That's not what I am."

It was from where he was standing.

"I didn't grow up like everyone else. My dad was always moving us around. I wasn't ever in a regular school. He always had tutors for us. And the art..." She licked her lower lip. "It was all I ever knew. My father was amazing. *His* talent was incredible. He wanted Remy and I to be as good as he was, but he never failed to let us know when we came up short." An echo of pain. "When I was younger, I came up short a lot. I wanted to make my own style. Not just paint what he ordered."

Her father had freaking raised her to work in the art underground? What in the hell?

"I had talent. Remy had talent. But instead of using it to grow, we just...became..." Her gaze darted to the blank canvas. "Something else."

She seemed lost, and he hated that. "This is going to be over soon." A promise. "When it is, you can create any damn art you want."

Her stare returned to him. "I thought that before, but here I am."

Hell.

"Sometimes, the past just won't let go."

"Then you just have to bury that shit deep so that it can never try to reach you again." His fingers caressed her delicate shoulders. "I happen to come equipped with my own shovel, so I know how to bury things."

She searched his gaze. "Why are you being so good to me? You—you didn't have to do *any* of this. You didn't have to come with me and be forced into this house. You could have walked away at any point."

She didn't get him at all. Not yet. She would. "Walking away was never an option." Not from the minute he'd looked up and seen her standing framed with the light trailing around her and falling on her hair. *The first time I ever saw you, Iris, and you took my breath away.* As far as he was concerned, she was the real work of art.

"I won't ever be able to repay you."

She had forgotten that they were being watched. He hadn't. The minute he'd stepped into the room, he'd tagged the video camera in the far-right corner. They were being watched, and no doubt, the audio of their conversation was being received by someone, too.

"You don't repay a lover," he told her deliberately. With his eyes, he said, *Baby, watch it.*

Her lashes flickered. "I've never had someone stay at my side the way you do." Slow. Soft. "You're not like anyone I've been with before."

She'd gotten the message and was using more care for their watchers. Playing the game. But at her words, his instant thought was…

I'm not like the bastards before. And if I have my way, you will never think of them again. It was the helluva wrong time, but a surge of jealousy rocked through him. He didn't want to think of Iris with other men. Didn't want to think that this case could end, and she'd walk away. He wanted to be close not just for her protection. Not for show.

Because he wanted her.

"Remember what I said before?" Pierce rasped.

Her lips parted.

"I always mean it." His mouth took hers. A hot, deep kiss. His tongue dipped inside. Tasted her. Savored her. His hands dropped to her hips as he hauled her closer. He lifted her up, holding her easily so that he could get better access to her mouth. To her.

She gave a little moan and locked her arms around him. She kissed him deeper. Met the thrust of his tongue. Tasted him back, and savage need tore through him. Pierce wanted their clothes gone. He wanted to be skin to skin with her. He wanted to thrust deep into her and hear her cry out his name as pleasure lashed through her.

But what he *didn't* want? An audience. No one else would see Iris that way.

Protect her. Always.

Protection first, pleasure second.

Carefully, he lowered Iris until her sneaker-clad feet touched the floor. Another kiss. Softer. Then he let her go.

Her hands slid back to her sides. Her lips were swollen. Her eyes big and wide and even darker with her need.

His cock ached. His body burned with tension. And her taste was so good he wanted to gobble her right up. *Soon enough, I will.*

"I'm going to check the house." Every inch of it.

"And I'll get to work." Husky. Her gaze lingered on him.

He had to pull his from her. With a major freaking effort. *Focus on the job, dumbass.* He turned. Glanced toward the camera with its little, red dot glowing underneath. He stared into that camera.

Someone had just gotten a show. That someone would know that Pierce was serious about Iris. Because he was. Deadly serious.

With slow, deliberate steps, Pierce walked to the camera. When he stood about three feet away, he smiled up at the lens. "Even think of ever hurting her, and I truly will bury you." He hadn't been making an empty threat when he talked about his shovel. Someone came for Iris?

He'd put them in the ground.

***

"What do we know about that bastard?"

Pierce had just flipped him the bird before slowly turning and walking away. What an arrogant prick.

He gripped the phone in his hand as he glared at the monitor before him.

"I'm digging deeper into his life as fast as I can, but some of the military records are proving elusive." Constantine's cautious reply. He knew Constantine was in his car, could hear the faint hum of traffic around him. "He works for Wilde. It's a protection firm, but I thought he was a pencil pusher there."

No freaking way. That bruiser was the physical type. His two broken men could attest to that fact.

"He's her neighbor," Constantine continued. His voice drifted in and out, as if he had a slightly bad connection. "I think he fell for her. Now he won't leave her side."

"Doesn't that seem fucking convenient?" he snarled back. "If he works for this Wilde firm—"

"It's probably just a bonus in her eyes. She meets this big hulk, she winds him around her finger—Iris could always get anyone to do what she wanted, even when she was a kid—and now she's got a professional who will walk through fire for her. I'm sure she sees it as win-win."

What a lucky break for Iris. "I want everything you can get on him." You couldn't truly understand an enemy until you knew the other person's weakness.

"It will take time to get more—"

Time was something he didn't have. "Can she do the work?"

"Aren't you watching right now?"

Yes, he was. Because that was all part of her test. He wanted to see her in action. He needed to see just how quickly she could recreate the work—and at what skill level. At seventeen, she'd been brilliant. But years had passed. She wasn't a kid any longer. She was a woman. Either her skills had turned to shit in the intervening years because she'd turned her back on the craft she'd been taught since childhood or...

Or you kept at it. You just got better and better. "Go to her place. Search it."

"Uh, excuse me?"

"Search her place. And his. Every inch." While they were occupied, this was the perfect opportunity to pry.

"That's breaking and entering."

Fucking seriously? He pinched the bridge of his nose. "Then don't get caught."

Constantine sputtered.

"If you can't handle this..." The guy kept balking at the weirdest stuff. *Amateur* hour. After the incident at the park, he had considered ditching Constantine. For the moment, the man still had his uses.

"I can." A grudging response from Constantine. "I can handle it, but I don't like it."

His eyes rolled. "Your conscience annoys the hell out of me." It was a weird-ass conscience. The man was fine with art theft, but a little kidnapping attempt had him exploding like a volcano.

"Maybe if you got a conscience, you'd understand where I'm coming from."

Screw that. A conscience just would slow down his business. He knew the price of having morals. Of caring about what happened to others.

They just burn you down with them.

"What am I even looking for in their places?" Constantine growled.

"You'll know it when you see it." An instinct he had—his gut told him the search needed to be done. *Mostly because I don't trust anyone.*

"That is a very vague set of instructions, boss."

"Constantine?"

"Yes?"

"Get the job done." He hung up. Kept staring at the screen. The asshole boyfriend was gone. He could click another button and check a feed from a different part of the house to see Pierce Jennings but...

He was enjoying his current view. Iris had picked up a brush. She was starting his masterpiece.

Don't let me down, Iris.

For her, failure truly wasn't an option.

CHAPTER NINE

He'd been watching her for the last hour. She hadn't looked up from the painting, well, not looked at him, anyway. She'd gotten more paint. Added colors to the canvas. Used careful brush strokes. A faint line had appeared between her delicate brows as she worked.

Six hours so far. She'd been working non-stop for six hours.

Exhaustion had to be pulling at her, but Iris seemed completely focused on the art. Her gaze burned with a dark intensity, and she seemed almost possessed as she kept—

"I think that's it." Soft. A breath rustled from her as Iris's shoulders sagged. "That's as good as I can make it." She put down her brush. Looked over at him. Frowned. "Pierce?"

"Hey, sweetheart." He hadn't looked directly at her canvas. He'd been staring at her. Locked on her.

"How long did it take me?"

He checked his watch. "Six hours, two minutes, and thirty-one seconds." He'd started the timer right after she'd begun.

Her fingers stretched and fisted, as if trying to work out cramps. He figured she had to be aching. He crossed to her, still not looking at the painting, and took her right hand in his.

She jerked.

"It's okay. I just want to help."

"I-I have paint on my fingers." Her voice was dazed, her eyes slightly unfocused.

He sent her a half-smile. "I don't mind." His fingers stretched hers, then carefully began to knead her palm.

She sucked in a gasp of air.

"Hurt?"

"No. It feels good." Her lashes flickered. "You haven't looked at it."

Now he did, even as his fingers kept carefully stroking her. And, no, it didn't take a dozen of art degrees to realize he was staring at something special. "Damn."

"Do you think it will be good enough?"

He knew they were still being monitored. His head turned toward the camera's lens. "It had better be or the guy running this circus is an idiot."

"Pierce..." A thread of worry.

"She's going to sleep now," he said to the camera. "So fuck off."

"Pierce!"

He scooped her into his arms. He felt the shock roll through her.

"What are you doing?"

"Taking care of you. You just painted for six hours straight, and you're exhausted. Tell me what you want first. Shower or bed?"

"Shower?" Iris made it sound like a question.

But he nodded. "Then shower it is." He'd scoped out the entire property while she worked. Constantine hadn't been lying. There were guards patrolling the perimeter. Armed bastards. He could have taken them out, even had the perfect strategy for it. But he hadn't because he knew they were supposed to play out this mad scene.

He'd located every security camera in the house. Knew exactly where they were placed, and because of that, he knew that the shower in the master bedroom was safe. There were no cameras in that bathroom. The evil boss had apparently balked at watching someone in that particular space.

Good to know.

There *was* a camera in the master bedroom, though. A camera in all the bedrooms. When it came time for Iris to sleep, he would be disconnecting that device.

"I can walk."

"But carrying you is so much fun." It actually was. He liked carrying her. Liked the way she felt in his arms. The warmth of her body. Her scent. His grip remained steady on her as he strode through the master bedroom. A room almost as big as his place in their building. Then he kicked open the bathroom door.

A giant, claw-foot tub. A shower big enough for four. Marble every-freaking-where.

When you had money to burn, kidnapping an artist was just a lifestyle choice, apparently. *A lifestyle choice you will regret.*

He slowly lowered Iris to her feet. "There's a robe hanging on the hook behind the door. When you're done, you can put that on." Because her clothes were covered in paint, too.

Constantine had told them that clothes and necessities were waiting. He'd been telling the truth with that statement, too. Though only one pair of sweats had been left for Pierce, while there was a whole closet full of clothes for Iris. Everything seemingly perfectly sized for her.

You planned this for a while.

Something that put him on edge.

"I'll be right outside," he promised as he turned for the door.

"Wait!" Her hand flew out and clamped around his arm.

Pierce looked back at her.

"Can he...can anyone see me in here?"

"No, baby, you're safe. I checked this room thoroughly. No cameras." He didn't say no listening devices because there was a chance a small piece of tech could be hidden, but once she turned on the shower, the sounds would be muted, anyway.

"You're sure?" Fear flickered in her gaze. "I don't want someone watching me while I'm naked."

His jaw locked. "Trust me, I don't want that, either. No one else will have eyes on you. And I will be right outside the door every single second."

Her breath released on a quick sigh. "Thank you."

He didn't want her thanks. Hadn't they already covered that? "Take your shower." Gruff. "The hot water will help your tired muscles. Then you can crash in bed with me."

"With...you?"

Oh, yes. "With me."

"Pierce?"

"Where else would you sleep?" he murmured. "But safely in your lover's arms?" Once more, he turned away.

"I do feel safe with you." Soft. "Safer than I've ever felt at any other time in my life."

Damn. The woman must be trying to break him. With confessions like that one...*Fuck. Just keep your control in place. Be what she needs now.* "You will always be safe with me." He slipped out. Shut the door. Stood there a moment until he heard the shower turn on with a roar. His gaze slid around the room.

Locked on the camera. With determined steps, he headed straight for it. "Hey, asshole." He didn't offer a taunting grin, not this time. Because he wasn't taunting. He was stating facts. "I'm shutting down the view for the rest of the night. You don't have this part of her. You don't have any fucking part of her. She did the painting. You can collect it *after* she rests. You'll be satisfied, I'm sure. Then you'll drag your ass out of the shadows and come meet us face to face if you want to proceed. We'll decide if *we* are interested or not. Oh, and one more thing." He tapped his chin. "The price just went up. Because I don't like being a fish in a bowl, even if the bowl is this fancy-ass mansion." Then he reached up and yanked the camera right off the wall. He pulled hard and all the wires shot out with it. Drywall fell. Dust fluttered in the air.

He tossed the camera onto the floor.

***

The image had gone dark.

Sonofabitch.

He quite hated that prick. Even as he glared at the screen, his phone rang. He picked it up with a casual hand. "Hello, Constantine."

"Uh, yeah, hey."

"Did you finish the search?"

"I did."

"And...?"

"And she's been keeping up her skills. I found several finished Monet canvases, but she'd slashed them all. I mean, hell, looked like a horror show the way she'd gone at them. Why would she do that? Those could have been useful to us."

A soft laugh. "That's probably exactly why she *did* slash them. Because she didn't want them to fall into the wrong hands."

"Why the hell would she do them in the first place?"

"Because art is an addiction to Iris. It was the same addiction that her father possessed. The images call to her, and she answers."

"She could paint something else." A mutter.

Constantine didn't understand. He didn't know how Iris had been trained by her father. How when she'd been younger, she'd been forced to paint those images even as tears slid down her cheeks. She'd loved and hated the art. Been drawn to it even as she wanted to destroy her creations.

"What do you want me to do with the paintings?" Constantine asked.

"Put them in the boyfriend's place."

"Why?"

Why the hell was the hired help questioning him? "Because let's see if he knows what she's been doing." He didn't have a clear handle on Pierce yet. Couldn't decide if he had truly fallen for Iris or if he was some sort of plant from the government. He wouldn't put that past the Feds. To move Pierce into Iris's building. To push him close to her. And poor Iris, always so desperate for affection and acceptance—she would have fallen right into his hands.

"Yeah, whatever," Constantine groused.

"I may need to kill him."

Silence.

His finger tapped along the edge of the phone.

"Want to say that again?" Constantine asked. "I don't think I caught your—"

"Iris is going to sleep soon. Give her eight hours. She deserves her rest."

"That's nice of you." A grumble.

"I can be nice. I can also be incredibly cruel. But isn't that how all humans are? It really just depends on the moment." For this moment, he was feeling generous. Iris had completed his test. "Give her eight hours, then you can go in and pick her up. She's finished ahead of schedule."

***

The robe swallowed her. It felt like the softest cotton in the world, and it brushed gently over her skin. The bathroom door creaked softly when she opened it, and steam drifted lightly in the air. Extremely hot showers were her guilty pleasure, and normally, she would have basked under that warmth for a very long time.

But she'd been afraid, so she'd hurried out.

The covers had been drawn back on the massive bed. And a broken security camera flopped on the carpet. Her toes curled into the carpeting as she looked at the discarded camera. "Was that the only one in the room?"

"I think so." Deep. Low. Coming from the bed. Because he was in the bed. Waiting for her.

Her toes curled a little more. The lamp near the bed cast a soft glow over the space. It was the only light in the room. Had he left it on for her? Because he'd noticed she kept his bedroom lamp on while she slept? "How can you be sure? That one was wired in, but these days, you don't have to wire things, do you?" She was rambling. So what? "And I saw this special report on the news about how you can have these teeny, tiny cameras that most people wouldn't spot."

"I'm not most people."

No, he wasn't.

"I know how to do a search, Iris. I spent a great deal of time searching this room while you were working because I wanted you to have a safe place to crash. He's not going to be watching you sleep. I'll be beside you."

The thought of Pierce being beside her unnerved Iris plenty. She forced herself to step forward and go toward the bed. "So, how are we going to do this?" Would he put a pillow between their bodies? Would he twist up a sheet and use it as a line to separate them? Her side of the bed? His? "What's the—"

His hand flew out, curled around her wrist, and he tugged her on to the bed. She tumbled down and fell straight into his arms.

"That's one option," she mumbled. Her chest was on top of his, and Iris very much feared that the top of the robe might be gaping open. One of her legs had slid between his, and she shifted a bit only to feel...*Oh, hello, there.*

"I want you."

Her head whipped up.

"Guessing that's pretty obvious."

It certainly *felt* pretty obvious to her.

His hands slid down her body. Curled around her hips. Then he gently lifted her up and off him. He eased her to the left and maneuvered so that—

"I'll be on the side of the bed that faces the door. Anybody coming in will have to go through me to get to you."

He was back in bodyguard mode. Apparently, just ignoring his body's physical response to her. Being all calm and collected. Was she supposed to act the same way? Because her heart was racing, and her body felt singed from the brief contact she'd had with him. Calm and collected did not describe her state of mind.

He grabbed the cover. Hauled it up and over her. "Good night."

"What?" She shoved the cover down because he'd had the dang thing all the way to her neck. "That's it? That's all you have to say?"

He'd rolled onto his side to face her. "What else did you have in mind?"

"I—" *I don't know.* "I think you should turn out the light."

"I thought you liked the light."

So he *had* remembered that she slept with it on. Normally, she would have kept it on. But, this wasn't a normal situation. "You're with me. I don't need the light." And if he had missed a camera, the darkness would provide her with a little extra protection.

He moved to turn it off, but in order to reach the lamp, he had to stretch over her body. Iris sucked in a breath and pretty much forgot to let it out until he lifted off her.

Could he hear the fast drumming of her heart? It was so loud that she feared he might.

"I locked the bedroom door," Pierce informed her, his voice slightly gruff. "Even put a chair under it. Didn't want us having unexpected company."

He'd locked the door. Chaired it—a technique she used, too. *And* now he was putting himself closest to that door. He certainly took his bodyguard work very seriously.

She should be thrilled with that development. Correction, she was thrilled. Not like she wanted some amateur-hour routine. But, still...

I want you. "Why don't you do anything about it?" A breathy whisper.

He shifted a little closer. "Sweetheart..."

Butterflies must have some sort of rave going on in her stomach with the crazy way it kept fluttering. Did he get how low and sexy that rumble of his voice could be? And hadn't they talked about the endearments? It did weird things to her when he acted like he cared.

"What are you talking about?" he finished.

She should stop while she was ahead. She didn't. "You said you wanted me, but you're not doing anything about it." She turned onto her side, too. "Why is that?"

He was a big, dangerous shadow. She couldn't see his features clearly, and the bonus of that situation was that he couldn't see hers, either. Because if he could see her, he'd realize that her cheeks had flushed a dark red. She could feel the heat on her face.

"You *want* me to do something?" Even lower. Even rougher.

"I..." *God, yes.* Maybe that was the adrenaline talking. It was a crazy situation. No doubt. Not every day that you were whisked away in a limo and transported to the fanciest prison on the planet. And after she completed her artwork, there was always a certain rush that fueled her body. A giddiness that made her skin feel almost electric. A euphoria that danced along the edges of her nerves.

But blaming the adrenaline or blaming the art rush—all of that would just be her pretending. Why not simply admit the truth? "I wanted you the first day I saw you."

She thought his body might have tensed. *Confession time. In the dark. Where it's safe.* She kept her voice low, though, barely above a whisper. He seemed confident no one was listening to them, but...

"You're telling me this shit *now?*" His voice wasn't so low.

"Shhh." First, she didn't think it was shit. She thought this was an important topic. Second, why not now? "Better now than never." She didn't know what might happen next. The Feds wanted to spirit her away, and, apparently, that was just a thing that happened in her life now. People took her to random locations.

"Fuck."

She wasn't asking him to fuck, per se. Just explaining to Pierce that she wanted him. "I'm sure you get told by lots of women that you're attractive."

"You didn't *say* I was attractive, baby. You said you wanted me. Day one, you wanted me. *Fucking fuck.*"

Now she inched back and pulled the cover up a little higher. "You seem mad." Not exactly the reaction she'd hoped to get.

"I *am*."

His anger hadn't been her end goal. "Forget I said anything, would you?" She had to blink quickly. *God, this is so embarrassing.* But they'd shared that kiss at her apartment, and she'd started to think that—

He wrapped his hands around the cover she'd been tugging toward her. He tugged them—and her—back. Brought her closer, inch by inch. "I will not forget a word."

Why was he pulling her closer?

"Thought you'd friend-zoned me," he rasped.

Oh. About that. "I had." Only inches separated them. Inches that were thick with tension and heat, and her heart just kept drumming faster and faster.

"Why?"

Because I wanted you too much. "Look at where we are." Wasn't the why obvious? "I didn't want to bring my trouble to your door." But she had.

"I'm exactly where I want to be."

He was?

"In bed. With you."

She wanted his mouth. She wanted his hands on her. Wanted his body surrounding hers. "It's dangerous to get involved with me." He had to understand that. The danger should be more than apparent.

But Pierce just laughed. "I don't mind some danger."

What if it wasn't just *some* danger? What if it was a whole lot of serious, terrifying danger?

"You wanted me..." Such a hard growl from Pierce. "The first day?"

"You were wearing a black t-shirt. Hauling up some boxes and your muscles were flexing like crazy. I opened my door, saw you, and my jaw nearly hit the floor." Probably not the right confession to make. She was definitely not playing it calm and collected.

"Such a waste of time."

Her eyes narrowed as she strained to see him in the dark. "Excuse me?"

"You were wearing your old cut-offs. Your legs were the sexiest things I'd ever seen. You had on a light blue top, and I almost dropped every box I was carrying because seeing you hit me like a punch to the gut."

Was he serious?

His hand rose and cupped her jaw. His touch seemed scorching, but a shiver still skated over her body.

"The tattoo on your thigh drove me crazy. *You* drove me crazy. I'd never seen anyone and had such an instant, primitive reaction." His thumb feathered over her jaw.

"Wh-what was your reaction, exactly?" Her voice had gone even softer. Extra breathy. Not intentional. There just didn't seem to be enough air in the bedroom.

"I got hard with a glance. I wanted to go to you, pull you into my arms, and take you."

She swallowed.

"I looked at you and thought...*mine*. I want her to be mine."

She needed to kick the bedding away. The room was way too hot.

"What about you?" Still a growl. A growl that made her ache and quake inside. "What did you think when you saw me?"

She didn't even stop to think about her response. What would be the point in holding back now? "I thought...I would like to lick every inch of him."

"*Fuck me.*" He dragged her close, and his mouth crashed down on hers.

CHAPTER TEN

He clawed for control, but it was barely hanging on. Savage need tore through him as his mouth feasted on hers.

I thought...I would like to lick every inch of him. Those low, husky words had wrecked him. His dick had already been hard and aching. When Iris appeared before him in a robe, when he'd been in bed waiting for her, there had been no way for his body not to have a fierce, physical reaction. Pretty much whenever he was near her, he wanted.

He ached.

He craved.

He wanted to touch and take and possess. And she...she felt the same way.

His tongue thrust into her mouth. She moaned for him, and he shoved against the covers that were between them. She smelled sweet, and her body was so soft. Her skin was still slightly damp from the shower, and he damn well knew that she was naked beneath the robe. His hand had already moved between their bodies. He had the edge of the belt's robe in his grasp. He could yank it open. He *could* touch. Every inch of her.

And if she wanted to lick—

Stop! The cry came from the last vestige of sanity in his lust-obsessed mind. *You're in a golden prison. This isn't a safe place for her.* Or for the things he wanted to do with her. Because if he sank between her thighs, if he thrust into her tight, hot core, the freaking bedroom could catch on fire around him, and Pierce wasn't sure he'd notice.

So some bad guys rushing in and shooting him while he was utterly lost in her? *Freaking possibility.*

Her nails sank into his shoulders. He wasn't wearing a shirt. Just the sweats. They did nothing to contain his erection as it shoved toward her. When her hand slid down, when her hand eased between them, too, and went for his aching cock—

He let go of the belt to close his fingers around her delicate wrist. "You touch me there..." Savage. Because he *was* savage. "And I won't be able to stop. I'll be in you so deep that you'll taste me."

Her breath hitched. "Is that a promise?"

His eyes squeezed shut. He almost lost it. That thin thread of control. Almost fell over the edge and didn't care. He could imagine tearing open her robe. Shoving apart her thighs. Putting his mouth on her sex and driving his tongue into her until she screamed. He'd do that, first, to get her ready. To make sure she was wet and hot, and then he'd slam as deep into her as he could—

His fingers tightened around her wrist. "It's not...safe. Not here. Not...not for the things I want to do with you." *To you.* His eyes opened. His nostrils flared, and he pulled in more of her scent. Enough to make him drunk. "As soon as we are home, you are *mine*." He took her mouth again. Another drugging kiss as his heart jackhammered in his chest. "*Mine.*" Locking his jaw, Pierce eased back. Returned to his side of the bed.

But wanted to pounce again.

"Pierce?"

He glared at the ceiling. Tried to tell his aching dick to settle the hell down. His dick didn't want to listen. He just wanted Iris.

"I...I'm...I haven't felt like this with anyone else, Pierce. Haven't wanted someone so much. It almost hurts because I want you so badly." A hushed confession.

Oh, fuck. He couldn't leave her hurting, now, could he? Iris thought he was a good guy, and good guys didn't leave a lady aching. "Spread your legs." Guttural.

"But...you said..."

"I'm not fucking you." Not here. *Keep the control. Keep it.* "Just gonna give you a little touch."

But he made sure the covers were up and covering her body. Just in case he'd been wrong about the cameras. He didn't usually make mistakes but...

No other bastard will see her.

He edged closer to her. Slid his hand down her body. She'd spread her legs. And it was so easy to dip between the edges of her robe. So easy to slide up and touch smooth, silken skin.

A gasp ripped from her lips.

He stroked her. Parted her. Found her wet. Hot. "Let's start with one," he whispered. Pierce slid one finger into her. God, she was... "Tight."

"It's...ah, been a while."

His heartbeat sounded like fireworks in his ears. "How long." Not a question. A rough demand.

"Almost...two years."

He withdrew his finger. Thrust it back into her. Let his thumb drag over her clit.

Another gasp from Iris.

"I-I haven't come this way." So low that he barely heard her. "Not with someone just—just touching—"

"You will," he promised. His thumb kept working her clit and slowly, he slid a second finger into her. *Tight.* She would feel insane around his cock. He'd drive into her and lose his mind. Pierce was sure of it. His sanity would be blown straight to hell.

Her hips arched, pressed against his hand. She jerked her hips in a quick rhythm to match his thrusting fingers.

She thought she wouldn't come this way? Oh, she'd come. She'd come hard. He'd make sure of it. He eased his fingers out of her. Went to her clit. Strummed her. Stoked. Played with sensual skill. When her body tensed, he worked her harder. Faster. Caressing the sensitive heart of her, then sliding one finger, then another into her. Pulling out. Strumming her clit once more Squeezing her with his slick fingers. Working her faster and faster—

Her whole body arched on the bed. She opened her mouth.

He kissed her and stole her cry of release. Iris shuddered against him. His fingers pushed into her. Felt the hot contractions of her core.

Control. Hold it. Hold. It.
His tongue thrust into her mouth.
Her sex squeezed his fingers.
So fucking hot.
His head lifted. His fingers slid out of her.
"Oh, damn," Iris whispered. "Damn."
She was fucking adorable.
She was *so* fuckable.
"But you—you didn't, you—"

No, he hadn't. He was painfully aware of that fact. "I won't. Not until I'm in you." Then it wouldn't be just one time that he came. When he plunged into her, one time wasn't going to satisfy him. The need was too savage and sharp. The hunger too primal. "I'll want you for a very long time."

Once more, he moved back to his side of the bed. His dick had tented his sweats—and the bed covers. His fingers were trembling. Pierce could not ever remember wanting someone so much.

"Let me do something for you," she whispered.

She didn't get it. "You touch me, and I'm done." He'd be in her two seconds later. His head turned on the pillow. His eyes had adjusted to the darkness, and it was easy to see that she'd turned her head to face him, too. "And you did do something, baby."

"I came." Another whisper. "You didn't."

"That's the something," he murmured even as a rush of possessive satisfaction filled him. "First time that way, huh?"

"Oh, God. You will never forget me saying that, will you?"

Not a chance. "What other firsts are you waiting for?" Because he'd be the one to deliver them.

"No one has ever gone down on me."

Fuck. He fisted the sheets. Nearly ripped them to shreds. "I *will* be doing that."

"And I've never gone down on anyone. I, um, would like to—"

"Stop!" A low warning.

"No, I didn't want to stop. You did. If I had my way, you'd be in me right now."

She is destroying me. "Baby, I'm trying not to pounce. But just so you know…I want your mouth on me. That *will* be happening." The images. The need. He was so close to coming. "Go to sleep," he growled.

"I'll probably just dream about you." A tired yawn. Her words were slurring. "I've done that before."

He heard fabric tear. The sheets. His fists had ripped them apart.

"Have you ever dreamed about me?" A soft murmur from Iris.

He didn't answer. He was too busy keeping his hands off her.

When we get home, I am going to fuck her so hard. In so many ways…

When she was safe. When he had her in his home. When he had her legs locked around him and her arms holding him tight…But until then…

This was going to be the longest night of his life.

Heaven and hell all rolled into one.

***

She felt good. Warm. Comfy. Safe.

Iris's eyes flickered open. Sunlight trailed through the windows, and the beautiful, flowing beams fell on—

Pierce.

An awake, hard-eyed Pierce who lay right beside her. Her body had actually curled around his. Her leg had hooked over his, and one of her hands pressed to his chest. His gaze was oh-so-aware. Feverishly aware. Bright with a burning need in those baby blues that had her swallowing.

And then flushing as she remembered just what she'd done with him before exhaustion had claimed her. "I—"

His jaw hardened. His nostrils flared.

"Good…morning?" Iris tried carefully.

"Thought it would be heaven and hell. Turned out it was just hell."

What was he talking about? Her brow furrowed.

"All I want to do is fuck you," he added, voice little more than a hungry rumble.

All I want to do is fuck you.

Oh. That was—

She heard something. The distant groan of an engine. The crunch of gravel beneath tires. Her body stiffened, then she shot up, only to realize that her robe had gaped open, and her breasts were peeking out to say good morning to Pierce, too, and he was—

"Fucking fuck."

He liked to do that, she'd noticed. Say double fucks.

In the next instant, he jumped out of bed. She had a fast flash of a very big tent in his sweats, then he was grabbing for his discarded shirt. "We're getting out of here. Get dressed as quickly as you can."

"The twenty-four hours aren't up." The only thing her still sleepy mind could pull together.

"My guess is that you aren't getting the full twenty-four. You did your job, now your buddy Constantine is back."

She slid from the bed. "He's not my buddy." Never had been. She'd once thought that he was tight with Remy, but she'd been wrong. Because if he'd been close to her brother, truly close, he never would have done this to her. He wouldn't have put her in danger. Or sold her out to his mystery boss.

Iris grabbed her paint-stained clothes from earlier. She had no intention of wearing anything that had been placed in the house. Maybe it was weird—

I used the soap. I used the shampoo but...

But she didn't want to take anything with her. She wanted to go and just leave this place in her rearview. So she dressed in a hurry. Yanked on everything as fast as she could. Then when she looked up—

Pierce was watching her. She'd never seen someone stare at her with such hard need. She rocked back half a step. "Pierce?"

He offered his hand to her. "I'll be with you every bit of the way." The words were a promise.

Her fingers curled around his.

Together, they made their way down the stairs. Just as they stepped into the foyer, the front door opened. Constantine swept them both with an assessing glance. "Guess you didn't need twenty-four hours." He looked toward the second level. "The painting up there?"

"Yes, but it's still wet, so if you plan to transport it, be very careful." She gave him a steely smile. "I'd hate for you to smudge my brilliant work."

"Don't move." A quick order. Then he bounded past them. Headed up the stairs.

She moved—deliberately—turning around and even taking a few steps to the side just to defy him. "It was like he didn't even hear my warning."

"He's an asshole," Pierce decided.

"Yes."

"How long have you known him?" Pierce added.

"Since I was about sixteen." Jeez, she'd even once had a crush on him. Talk about awkward and being *wrong*. Back then, she'd thought Constantine was one of the coolest guys she'd ever met. Whenever Remy had teased her, Constantine had always stepped up to her defense.

Those days were long gone.

Constantine's heavy footsteps thudded on the stairs as he hurried back toward them. "Iris, you painted the dress the wrong damn color."

She smiled. "No, I didn't."

"She's wearing *purple* in your picture. That's not what she's supposed to—"

"I painted the color I wanted. I also signed the work, as I'm sure you noticed."

"Hard to miss your big-ass signature," he grumbled as he jumped off the stairs.

Her shoulders straightened. "I didn't want your boss trying to use that painting." Iris then allowed a delicate pause because she had a role to play. When the silence had stretched *just* enough, she added, "Not without providing me with proper compensation. So if he wanted this paint show to be a test, then test it was. He'll be able to see I can get the job done, no problem." He also wouldn't be able to use the painting for any illegal purposes. Well, she hoped not, anyway.

A muscle flexed along Constantine's jaw. "The limo is waiting outside."

"And when will I be hearing from your boss?" she asked sweetly.

"Soon." His curt reply.

Pierce took an aggressive step toward him. "Yeah, that doesn't work for us."

"Man, you don't even need to be involved. She's the talent." Constantine made a shooing motion with his hand toward Pierce. "Why don't you just go back to protecting celebrities or whatever it is that you do at Wilde?"

"I'm involved because she is."

Constantine squinted. "I am so trying to figure you out." His head cocked. "You're involved because she paid you?"

Iris opened her mouth to reply.

"She hasn't paid me a dime," Pierce responded.

Technically, that was true. She hadn't. She *had* signed the contract, though, one with a negotiable fee. Which, yes, that was weird, she got it. Surely Wilde normally stipulated an upfront fee for clients? Maybe Pierce was giving her special treatment?

Constantine turned his squinty stare on her. "You have some street smarts now, yes? I remember you were a naive as hell kid. Remy always thought it was cute. I figured it was dangerous."

Her stomach clenched. "What are you talking about?"

He rubbed the back of his neck. "You get that Remy understood what your dad was doing in the old days, right? Remy was five years older than you. Of course, he knew. And like I said, he thought it was cute that you didn't. Or maybe..." His hand dropped. "Maybe he just liked that you thought he was some kind of freaking perfect hero. He wasn't, though. Not even close." A long exhale. "Did you ever wonder why Remy vanished the night your dad died?"

The clenching in her stomach got worse. "He's not dead." She would not believe that her brother had been killed, too. *Not Remy.*

"No, I never said he was." He watched her carefully. "But who is it that you think killed your father?"

She could actually feel every bit of blood draining from her face. Iris swayed. "No." She understood exactly what he was insinuating, and Constantine was *wrong*. "No!"

A shrug. "Just food for thought. I wasn't there. I wasn't in the room with your dad that night. But I was supposed to meet Remy at that location. I arrived too late. Saw you—saw you crying and covered in your father's blood. I ducked out right before the police arrived." His gaze never left her face. "From what I gathered, Remy never did show up. Or maybe—maybe he showed up *early*. Maybe he even beat me to the scene. Maybe he was long gone by the time I arrived. By the time you arrived. Maybe he was there with your dad—"

"*No!*" Almost a shout. "Remy wouldn't do that. He wouldn't kill our dad!" She could feel Pierce watching her, but he wasn't saying a word.

"*Rembrandt* always looked out for himself," Constantine snapped back. "And like I said, he knew exactly what your father was." He lifted his hand again, and she saw the wet paint on his fingers. He'd smudged her work.

And he's trying to make me believe my brother is a murderer.

Constantine's expression seemed almost pitying as he asked, "If you couldn't trust your own brother, why the hell would you trust this guy?" He pointed at Pierce. "You just met him. And isn't it ever-so-convenient that he showed up just when I did? That he just slipped into your life as if...as if he had been *planted* there by someone?"

"You sonofabitch," Pierce snapped. "You're trying to make her doubt me. Not gonna work."

Constantine didn't appear concerned. "Like I said, the limo is waiting."

"Tell your boss that we want twenty grand for last night's work." Pierce took Iris's hand in his. Squeezed her fingers. "I expect a delivery at Iris's place by the end of the day. If we don't get the payment, there will be no more work."

"Ah. So you're interested in the money. It has priority for you. Good to know. See, Iris, a person's true motives will always show."

She glared at him. "Fuck off." Anger burned through her. "Remy isn't a killer. He didn't stab my father in the chest and leave him to die in my arms. That didn't happen."

"Keep telling yourself that," Constantine advised.

"I *will*." She had to get out of there. Away from him. Out of the mansion that felt like a prison. She yanked Pierce's hand with hers as she spun for the door. When they burst outside, the light seemed too bright. The sunlight hit her in the face as she practically ran for the limo.

Iris jumped into the back. Pierce followed right behind her.

The door slammed. A moment later, the car rolled forward. She looked back at the house and saw that Constantine had followed them outside. He stood watching her, raising his hand to shield his face from the sun's glare.

"Your brother is named Rembrandt," Pierce spoke slowly.

"Remy for short. He always hated being called Rembrandt." She stopped looking back. What was the point? Iris faced forward. "Rembrandt was my dad's favorite all-time artist, but he also really loved the irises that Van Gogh painted after he entered the asylum in Saint-Remy. Van Gogh painted the irises that he saw in the asylum's garden." Her voice came out so low. Each word seemed an effort. "That's where my father got my name."

Before, Pierce had warned her to be careful talking in the limo. Iris was certain that same rule still applied. But talking about names? Hardly seemed dangerous.

"Did your mother like art?"

"She was a curator. She loved to collect art. My dad loved to remake it." She only had a few random memories of her mom. More flashes than anything else. "Fingerpainting," Iris whispered.

He still held her hand. Loosely, carefully. "What about fingerpainting?"

"I remember doing it with my mom. Just—like vague images." She smiled. "Yellow paint. I'm pretty sure it was all over me and not on the page. And I...I can sometimes still hear my mom's laugh."

"I'm sorry."

"It's okay." Her gaze had fallen to their joined hands. "I've been alone a long time now." Remy had never come back.

Because he killed our dad?

She slammed the door on that thought. *No, no.* Remy would not have done that. Yes, Remy and their father had argued plenty. She'd seen them do it, and she'd caught one particularly vicious bout about a day before her dad's death.

"You won't take her!" Remy's yell.

She'd walked in on them. Remembered smiling uncertainly. *"Won't take who?"*

They'd both stared at her.

Goose bumps rose on her arms as the memory slipped away.

"You're not alone anymore," Pierce told her.

She wanted his words to be true. But...they were probably deliberate. For whoever was listening. Part of the cover job. Just to make sure that their relationship seemed believable. He was playing the role of the concerned lover. The caring partner.

A pang pierced her heart, and she tugged her hand from his.

"Iris?"

She leaned her head back against the seat. "I'm really tired." No, she wasn't. What she was? *Terrified.* Constantine had just been trying to manipulate her. He was wrong about Remy. He had to be.

The brother she was risking everything to protect...he *couldn't* be a killer. He couldn't be the one who had destroyed her life.

***

She'd shut him out. Iris sat right next to him. Mere inches separated their bodies, but she had left him. Pierce could feel the distance.

Her eyes were closed. *Another way to shut me out.* She'd pulled away—physically and mentally—and he hated that withdrawal. Constantine had tried to make her doubt him. He'd wanted her to doubt Pierce and her own brother.

Isolate your prey. A basic warfare technique. He had underestimated Constantine. Pierce wouldn't be making that mistake again. As soon as he and Iris were alone, he'd be sure to regain his ground with her. No way would she be able to put walls between them.

Reason one...that would be too damn dangerous. If Constantine succeeded in getting her away from Pierce...*Oh, no, not happening.*

Reason two...*I need her too much.* He'd spent the night in hell, having the person he wanted most just inches away from him. He wasn't going to give her up now.

He'd briefed Colt about the case before they'd ever gotten into the limo. The guy had been given orders to watch Iris and Pierce's building while they were away. Once they were back home, Pierce would be checking in with his buddy ASAP.

Because if I were Constantine, I would have searched our homes. Maybe put in some listening devices and video surveillance equipment. It would be Colt's job to make sure that any and all surveillance tech was disabled—or jammed. Wilde had some very nice jamming products.

Speaking of tech...Constantine had left his scanner on the billiard table. So while Iris had been painting, Pierce had taken the liberty of pocketing the device. He wasn't familiar with the tech, and he wanted to know just what the hell it could do. The Feds *were* planning to send them in tagged with devices, and the last thing he wanted to do was get caught and have a gun shoved into his face.

Or, heaven forbid, into hers.

"I'm going to keep you safe, Iris," he promised.

She sucked in a breath. "Because you have a lot of experience at this sort of thing?"

He had experience at kicking ass. At getting in and out of dangerous situations. At taking down targets in bloody and violent ways. He didn't want to tell Iris about those dark parts of his past. Not now. Preferably not ever. Pierce didn't want her afraid of him. He wanted—

Maybe he just liked that you thought he was some kind of freaking perfect hero. He wasn't. Constantine's words rang through his mind. Hell. Maybe Pierce was just as bad as her missing brother. Because, if possible, Pierce wanted to keep his secrets from Iris. He wanted her to think he was hero material.

Even if he really wasn't.

CHAPTER ELEVEN

"Thanks for the ride," Pierce drawled to the stony-faced limo driver. "Total thrill." His hand pressed to the base of Iris's back. He urged her forward. The sooner they got away from the driver and into the security of his home, the better.

In moments, they were stepping into the elevator. An elevator that was occupied by a waiting Colt.

Pierce's brows lifted in surprise when he saw his partner, and Colt winked in response.

Colt pushed the button to close the doors. Then immediately halted the elevator with another press of a button. "You two can speak freely at Pierce's place and in here. Did a thorough sweep with Wilde tech after the crew left."

"The crew?" Iris rested her shoulders against the elevator's back wall. "What crew?"

"The crew that came after you departed. Weird team. They took some paintings from your place, covered them in sheets, and then transferred them to Pierce's place." He tapped his foot. "Didn't see anything else disturbed. I want to personally do another sweep of your place before you go in there, Iris. But like I said, Pierce's home is clear."

Worry flashed on her face. "Didn't they see you doing all this?"

"No one saw me enter the building. And they have no idea I'm even in this elevator now." He spoke with total confidence.

Her brow furrowed. "You're that good?"

"You have no idea."

Pierce's eyes narrowed. "Stop bragging and just tell us what else we need to know."

"Sure. They wore gloves. They were fast. Obviously, not a first-ballgame situation. And the Feds saw them do it all. They are watching from across the street, by the way. Now *that* is amateur hour. I swear, I caught one guy actually standing in front of the window with binoculars as he peered over at Iris's home. He might as well have been shining a neon-light. Maybe someone can give the guy a head's up that he's going to screw up this whole scene if he's not careful?" A frustrated sigh escaped Colt.

"I'll take care of it," Pierce promised.

"I suspected you would." His foot stopped tapping. "Any problems last night? FYI, I really don't like it when you go all radio dark on me."

Iris's alarmed gaze immediately flew to Pierce.

"It's an expression," he assured her. "I wasn't wearing any wires." Which reminded him... Pierce shoved his hand into his pocket and hauled out the scanner. "Got some tech I want analyzed." He tossed it to Colt.

Colt caught it. Frowned. "What in the hell is this supposed to be?"

"He used it to scan us," Iris said. "Constantine did. He said he was making sure we weren't wearing any listening devices." She turned on

Pierce. "Don't you think Constantine will notice that you took it?"

Did he care? "If he didn't want me to take it, then he shouldn't have just left it lying around." He leaned forward and shoved the button to get the elevator moving. "I need to talk to Iris, alone. Call me when you find out something useful."

"Will do." Colt's gaze lingered on Iris for just a moment.

"Asshole took my gun," Pierce groused, almost as an afterthought. "But I have plenty of backups at my place."

The doors opened. Pierce and Iris headed down the hallway together, and Iris paused briefly by her own door.

The first time he'd seen her, she'd been standing in that doorway, with light all around her. The most beautiful woman he'd ever seen. It was truly a miracle he hadn't dropped his boxes and broken every dish he owned. He'd barely been able to breathe when he first locked eyes on her.

"Why do you think he moved your paintings into my place?" he asked, mostly just to have something to say.

But at his words, she gave a little jolt. Her cheeks flushed. "I may have an idea." Her chin lifted and her shoulders straightened as she picked up her pace and hurried to his door.

He followed behind her, a little slower. A little more thoughtfully.

She waited while he opened the door. As soon as they stepped inside, he saw the paintings that were waiting for him. Covered in heavy cloths and perched near his couch. Almost waiting like some sort of surprise presents.

"I didn't intend anything illegal." Iris's words rushed out. "I get that you probably won't believe me. And, yes, this will look bad. I don't even know why I did it. It was like a compulsion. I just—I had to paint. Then I'd hate myself when I did and—" She blew out a breath. "Screw it." Iris marched to the paintings. Ripped off the coverings. One by one by one.

Then she stood there, with her hands fisted on her hips, and her dark gaze blazed as she waited for his reaction.

He looked at the canvases. "They destroyed your art." Deep slashes cut across the canvases.

"No, I did that. I sliced each one of them."

A frown pulled at his brows. "Why the hell would you do that?"

"Because I didn't want someone coming along and trying to take them. Crazy, isn't it? As crazy as everything else in my life, and now I've gone and yanked you into my madness."

"Aren't we all a little mad?" he mused.

"Yes, Alice," she replied without missing a beat, "welcome to my wonderland. Bet you never expected to fall down this particular rabbit hole when you met me, did you?"

No, he hadn't. "I like the unexpected." Even with the slashes in the work, he could tell he was looking at talent. "More Monet?"

"He is my specialty."

A nod. "But you do like to branch out." He glanced away from the paintings. "Thus, the idiot wannabe male model who was sniffing around you the other day. Bentley something?"

Her lips parted. "I...yes. I like to branch out. I want to have my own style. My voice. My passion."

"Um." He wanted to touch her. Feel all her passion. "The offer still stands, you know."

"What offer?"

"My modeling services. I'll get naked for you whenever you want. No charge at all. No need for Bentley."

She blinked. Shook her head. Then stalked to the paintings. She grabbed one. Lifted it up. "Did you see this?"

"Yes, I did. Hard to miss since it's in front of my new couch."

"I'm a forger."

"I have heard that rumor."

Her hold tightened on the painting. "It's not a rumor. It's the truth. I'm a forger. I was raised to be a forger. Trained by another freaking forger who happened to be my father." She shoved down the painting. Her chest rose and fell rapidly as spots of red stained her cheeks. "My brother was a forger. And, apparently, he was also a liar, just like my dad. They stole art. They sold their talents out to the highest bidder—they sold me." Her nostrils flared. "I'm just like them."

"I don't think so."

"*Look* at what I've been doing! I should have gone to jail when I was a teen—"

"No. You were a kid. You were used. You were—"

"I shouldn't have pulled you into this mess. When I first turned to you, I was panicking. I was just thinking about protecting myself. About getting my brother back. I was selfish and cold, and that wasn't right." Her words came even faster. "You've been nothing but kind to me since the moment we first met. Nothing but good. I thought it was the luckiest day of my life when I met you. I don't meet a lot of *good* people. Everyone else close in my life has wanted to use me. You were the first one who was different."

He *hated* her pain.

"You were different, but then what did I do?" Her hand lifted to shove back a lock of her hair that had tumbled over her forehead. "I proved I was just like them."

What was she talking about?

"I used you," Iris concluded sadly. "I used our friendship."

Hell, were they back to that?

"I used your goodness."

Um, his what now?

"I took advantage of you."

Take advantage all night long.

"You're a good person, Pierce. I'm trouble. I panicked, and I came to you when I shouldn't have."

Oh, he did not like where this conversation might be going.

"But I'm not going to have you vanish with me again. The Feds are working the case." A bitter laugh. "Apparently, they are just across the street. They will be my backup. Everything will be fine.

I'll work the deal to help my brother, and I will keep you out of things from now on."

Back to the deal.

"Even if Remy did lie to me. Even if he did use me. Because he's family, the only family I have left." A slow exhale. "But I won't use you. We were a mistake, and from this moment forward, that mistake is over." Her shoulders sagged like she'd just shed a huge burden. Iris started walking forward, as if she'd walk out of his door. His life.

So he sidestepped and put himself directly in her path. She almost walked straight into him, but at the last moment, her head snapped up. Her steps staggered to a halt.

"That is fucking adorable," he told her, truly serious. "Precious even."

"Excuse me?"

"The fact that you think I've been helping you out of the kindness of my heart. That I helped you because of our *friendship*." His absolute, least favorite F-word ever. "That you think I'm good. Some nice little helper who just does good deeds for fun."

She rocked back a little. "I don't understand."

"Obviously, and that is entirely my fault. I was trying to hold back so I didn't scare you off, and apparently, I held back too much. Now you think I'm the friendly neighborhood bodyguard while I am actually something very, very different."

"What?"

"Constantine called you naive. I think you're too trusting."

Red flashed more in her cheeks. "Excuse me?"

"You kind of remind me of Little Red Riding Hood." Brutal truth time. "You came walking into the woods, swinging your basket. The wolf saw you, and he figured that in order to get close, he had to pretend to be something he wasn't."

She swallowed. "In this little story, I'm guessing you're the wolf?"

Fuck, yeah, baby. I'm the wolf. "The wolf didn't want to scare you away. After all, if you took one look and saw his big teeth and big claws..." *And big, eager dick.* "You'd run. He didn't want that."

"I...should tell you I don't know a lot about Little Red Riding Hood. Remy read *Alice in Wonderland* to me when I was a kid, but I don't know a whole lot of—of fairytales. My dad wanted me painting. There wasn't a lot of time for other things."

The more he learned about her dad, the more pissed Pierce became. "That's okay. I'll tell you how the story ends."

Her breathing came a little faster.

That lock of her hair fell forward again. This time, he reached out and slid it back. His knuckles brushed over the silk of her cheek. "The wolf pretended he was harmless. No threat at all. And so you got closer to the wolf." *My, my, what big, dark eyes you have.* He could get lost staring into her eyes. "You spent time with him. Curled up with the wolf on his couch. Laughed and teased. The wolf slipped right past your guard, and you never even realized you'd been sharing your life with a beast."

"No." She stepped back. "You're not some wolf. I know bad guys. You are not bad. You would never hurt me."

"I would not." *But I would fight like hell to protect you.* "That doesn't mean I am not well acquainted with bad. And, baby, I can be so very bad."

"I'm...I'm going to my place."

Not yet. "I wanted to fuck you all night long. When you were sleeping in bed with me last night? I wanted to take and take."

Another step back. "But you didn't."

"Wrong place. Wrong time. When I'm buried balls deep in you, I want you screaming my name, slamming your hips into mine, and not worrying that someone you don't know might be listening or preparing to rush into the room."

Her cheeks were dark crimson. "Yes, that would...be, ahem, not the most ideal situation. Getting interrupted, that is."

Her voice had gone husky. A good sign. Her backing up? Not good. He wanted her to surge toward him. To put her hot little hands all over him.

So he told her, "I wanted to kiss you the first day I saw you."

"You didn't." Even breathier.

"Kiss you. Caress you. Fuck you. Like I said, the wolf needed to get close. I was hungry for you from the first moment, so I just played the role you wanted."

Her brows scrunched. "What role would that be?"

He'd played several roles. "Friend first. You wanted someone who would hang out with you. You were lonely."

Her mouth dropped open, but Iris quickly snapped it closed. "You felt *sorry* for me?"

"No. I felt like I wanted to fuck you."

"*Stop* saying that!" She fanned herself. "What is happening here?"

"You're trying to run away because you have this weird idea that by leaving, you'll somehow protect me. Like I told you before, it is adorable. I don't need protecting, though. Never have. Never will. Baby, I can kill a man in more ways than you can imagine."

A half-step back. "What?"

"I shouldn't have said that." He looked down at her feet. "I get that was some oversharing on my part. How about I qualify and say that I was trained in the military to be an effective hunter and soldier? Is that better?"

She inched toward him.

He smiled as his gaze lifted. But he must not have looked particularly harmless because uncertainty flickered over her beautiful features.

Are you seeing the wolf now, sweetheart?

"I played your friend. Then I played your bodyguard." A role he intended to keep playing. "I didn't have to take the job, you know. I could have assigned the case to someone else. Or I could have just said no."

"But you didn't." Soft. Thoughtful. Suspicious. "Because you were still trying to get close to me?"

I am close to you. So close that her honey and cream scent wrapped around him. So close that he still touched her cheek. "I like being close to you." He liked it when his fingers were *in* her tight sex. Liked it when she gave that hot little gasp from the back of her throat.

"Even knowing what I am?" Iris pushed.

What she was? "Knowing you're the sexiest woman I've ever met?"

"I'm a criminal. My art pieces are just frauds. I'm fake, I'm—"

"You're fucking perfect to me."

"No." A shake of her head. She started to rock back. "No—"

His hands moved to curl around her elbows. "You take a little half-step back when you're either lying or afraid."

Her eyes widened.

"Which is it this time?"

"Pierce..."

"Because you don't need to be afraid of me. Want to know an important fact about the big, bad wolf?"

She stared at him with her big, deep, and dark eyes.

His gaze devoured her. "He protects his own. And, you, sweetheart, are most definitely mine." He let his mask fall. He let all his hunger, his need, his dark lust for her show.

And she—

She surged up onto her toes. Surged toward him. Her hands grabbed him as she hauled Pierce close and kissed him.

CHAPTER TWELVE

Desire exploded through her. She kissed him frantically, and he kissed her back the same way. There was no restraint. No gentle touches. Her nails dug into him even as he hauled her up against him. His hands were tight on her waist, and her legs locked around him. Much like they had when she'd kissed him in her apartment and need had ripped through her control.

The same need rode her now, except...

Except she knew that she could let go with him. She knew what waited. She knew he'd be giving her oh, so much pleasure.

"Baby..." His mouth tore from hers, and he began to kiss a blazing path down her neck. "I am going to eat you up."

Was that what the wolf would do?

Then he hit a particularly sensitive spot on her neck, and she moaned as her eyes squeezed shut. The world seemed to shift, and she realized they were moving. He took fast steps, and her eyes opened to see that they were in his bedroom.

He put her down near the edge of the bed. Proceeded to strip. All the moisture left her mouth as she just enjoyed the spectacular view.

His t-shirt hit the floor. Muscles and muscles and muscles. He kicked out of his shoes, ditched his socks, then his tanned hands shoved down the waistband of his—

Her eyes widened. *Wow.*

"This will work so much better if you strip, too."

He was thickly aroused. Long. Hard. Heavy. "You are *way* bigger than the guys I've been with before."

A growl.

Her eyes flew to his.

"First, thank you." His nostrils flared. "Second, let's not ever talk about them the fucking fuck again, okay?"

Fine by her.

He reached for the hem of her shirt. "You are still dressed." He yanked the shirt over her head. Tossed it onto the floor next to his. "I'll help with that problem."

She squirmed and kicked off her shoes. He tugged down her paint-stained jeans, and his fingers burned a path down her hips and over her thighs. Then the jeans were in the corner, and he'd managed to take her socks with them.

She still wore her bra. Her panties. Both were blue.

"Sexy. Love that color."

Should she tell him that her favorite color was blue? Just like his eyes?

"You taking them off? Or am I?"

Her hands fluttered in the air ever so uselessly.

"Got it." *His* hand moved behind her. Deftly unhooked her bra. It fell to the floor between them as he eased back to stare down at her chest.

She was on the small side. Always had been. Yes, it would be fabulous to have big, beautiful breasts, but that hadn't been in the cards for her, and maybe she was not—

"Fucking gorgeous."

Her back *may* have arched the tiniest bit right before his fingers closed over her nipples.

Her breath hissed out.

In the next instant, he lifted her up. High and easily. His mouth covered one nipple, and he lashed her with his tongue. It was such a good thing that he held her because otherwise, her knees probably would have done a crazy jiggle. He licked and sucked, and a moan broke from her.

He lowered her onto the bed. Licked her other nipple. Sucked her strong and hard, and her eyes pretty much rolled back into her head.

"That tattoo is sexy as hell."

She levered up her head enough to see that he was staring at the tattoo below her breasts.

A crescent moon surrounded by faint stars. Small, curving with elegant lines. Her own version of a starry night. An image that she'd created to remind herself that there was always a little bit of light even in the dark.

He kissed a path over the tattoo. Down her stomach. Down...down...

Her breath caught. She'd told him before that no one had ever gone down on her. Iris had the feeling she was seconds away from another first with Pierce.

He caught her panties. Didn't pull them down. Just ripped them away.

"That was, um, unnecessary," she managed. But hot, dammit. *Hot.*

"It was also faster. And fun." His gaze was on her sex. "Spread your legs."

She did.

He smiled.

"You—ah, you don't have to—"

"I one hundred percent do."

His mouth took her. Rational thought ended. His tongue lashed her, he teased, he thrust that slick tongue into her, then withdrew it. He worked her clit—over and over with strokes of his tongue. First slow, then fast. Soft. Hard. She bit her lower lip to hold back her cries.

"I want to hear everything. It's only for me. *Me.*"

Her lips parted, and she cried out his name when he pushed two fingers into her. Fingers in her core even as his tongue slid over her clit. Again and again.

She came. Felt the tension break apart inside of her like a tidal wave crashing.

"Hell, yes." She *felt* his words against her. "*Yes.*" His fingers were gone. His tongue thrust inside of her. Her hips bucked off the bed, but he held her with one hand so she didn't go flying.

No, I am flying. It felt as if she was soaring and bursting through the clouds as pleasure rushed through her. And when he rose above her moments later, she was still gasping. Shuddering.

His eyes—her heart beat even faster as she stared up at him. His eyes *burned.* The blue seared Iris straight to her soul. He leaned over. Yanked open the nightstand and pulled something out. A condom. She fought to catch her breath while he tore open the packet and shoved on the condom.

This is it. This is happening.

He positioned his cock at the entrance of her body. She pushed against him eagerly, wanting him inside.

"Never going back to the friend zone." A growl.

Iris arched her hips against him, shoved up, and took him inside of her. There was a brief flash of resistance, she felt her muscles strain around him, then her sex clamped greedily—eagerly—around his dick.

"Fucking fuck."

She would have smiled at his double curse but need spiraled in her again. Her body strained against him, and there was no way she could speak. He drove into her again and again, seemingly with an unquenchable hunger. She held on tightly. Locked her legs around him. Let the pleasure take over.

This time, she yelled his name. A strong, powerful yell.

And, moments later, his hips pistoned even harder against hers. She stared in his eyes, saw the blue go blind with pleasure right before...

"Iris!" A roar.

***

His phone rang.

Pierce opened one eye, glared, and seriously thought about ignoring the damn thing.

Except...the ringtone—the weird, extraterrestrial music—belonged to Colt. And if his partner was calling, it had to be important.

He slipped from the bed. Where the hell was his phone? *Ah. There.* On the floor. Figured.

"What's happening?" Iris's sleepy voice. They'd both dozed after the sex. *The best damn sex ever.* Not just one bout. It had taken two before he'd been able to get his control back enough to get his dick to calm down.

"Colt." He swiped up the phone. Put it to his ear. "Missing me already?"

"Company is headed your way. Thought you might appreciate a heads-up." Colt's voice was mild. "Didn't want anyone bursting into your home at a super awkward time." He cleared his throat. "The way you were eyeing Iris told me that you planned to have an, ahem, very in-depth conversation with her ASAP. Not the kind of conversation you want the Feds witnessing."

The Feds. Hell. He marched to the window. Peered outside. Saw Bryce in his cheap suit hurrying across the street.

"Like I said," Colt murmured. "Those fellows have no good idea about how to keep a low profile. I sincerely hope all FBI agents are not that clueless. Anyone watching the building will see you get a visit. So if I were you, I'd keep that in mind and play the scene just right."

"Have you spotted any other people I need to be aware of?"

"Not yet. Doesn't mean they aren't there."

Absolutely. "Thanks for the heads-up." He ended the call. Turned back toward Iris. Just had to stop and stare.

She'd sat up in the bed. Her hair tangled around her face. Her eyes looked extra dark and deep. Her lips were slightly swollen from his kisses.

Before he'd let her doze, he'd kissed nearly every inch of her. Tasted all of her. *And I want to do it again.*

Unfortunately, company was coming. "Your FBI buddy is on his way up."

She sucked in a breath. "Probably wants an update on our meeting last night."

Pierce figured that what Bryce wanted was to keep using Iris in his master plan to take down the art ring.

She jumped from the bed. Tugged the sheet with her. Looked at the clothes scattered on the floor. Glanced back up at Pierce. Bit her lip.

He smiled at her.

"We should...talk about what happened, shouldn't we?" Iris began, obviously flustered and nervous.

So freaking cute. "If you want."

Her gaze cut to the door. "But Bryce will be here soon."

"It would seem so." He wasn't overly concerned about the Fed.

"I need to go to my place. Get dressed in fresh clothes." Her hand rose to touch her hair. "Oh, God, it's a mess, isn't it?"

"You're never a mess." She looked hot. Sensual.

Her hand moved to her lips. Her eyes widened. "Do I look like I just had sex?"

"No."

Her shoulders sagged.

"You look like you just had sex *twice*. Got that gorgeous, after-sex glow going on."

Her shoulders snapped right back up. "That is not helpful."

Wasn't it?

She dropped the sheet. Gave him the sensational view he loved before throwing on her clothes as fast as she could. Most of her clothes, anyway. Her panties were ruined. "Stall him, will you? I'll go back to my place, change, and—"

"He's on his way up. Probably in the elevator now." Because the Fed just kept making himself at home in the building. *Where did that all-access pass magically come from?* "Don't think there is going to be time for you to rush down the hall and find fresh clothing."

She grabbed her hair. Attempted to smooth it back. Didn't achieve that goal, but just made herself look sexier. "You should get dressed, too."

If she insisted. He grabbed a pair of clean jeans. Tugged them on. Dragged on a black t-shirt. Even toed into shoes.

And heard the pounding at his door.

Someone had been fast.

Pierce took his time heading for the door. Iris's bare feet padded on the floor behind him. He peered through the peephole. Saw the agent glaring impatiently. For fun, Pierce counted to five, giving Bryce a little longer to wait and cool his heels.

"Why aren't you opening the door?" Iris whispered.

For shits and giggles probably wasn't the best response. He glanced back at her. "Do you trust him?"

The question seemed to give her pause. "He's an FBI agent."

That wasn't really an answer. "Does he know about all those canvases behind me?"

She slipped back half a—

He caught her wrist. "I'll take that as a no. How about we move them into the bedroom?"

She spun and immediately grabbed a canvas. For a moment, he watched her. *Iris doesn't trust Bryce. If she did, she wouldn't be scrambling to hide this part of herself. But then again...she hid it from me, too. Does that mean she doesn't trust me, either?*

More pounding shook the door. He ignored it and helped Iris move the paintings. She yanked the bedroom door shut, slamming it a little too hard, and then they finally let the FBI agent in Pierce's home.

"What in the hell took you so long?" Bryce demanded. His gaze swept between them. Narrowed. Understanding dawned and his lips thinned. "I do not need this personal crap between you two messing up my case."

"Right," Pierce responded easily. "Especially since you are doing such a thorough job of screwing things up on your own without any assistance from us."

Bryce glared at him. "What in the hell is that supposed to mean?"

"Well, Captain Way Too Obvious, have you thought that doing a stake-out right across the street isn't the best plan? Or that just strolling over *in broad daylight* might attract attention? Did they not teach any low-profile skills to you at Quantico?"

Bryce's cheeks puffed out. "No one noticed me come into the building."

Not even half true. "My partner noticed you and your whole FBI crew. That's how I knew you were across the street. *And* he saw you heading this way moments ago. If he saw you, that means others did, too. You need to play your game way better." He considered the situation. "Or are you actively *trying* to scare off the target that Iris is supposed to be catching?" A worrisome thought.

"I had to come in! I need to talk to Iris."

Pierce didn't buy his story. "And a phone call just wouldn't do the trick?"

"Asshole, there are some things that need to be said in person." Bryce stalked closer to Iris. Jerked a hand through his hair. "I...shit. I'm sorry, Iris."

"Sorry?" A little line appeared between her brows. "For what?"

Pierce could name plenty of reasons the guy should be sorry. *How about for dragging you into this mess, for—*

"The body was found a few days ago. It just—it took some time to identify him, or I would have told you the news sooner."

All the color bled from Iris's face. "Remy?"

Shit. *No, do not be—*

"No. It's not your brother," Bryce rushed to say.

A breath shuddered from her.

Bryce wrapped his hands around her shoulders. "It was Franco Lopez."

Who the hell was that?

"My handler?" Her eyes widened.

"Franco was still working with the U.S. Marshals. Everyone thought he was on a case. Like I said, it took some time to identify the body. We were trying to figure out how our target had found your location, and it seems..." His words trailed away.

"Wait." She broke from his grasp. "You're saying Franco was killed because someone wanted to find me? *OhmyGod, when I said he'd ghosted me...you're telling me that Franco was dead?*"

A grim nod. "Your case files are missing from his office. The current idea is that he was...he was going to sell them. Give the buyer your location." His features tightened. "It's suspected that after the buyer got what he wanted, he killed Franco."

Sonofabitch. This was a clusterfuck of a nightmare. Pierce felt his temples begin to throb. "Now you're panicking because you suspect the same thing is going to happen to her," Pierce blasted. *Oh, the hell, no, it will not.* He wouldn't let it happen.

Iris's head whipped toward him. "What do you—you think they're going to kill me?"

After you do their job, they might try. It was obvious Bryce feared the same thing. There were secrets in Bryce's eyes. Hell, Pierce could practically smell the stench of lies coming from the agent. "What else haven't you told us?"

"I-I just found out about Franco—"

"Do I look like I enjoy BS? The Feds are all-in on this case. You're practically salivating. If a U.S. Marshal has been murdered, that means we are playing in the big leagues. This isn't just about art. It's about homicides. How many?"

Bryce darted a glance at Iris. A glance laced with guilt.

Oh, fuck. "Her father?"

Iris shook her head. Hard. "Wait. Stop. Just back up." She stepped away from Bryce. "You think the same person who killed my dad also killed the U.S. Marshal? But why?"

Bryce's jaw locked. "I'm not at liberty to discuss specific details."

What the actual hell? The Fed kept pushing all of Pierce's buttons. "You're at liberty to use her. To toss her into your investigation and leave her dangling in the wind, but you can't tell her how those two murders are linked? Why the hell not?" But Pierce had already realized one very important fact. How could he not? It was staring him right in the face.

She's the link. The link to her father. The link to the Marshal. His spine stiffened. "How many more?"

"How many more what?" Iris asked, frowning.

But the Fed knew what he meant. It was on his face. In his eyes.

How many more bodies?

"I've said everything I can," Bryce stiffly declared. "I know Iris liked Franco. I wanted her to know what happened to him." Once more, he ran his hand through his hair. "And I do need that update. Tell me...did you see the ringleader? Face-to-face? Can you identify him? Was he with you last night?"

"We only saw Constantine," Iris told him.

The lines near Bryce's mouth bracketed. "That jerk is always in the way."

Tell me about it. Not like Pierce was a Constantine fan.

"You followed us to the location," Iris noted as her head tilted slightly. "You must have. Did *you* see any sign of the elusive boss?"

"Didn't need to follow too closely. I tracked your phones. And, no, we didn't see our target."

Her eyelashes flickered.

"Who owns the house?" Pierce wanted to know. "The place was expensive as hell. So whoever owns it—odds are he is either the guy you're after or he's tangled deep with him."

Bryce coughed. "About the house...here's the thing—no one owns it. The previous owner died last year. The property is listed for sale. Our target knew it was empty. He got you in there because it was the perfect place—"

"For his test," Iris concluded. Her voice was a little raspy, haunted, and shadows darkened her eyes.

She's thinking about Franco. About her father.

"It was perfect for his test." She wrapped her arms around her stomach.

"He wanted you to paint?" Bryce asked.

Pierce fired the Fed a look of disgust. "No, he wanted her to dance a freaking jig. What the fuck else would he have wanted?"

Bryce flipped him off.

Iris quietly said, "Yes. Painting on site was his test. He had cameras set up, and he wanted to see me in action."

"And did you pass the test?"

"Of course." A bitter smile curled her lips. "I'm very good at my work."

Pierce could feel her pain. He hated it. He moved closer to her so that their shoulders brushed. "As long as you and your FBI buddies don't scare him off," he told Bryce, "he'll take the bait. That means you need to start keeping a low profile." If it wasn't already too late for that. Rage blasted through him as he charged, "Except now I'm realizing you're sending her in to face a killer."

"Oh, what? Like you thought these were the type of bad guys who spent their days baking cookies?" A snort from Bryce. "Like *you're* the kind of guy who does that crap? The stakes are huge. The danger is high." His stare lingered on Iris. "But the payout is worth it. We close this case, you get us the info we need, and we can stop these bastards. We can take out the ringleader."

Iris frowned. "You take him out, *and* my brother gets his freedom. He doesn't have to run any longer. That was the deal."

"Right. Sure. Your brother." A nod.

You are such a liar, Agent Robertson. Pierce wasn't going to let the jerk get away with BS. "You made a deal about her brother. Iris gives you the evidence you need, and her brother *will* get his freedom."

"Remy will not be charged with forgery cases." An immediate reply.

One that was far too slick for Pierce's liking. Because there were plenty of other crimes that the Feds could charge Remy with...things like murder.

Iris's gaze cut to Pierce. He saw the fear in her eyes. Fear and worry and dying hope. She feared this whole case was about her brother. About *him* being the mysterious ringleader. And she wanted to be wrong. Her attention swung back to Bryce. "Who killed my father?"

"You know we were never able to charge anyone—"

"Who were the suspects?"

Bryce's hands fisted. Released. "Honestly? You were one of them."

Shock filled her face. "What?"

"Your prints were on the knife, Iris. You had his blood on your body. You had motive. He'd been using you for years. He'd just entered an arrangement to have you create more forgeries—and you had finally realized how badly he'd misled you for your entire life."

Iris flinched.

"If you had lost it in that instant and attacked, I'm sure plenty of people would have understood."

Enough of this shit. Pierce leapt in front of her. "If you don't have anything else useful to tell us, how about you get the hell out?"

Bryce thrust up his chin. "What's your problem, buddy?"

"You are, obviously." *And I'm not your buddy.* "You think I don't get what you're doing? It's like beginner FBI 101. You need to stop wasting your energy, though. You aren't going to convince Iris to make some big confession to you by acting like you understand her. That you get her pain or some other crap."

Bryce's eyes lit up. "Does she have a confession to make?"

Pierce made sure to keep his body between Iris and the Fed. "No. Iris isn't a killer. But you knew that when she was just seventeen or you would have charged her with something back then. So don't try your manipulation bullshit now. It won't work." A disgusted shake of his head. "I'm sure you realized she wasn't guilty at the scene with her father. She was probably wrecked with grief. Crying uncontrollably. She was in pain, and you took advantage of—"

"Actually, Iris didn't shed a single tear that night. One of the things that stood out to everyone. She had her father's blood on her, and she—"

"It's called *shock,* asshole," Iris gritted out. "It's what happens when your father dies in your arms and his blood covers you and your whole soul *screams.*" She jumped from behind Pierce and lunged for the Fed.

CHAPTER THIRTEEN

She swung toward Bryce's face with her hand clenched into a tight fist.

"Can't let you do it." Pierce locked his arms around her waist and just seemed to pluck her from the air. He hauled her back against him and her swinging fist missed its target by a good two feet.

What in the hell?

"Tempting, I know, but you hit him, then maybe he arrests you for assaulting an agent. He tries to take you into custody, tries to take you from me, then I basically have to burn the world down to get you back." Pierce's hold was strong, but he didn't hurt her, not even a little. "I'd do it, of course, but I'm sure there is an easier way to go about things. A way that doesn't involve me being separated from you."

Since when was Pierce the cool and collected one? He'd been swinging plenty at Constantine. And at those creeps in the park and...

What happened to those creeps? Where were they? Still in custody? She certainly hoped so. The Feds seemed to have made them vanish.

Bryce straightened his dark gray suit. "I get that emotions are running high." A sniff. "Been a big twenty-four hours."

Running high? She twisted in Pierce's grip. "Let me go."

He didn't. "If I do, you'll go straight for him again. We both know it."

She seethed. He was right.

"You were a suspect," Bryce continued doggedly as he beetled his bushy brows at her. "I'm the one who pushed for the others to believe that you were innocent *and* finally got you a new identity in a new city. So maybe remember that stuff when you have your rage moments? You and Remy were both always so high strung. Must be an artist thing. He could never control his temper, either. He—" Bryce broke off. Pressed his lips together.

"Do not stop now." She could actually hear the rush of her blood in her ears. "Keep going. Is this where you say that Remy was also a suspect?"

His head tilted. "Do you think your brother killed your father?"

"I asked you the question first!"

"Yes, but I'm not the one who knew Remy the best. You are. You're his prized sister. The one he would do anything in the world to protect. Just as you would do anything for him." A pause. "After all, look what you're doing for him now. He's abandoned you for years, and yet you are still willing to risk everything for him. That's quite the deep bond. Got to say, part of me envies it. I'm an only child. Never had a sibling who would fight so hard for me. But I guess that's what Remy did for you, huh? Always protected you. Always shielded you from all the harsh realities of life."

The rush in her ears got worse. "You're saying he knew what my father was doing. That he lied to me."

His eyes widened. "Is that what I'm saying? Sounds to me like it's what *you* are saying."

It was what that jerk Constantine had said.

"You're not a kid any longer." Bryce's voice deepened. "You don't get to sit on the bench while the adults play the game. You have to open your eyes and see what's right in front of you."

She saw an FBI agent in front of her. A man who'd kept plenty of secrets over the years. "I'd rather look at what's behind me." An admission that just slipped out even as her head turned.

Pierce's arms still caged her. He held her with his easy strength, and when she looked back, he was what she saw. His eyes were bright with emotion, but she couldn't quite read all the tangle of feelings in his gaze. Rage. Worry. Yes, but—

"I've got your back, baby," Pierce assured her. "Don't worry about that."

Bryce laughed. "Behind you? A lying father and a brother with criminal ties—that is what waits behind you. That is your past. I'm offering you a future. A clean slate. All you have to do is finish one job for me."

Her head angled back toward him.

Bryce scratched his chin. "If your work was good enough, he'll call you. Guess we're in a waiting game."

It was more than good enough. It was almost insulting for him to suggest otherwise.

"He's going to bring her a cash payment first," Pierce's voice rumbled. It was a rumble that she felt run the length of her body. "Baby..." His breath rustled against her hair. "If I let go, are you attacking again?"

No, she was better now. For the moment. "I'm good." Mostly.

His arms slowly released her. "We demanded twenty grand for the test run. When we get the money, you can trace it back to the owner. We might not need to continue this charade at all. Job done."

Bryce gaped as if Pierce had just said something insane. "You demanded twenty grand? And you think he's just going to jump to do your bidding?"

"I think if he wants Iris badly enough, he will. Your Feds are watching the building. My partner has eyes on it, too. I think when payment comes calling, we'll know. I said I wanted the cash delivered by the end of the day. When we get it, we can check—"

"Serial numbers," Iris murmured.

"Exactly. We can try tracing him via those numbers."

Bryce laughed. A loud and grating sound. "That's not going to happen. He's not going to make an amateur mistake." He pointed at them. "If you get paid, it will probably be in small, unmarked bills. Constantine will be the delivery driver, and if we nab Constantine, the whole project stops. We can't make that move, not yet."

It kept coming back to Constantine. Goose bumps rose on her arms. "Are we sure he isn't the one pulling the strings? Constantine? How do we know that there even is a real boss? Maybe it's just him." Maybe it had always been him.

Could Constantine have killed my father?

Bryce jerked back his head. "What?"

"Constantine is smart, he's dedicated, and he knows one hell of a lot about art." Remy had taught him plenty in the old days. "Are we sure Constantine isn't the man we're after?" The more she considered the option, the more suspicion Iris felt.

"He's a flunky. Just a cog in the wheel." A dismissive reply from Bryce. "Constantine has got a rap sheet a mile long from his youth."

His youth. She locked on that point. "What's he been doing since he's been an adult?"

Bryce frowned.

Pierce didn't speak. She was sure he was mulling over this possibility and considering angles.

"Has he been arrested in the last few years?" Iris pushed. Constantine hadn't been arrested at the time her world had gone to hell. In fact, Constantine had just...sort of appeared with her brother back in those days. Popped into their lives. Overnight, he'd seemingly become Remy's shadow. Fast friends, Remy had called it. *We met at the right time, in the right place.* But...

What if it was more? What if it had always been more?

"He's a minor player," Bryce muttered.

Maybe. Or maybe he just wanted to look minor.

"Look, you're off track." Bryce huffed out a hard breath. "Your job isn't to play junior PI. It's to just wear the wire. To give us the recordings that we need—"

"Yeah, that's gonna be tricky," Pierce cut in to say. "Because the first thing that Constantine did was check to make sure we weren't transmitting anything. So getting big confessions on the record for you isn't going to be a walk in the park."

Bryce's brow furrowed.

"Did you *seriously* not think they'd check us out?" Pierce asked silkily. "They don't trust us. Iris passed the painting test, but it's not like they're just gonna throw caution to the wind from here on out."

"The plan will work," Bryce insisted even as a flicker of uncertainty echoed in his voice. "We have access to some tech they might not expect. Not like the old days when you had to tape a long cord with a microphone to your chest. Things are tiny now. They transmit well and far."

"Yeah, we already saw some tech that we didn't recognize," Pierce tossed back. Iris noticed that he didn't mention that he'd taken the liberty of lifting that tech. When his fingers closed over her shoulder and he gave her a quick squeeze, she understood that he wanted her to keep quiet about it, too.

"We stay the course." Bryce was adamant. "This will work." He glanced at his watch. "I've got a meeting with my supervisor. I'll update him on everything that's gone down. But first..." His stare shifted to Iris. "We need to talk, alone."

A flash of foreboding slid over her. *As if things weren't already bad enough...*

"You keep doing that," Pierce drawled. "Like it's a thing. It's not. I stepped aside the first time, but I don't plan to do that again."

"It's need-to-know info, bodyguard," Bryce shot back. "If—after I talk with her—Iris wants you to know, she can tell you. Feel better?"

"Nope." A prompt reply.

"Too bad." Bryce jerked his thumb toward the door. "Iris, I need five minutes with you in your place. There are things we need to discuss without an avid audience."

What else could he possibly have to say?

"Iris..." Bryce's impatience bled into her name.

She felt plenty impatient, too. "Whatever it is, just say it in front of Pierce. I trust him." She did. More than she trusted anyone else.

"You're making a mistake," Bryce warned.

"I seem to make a lot of those."

A muscle flexed along his jaw. "Fine."

Why are you keeping me in suspense? The silence stretched. Did he not really have anything to say—

"Someone started digging into your background, Iris. Someone who was trying to access your classified history with the FBI."

"Well, sure, that's probably related to the case," she responded, not getting why this was such big, dramatic news.

"No, it's related to your new boyfriend." He pointed at Pierce. "The inquiry came from Wilde. He has his team tearing into your life, were you aware of that?"

All the breath seemed to leave her lungs in a fast rush. "What?"

"Your life, your family. Even *my* life. He's ripping your world apart and causing a whole lot of trouble. And, sure, you may trust him, but I have to wonder...why is he doing all this? And *why* did he start doing it even before you signed that contract at Wilde?"

Her feet had rooted to the floor.

"Because I did some digging on my own. The first attempts to access your FBI file were made *before* you signed that contract with Wilde. You know, the one that effectively locked you to this man? A man who, by the way, has a very interesting back story of his own. Did you know that while he was serving as a Ranger, he had over seven confirmed—"

"Stop." Her goose bumps were worse.

Bryce just spoke faster as he added, "He hired his services out after he left the military. Did work in the Middle East as—"

"Stop." Had he not heard her before?

Bryce surged toward her. *"You need to know who this man is.* You let him into your life, but he's a stranger. You might have jumped into bed with him, but great sex doesn't mean he's a great person. You have been walled off from the rest of the world for so long. Too long. Someone shows you a little kindness, and you just lap it up."

Her cheeks felt icy. "I'm so sick of people thinking I'm naive. That I don't know how to survive in this world. That I can't judge someone's character." So damn annoying. "I was cast out of the life I knew at seventeen. On my eighteenth birthday, Franco gave me a new ID. Same first name, different last. Said it was supposed to make it easier for me. Said that when people called out Iris, I would remember to turn. That people messed up more when they changed their first names." She hated the cold surrounding her body.

I hate all the things that happened. I hate I found my father dying. I hate I was trained to be a criminal. I hate I lost my brother. I hate that I just can't have a normal life like everyone else.

Iris sucked in a breath and tried to steady her voice. "I moved into my first place. Got a job as a waitress. A year later, Franco said I had to move. I had just started to make friends, but I packed up everything overnight. Started over. Six months later, I did it again. And I've done it over and over...I've started again more times than I can count. Each move terrified me, but I did it. I succeeded. Every single time. *I started over with nothing.* So don't act like I'm some clueless kid who can't handle the world. I can and I have, and I will continue to survive. I don't need you telling me about Pierce's life. I don't need you to tell me a damn thing about him."

Bryce took another step toward her. "Yes," he hissed softly. "You do. Because you weren't always alone. You had the Feds looking after you. You've always had us, and we've never let you down." His eyes burned with emotion.

"You need to back up," Pierce warned him flatly. "Now."

"You don't know who he really is." Bryce flickered a glance at Pierce, then looked back at Iris. *"Be careful."* But he retreated. "I'll be checking in again soon." He stormed for the door. An ever-so-dramatic exit.

She stared after him. Felt brittle. Cold on the outside but now oddly hot on the inside.

"Excuse me for a moment, sweetheart," Pierce murmured. His voice was a gentle as a breeze. "Just want to make sure the FBI asshat—I mean, agent—gets to the elevator all right. Be back before you can miss me."

And he just walked past her.

She shook her head. *What is happening here?*

It took her a moment too long to unroot her feet from the floor. She bounded forward. Yanked open the door.

The two men were at the elevator. Pierce turned toward her and flashed an easy smile. "He needs help getting downstairs."

That made no sense. "Pierce!"

Pierce shoved Bryce into the elevator. Both men vanished.

Her breath heaved in and out. Her fingers clenched and released. Clenched and released.

Pierce investigated me. Even before I hired him. She hadn't wanted to show how unnerved that discovery had made her, not in front of Bryce. Bryce had been looking for weaknesses.

But...she *was* unnerved. Confused. Why would Pierce investigate her even before she'd hired him?

Iris grabbed her keys. She'd dropped them on the table near his door—hell, she didn't even remember when she'd done that. Her steps were wooden as she marched for her place. She needed space. Fresh clothes. To *think*.

She unlocked her door. Stepped inside. The place was completely dark. Her blinds had been lowered to block out the sun, and every light was turned off. She reached for the light switch.

A hand flew out and curled around hers.

"You are in so much trouble."

CHAPTER FOURTEEN

"What is it with you and elevators?" Bryce wanted to know. "Do you just like hanging out in them or...?"

"It didn't work."

"Excuse me?"

Pierce slammed the button to halt the elevator. Colt had given him the perfect place for a one-on-one talk. Privacy and a trapped audience. Got to love that combination. "You tried to turn her against me. She told you to fucking fuck off."

"I tried to *warn* Iris about you. You're a dangerous man. A man who has obviously developed some sort of obsession with Iris. I wanted her to know that."

"Obsession," Pierce tasted the word. Was he obsessed? Definite possibility.

"You had her investigated even before she signed with your firm. You going to act like that's normal? Like that's typical behavior?" Bryce's lips twisted in a mocking smile. "Tell me, do you always investigate potential lovers before you take them to bed? Is that like your go-to method or something?"

Oh, did the FBI agent think he was being amusing? He wasn't. "I am dangerous."

"Glad we agree on that point."

"To everyone *but* Iris. I would never hurt her, but I would fight like hell burning to keep her safe."

Bryce snorted. "Is that supposed to intimidate me?"

Pierce sent the agent a cold smile. "I don't know. You're the one who apparently read my very long—and somehow now magically unclassified—background report." He waited a beat. "Are you intimidated, knowing what I have done? What I can easily do again if the mood hits me?"

Bryce swallowed. "Are you threatening a federal agent?"

"I'm asking a question. When I threaten you, you'll know." He stepped forward, going toe-to-toe with the jerk. "You're using her."

"We're using each other. A mutually beneficial situation. I get to take down someone very bad, and Iris gets her brother's record cleared. Win, win."

"Not quite. You left out the part where you were sending her after a killer. You *know* he killed her handler. You also suspect he killed her father—and, no doubt, others, too. We're looking at someone with a whole lot of power and reach. Someone who apparently plays in the million-dollar art theft ring."

"Some paintings are priceless. So it's not just a *million* we are talking about."

Pierce knew plenty of people would do anything if the payout was high enough. "I don't like that you won't name your suspect."

"Maybe it's because we *don't* have a name for him."

"Or maybe it's because a perp like him will have all kinds of reach. Enough reach to even have some Feds on his side."

"You're suggesting I'm on the take?" Bryce's voice sharpened. "Screw you, buddy."

"Not your buddy." Why did the Fed keep making that mistake? Maybe Pierce looked too friendly. Nah. Couldn't be the case.

"I helped Iris. I've been helping her for years. I've always stood by her. And I'm on no one's payroll except the U.S. government's. Don't believe me? Check my bank account." He jerked around Pierce and stabbed the button to get the elevator moving. "This talk is over. You shouldn't even be on this case. You shouldn't be involved at all!"

"Iris wants me involved. She wants me close. Where she wants me, I'll be."

"Because of your freaking obsession. You're a danger junkie, and she feeds your need because her life is so screwed up right now. Yes, I read your file. I know just how crazy you really are." The elevator doors opened. "Iris doesn't need someone like you in her life, not permanently. When the case is over, when she has her brother back, Iris will be cutting you out of her world as fast as she can, and we both know it."

Oh, he was an asshole. No question at all.

"Will your *obsession* let you deal with that?" Bryce taunted. "Or will you try to hold on when she doesn't need you anymore?" With that, the Fed stormed away.

Jaw locked, Pierce pulled out his phone and put it to his ear.

Colt answered immediately.

"You've got an agent exiting," Pierce told him. "Let me know where he goes, will you?"

"You sound pissed."

Astute observation. "Blame it on the Fed. I don't trust him." He needed the Wilde report on the fellow ASAP. Speaking of the reports from Wilde...hell, he had to do some serious explaining to Iris. Pierce ended the call with Colt. Rode the elevator back up to his floor. As he headed down the hallway, he sucked in some deep, gulping breaths.

Iris deserved an explanation. She'd stuck by him when Bryce was talking his shit, but Pierce knew he had to tell her why he'd asked for a background investigation on her.

Because I was worried. Because I wanted to help. Because I am a nosey bastard when it comes to you, baby, and I want to always keep you safe. But he'd overstepped, and Pierce knew it.

He entered his apartment. "Iris, I—"

The place felt too quiet.

"Iris?" He surged forward. Checked the bedroom—*all* the rooms. Whirling, he rushed back for the den. She'd been upset when he left. She probably had gone back to her place. *She's just in her apartment. Calm down. No big deal.*

But his feet practically flew down the hallway. He twisted the knob on her door. *Locked.* His hand lifted, and he rapped on her door. "Iris?"

Pierce called. "We need to talk." *I can try to explain, but...*

Nothing.

No pad of footsteps. The door didn't open.

His muscles tensed. "Iris?" He lifted his hand. Pounded again. He knew she hadn't left the building. If she had, Colt would have told him when they talked on the phone.

His gaze focused on the peephole. Had he just heard the quiet rush of steps inside her place? "Iris, I get that you're angry with me, but give me a chance to explain." The door didn't open. "Please," he forced out, voice gruff. Not a word he used often, but he'd use it with her. She couldn't shut him out.

The door slowly opened. Just a few inches. Iris ducked her head through that small opening. "I don't want to talk right now." Her words trembled faintly.

Because she was upset with him?

Or...

Something else?

His hand lifted and flattened against the door. "Let me come inside."

"No!" Too sharp. Too fast. She cleared her throat. "That's a bad idea."

"I just want to talk."

"I don't." Her gaze didn't quite meet his. "I think...I think it would actually be best if we just, ah, took a break for a bit."

"A break," Pierce repeated as his insides clenched.

"Yes." A quick nod. "You should take a break from me."

That was the last thing he wanted. "I can explain what happened at Wilde." He winced. Okay. It was still gonna sound bad and stalkerish and obsessive but... "I was worried about you. I contacted the team after you were nearly abducted because I wanted to protect you." He exhaled. "I have a background file on you. It's on my computer at my place right now. I got the intel because..." His words trailed off.

Her gaze had just darted back toward her apartment.

Now why would she be looking back all nervous-like? But he knew. His muscles tightened even more.

"Iris," he said her name deliberately.

Her stare swung to him.

"Is something wrong?" Soft. Careful.

"No. Yes. We're wrong," Iris said quickly. She inched back a little. That nervous half-step of hers. "I need time alone. And you should—you should stay away from me."

She started to swing the door shut.

Not happening because he'd slid his foot over the threshold, and the door couldn't close all the way. It just bounced off his foot. "Sweetheart," he said the endearment tenderly. "Not happening."

Her eyes widened in real alarm. "Pierce?"

"Get back, baby. Don't want you getting hurt."

"I—"

She didn't get back. Someone *pulled* her back. Yanked her back hard, and a snarl tore from Pierce's lips as he shoved the door all the way open and lunged after her.

His hands flew out because he wanted to get hold of Iris and pull her away from the threat he knew waited, but someone else already had her in a tight grip.

The light from the hallway spilled into Iris's place. Otherwise, it was dim in her home, with all the lights off and all the blinds tightly closed. But the illumination from the hallway was enough for Pierce to see the tall, muscled man who held Iris in a too-tight grip. His hair was a little long, thick, and he wore black—pants, shirt, and boots.

"Shut the door," the man snarled.

"Let her go," he returned.

"Pierce." Iris's voice was breathless. "You don't understand—"

"He doesn't *have* to understand," the man behind her snapped. "The boyfriend just has to do what the hell he's told. He has to follow my orders to the letter or you will—"

Pierce curled his hands into fists. "You won't do *anything* to her."

"No, you won't," Iris snapped at the same time. Then she slammed her elbow back into the male's midsection.

He grunted.

"Let me go!" Iris yelled. *"Now!"* She hit him again with her elbow.

His hold loosened.

Iris lurched away, only to immediately spin back toward him. "I just don't understand—" Iris began furiously.

Pierce understood plenty. Iris was being attacked. In her own home.

He caught her hand. Pulled her away from the clown and prepared to make the fool sorry he had—

Iris fought Pierce's hold. She jerked free and lunged right back to the man who'd broken into her home. And she put her body in front of his. Then Iris spun back to face Pierce as she seemingly shielded the other guy. "Don't hurt him!"

Pierce froze.

Iris was telling him not to hurt her attacker? "Uh, Iris? Generally, we don't play nicely with the people who break into our homes."

Her chest heaved with her panting breaths. "It's not what you think."

"Iris," the man behind her groaned. "Why did you hit me? Twice?"

"I didn't hit you, I elbowed you," she returned. "And you deserved it."

Another groan. Then, "Your boyfriend still hasn't shut the freaking door."

No, he hadn't. "Iris, move away from him."

She shook her head. "You need to leave, Pierce. Just turn and walk out and leave. This doesn't concern you."

He turned. Stalked toward the door. Grabbed the side and slammed it shut, sealing them all inside. He threw the locks back into place, then whirled to confront them.

Too dark.

His fingers hit the light switch. Illumination flooded on overhead from her recessed lights. Enough illumination for him to see the man behind Iris. A man who was close to Pierce's own height, but with dirty blond hair. A faint growth of stubble along his hard jaw. And...

Eyes far too similar to Iris's. Dark, deep brown and with those very distinct amber flecks burning brightly.

"You didn't leave," Iris whispered.

"I'm the bodyguard. I'm supposed to protect you, no matter what." No matter who presented the threat. Right then, it sure as hell seemed to Pierce that the greatest threat she faced came from the man behind her. "Hello, Rembrandt."

The man took a few steps away from Iris. He kept rubbing his mid-section. "I freaking hate that name."

Pierce shrugged. "Do you think I care?" Iris was still far too close to her brother for his peace of mind.

Iris glanced between the two of them. Pain flashed on her face, and her hands balled into small fists.

"Come to me, Iris," Pierce directed. He was afraid her brother might make another grab for her at any moment. Pierce held out his hand. Even offered her a smile. "Come closer."

She looked at his hand. Then her gaze jumped to his face. Lingered on his smile.

"*No.*" A snap from Remy—Rembrandt. "Don't get close to that guy, Iris. He's gonna try to take you away from me!"

Yes, he was. The long-lost brother was not wrong with his assessment. "My job is to keep Iris safe. I can't have her around people who will threaten her."

Iris stood between them. A few feet from her brother. A few feet from Pierce. "Remy wouldn't hurt me."

"No?" Pierce kept his voice steady. "You haven't seen him in a very long time. You don't know who he is any longer." A deliberate hesitation, then, he added, "And quite a few people are saying that you *never* knew him."

Iris flinched.

Remy swore. "Oh, hell, no, you don't get to try and drive a wedge between me and my sister—"

"I don't have to drive a wedge. You did that on your own. When you left her. She was just seventeen and you left her to hold your father while he died."

Remy leapt toward him. "You don't know a damn thing about me or my family!"

Iris put her hand on Remy's chest. "Don't! Just—*don't!* Pierce wants to help me!"

"From what I've gathered, Pierce just wants in your pants, Iris!" Spittle flew from his mouth. "He's been playing you because he wants to get you in bed, and you can't trust this jerk that you just met barely a week ago—" He locked his fingers around her wrist and hauled her toward him. "You are in serious trouble. Sharks are closing in, and you still can't see them. You could never see them! I'm here to get you out of this mess before it's too late. You're coming with me. We're leaving tonight, and they will never find you again. I can make you vanish."

"That's not going to happen." Pierce didn't move. He kept blocking the door. "Iris and I are a package deal. Got a signed contract that says where she goes, I go."

"Well, consider yourself fired," Remy snapped. "I can take care of my sister!"

"I don't think you can. I think you know how to abandon her, but I think you know jack shit about taking care of her."

Remy's head whipped toward him. "And you think *you* can take care of her?" He still had his fingers manacled around her wrist.

"Your hold is too tight," Pierce told him flatly. "If she bruises, I will be very upset. Iris has delicate skin, and, as a rule, she bruises easily."

"What?" Remy automatically glanced at Iris's wrist. "What are you—"

Pierce was on him two seconds later. He'd pulled Iris free of her brother's hold and had the guy pinned to the nearest wall. Pierce didn't hurt him, but he made sure the other man couldn't break free. "Iris, call the Feds."

Remy's eyes widened in horror. "*Iris, don't!*"

"Why not?" Pierce drawled, but her brother's response was exactly what he'd expected. After all, he'd just been bluffing. He didn't want the Feds rushing in on this scene. "Because you're a wanted man? Because the Feds are planning to lock you up and throw away the key?"

"No, because they want to kill me! Because they are on the take and Iris is in danger, and those guys are the ones we need to stop." He didn't fight Pierce's hold, just glared up at him. "Iris has enemies stretching a mile long. I'm here to help her!"

"Here...*now*." Pierce glared right back. "Where the hell have you been since she was seventeen? Where were you all that time when Iris needed you?"

Remy's lips clamped together. His dark eyes—so very much like Iris's—swirled with emotion.

"Stop it. Both of you." Iris's voice came out brittle. Too flat. Not like her at all. The floor creaked as she surged closer. Her hand lifted and touched Pierce's shoulder. "Let him go."

Slowly, he did. Then Pierce took her hand and lifted it up so he could carefully inspect her wrist.

"I didn't hurt my sister," Remy muttered.

"Yes," Pierce said. "You did. You've hurt her plenty." He just hadn't left bruises. Pierce threaded his fingers with hers and made sure to chain her to his side. He didn't trust Remy. Not one damn bit. "How the hell did you get inside?"

"I think this building has really shitty security," Iris mumbled. "Everyone is always coming in and out without—"

"It's my damn building," Remy revealed with a growl. "There's a tunnel beneath it that I use to gain entry. It connects to another place about a block over. I can come and go as I want."

His building. What the hell?

"I arranged for you to be brought here, Iris." Remy rolled back his shoulders. "I got Franco to move you to this location because I wanted to be able to keep a better eye on you."

A shudder ran the length of Iris's body. "You know Franco?"

Know. She'd used the present-tense. Probably because Iris hadn't yet adjusted to the fact that her handler was dead.

"I knew him." A curt reply. Past tense. Remy was already aware of the man's death.

Iris seemed to realize the same thing. Her gaze locked on her brother. "OhmyGod." A frantic shake of her head. "What have you done?"

Remy frowned at her, his brow furrowing. "You—you think I killed him?"

"She asked her question first," Pierce thundered.

"Go fuck yourself, bodyguard! I'm talking to my sister!"

"A sister you ignored for years." He made sure his body was close to her. "And don't yell at her. Iris has been through a rough-ass few days. Some jerks in the park tried to abduct her—"

"I *know.* That's why I came to her. Why I broke my rule so we could talk." His shoulders lifted, then fell. "And I'm not yelling at her—I'm yelling at you, you interfering asshole!"

Pierce bared his teeth in a come-and-get-me grin.

Remy glared, but then his features softened as he told Iris, "You need to vanish. Don't take the job the Feds are offering. Don't paint anything. You are in over your head. You can't handle what's happening."

"How do you know Franco is dead?" Her question came out hushed. Sad.

His lips thinned. "Franco was on my payroll. He had been, for a very long time."

Fabulous. This mess just went from bad to worse.

"Your...payroll?" Iris's voice notched up. "What does that even mean? You're sounding like some kind of—of—"

"The word is criminal," Pierce supplied helpfully for her. "But, actually, I don't believe your brother is some junior guy in any organization. I think he might be a ringleader. Someone with a lot of power and clout in the right circles." Or, rather, the wrong ones.

Remy gave him a cold smile. "You think you know so much..."

"I *think* I'm good at connecting dots. I think the Feds were always a little too careful when they told Iris about the deal they were making for you."

"Deal? What deal?"

"They were going to clear you of forgery charges. But Agent Robertson only said forgery, and I knew that left the door open to all sorts of other crimes." His head turned toward Iris. "You were willing to sacrifice so much, but it wouldn't have ever worked." There was no happy ending in sight, and she needed to realize that truth. "Your brother isn't going to walk away a free man. You're putting yourself in danger for nothing."

Tears swam in her gaze. "It's not nothing. He's my brother."

"*Iris.*" Remy's voice seemed strangled. "You're doing this for me?"

Her lower lip trembled as she looked at him. "Why else would I do it? I missed you, Remy. I lost everything that night, and I've tried to pick up the pieces, but you weren't there, and if I had the chance to get you back..."

Remy lifted his chin. "The bodyguard—or boyfriend or whatever the hell he is—he's right about me." Ice dripped from his words. "I'm a criminal. A monster. And you don't want to be anywhere near me."

CHAPTER FIFTEEN

She sucked in a sharp breath. "Did you kill our father?"

Remy staggered toward her.

Pierce got in his path. "Nope."

But Remy merely smiled back at him. "You think you can keep her safe from every bad thing out there?"

"I think I'll give it my best effort." *Yeah, I think I can handle whatever comes.*

"Who the hell are you really? What is she to you?"

"I'm the next-door neighbor. But I actually think you know plenty about me already...seeing as how I had to do a background check to get an apartment in this building." Which raised another question...why had Remy *let* him move in? Pierce would get to that, later. "As to what she is—"

"I'm his friend," Iris replied, voice trembling.

There she went with the F-word again.

But Remy's smile stretched a little more. "I don't think so."

"She's my client," Pierce returned. "I'm sure you're aware of Wilde's reputation. We always take care of our clients."

Remy seemed to weigh him. "Get her the hell out of the city. Get her far away from the people who want to use her. I tried to keep her separate from that world. Didn't matter, though. They still found her. They still plan to use her. Unless you want her to wind up with a knife in her heart, then you had better do your job very, very well." An exhale. "With that, I think it's time for my exit." He sidestepped and reached for the door.

"Remy..." Pain thickened his name as it came from Iris. "You're just going to leave me again?"

He stopped. His back was to her and Pierce. "I figure I have about two minutes before the place gets stormed. Both by the Feds and by Wilde agents. I saw lover boy send out a text when he first arrived."

Pierce *had* texted Colt. He'd been biding his time until his partner arrived. All he'd needed to do was text just one letter. *A*. It was a system he and his friend had. *A* for...*All hell is breaking loose. Get in, now.*

"I don't intend to be taken into custody by anyone. Won't suit my purposes." Remy opened the door. "How about you don't trust anyone too much, Iris? And that definitely includes me."

"You're my brother."

Finally, he glanced back. "No, I used to be your brother. He died a long time ago. You need to let him go."

"No." She lunged for him. Grabbed his arm. "No! I looked for you, I searched and searched, and I needed you—"

An alarm began to shriek. High-pitched. Wailing.

"Fire alarm." Remy's eyelids flickered. "Seeing as how *I* haven't set any fires in the building, I think we can assume someone else is staging an attack." His gaze shifted to Pierce. "It would be a great way to separate her from you. In all the confusion, if it were me, I'd just swoop in and take her."

Pierce jerked his head in understanding. He got exactly what Remy was saying.

"No one is taking me anywhere!" Iris shouted as the alarm blared. "This is ridiculous! Remy, I want to talk to you! I want to know where you've been—"

Smoke. Pierce could smell it drifting through the open door.

Fuck.

He grabbed Iris. Lifted her over his shoulder. "I'm sorry, baby."

"What? Pierce! Stop! Let me go!"

"Get her the hell out," Remy said. "Out of the building. Out of this town. *Get her away.*"

Iris heaved in his hold. "What in the hell are you doing? Put me down! There's no fire!"

Remy rushed away.

"Remy!" Iris yelled. "Dammit, Remy! Did you do it? Did you kill our father?" she shouted after him.

Pierce had to tighten his hold as she twisted her body. He rushed into the hallway and headed for the stairs.

"Stop it, Pierce! Put me down, *now!*"

He didn't. This building wasn't secure. Everyone and their brother—fucking literally—kept coming in. That meant it was time to relocate. He burst into the stairwell and nearly slammed straight into Colt.

"What's happening?" Colt demanded. "Dammit, I got in as fast as I could!"

"Put me down!" Iris bellowed.

"Tell me a car is waiting downstairs," Pierce snapped.

"A car is waiting downstairs."

The alarm was about to burst his eardrums. "Good."

"I want my brother!" Iris slammed her hands into his back. "This is not cool, Pierce! Friends don't do this to friends!"

He rushed down the stairs and made sure to keep his hold on her. "I thought we covered that we were way past the friend stage of the game."

"Did she say her 'brother'?" Colt asked as he scrambled to keep pace with them. "And do I smell smoke?"

The smoke was no doubt a diversionary tactic, just like the alarm. Was there an actual fire or was it all just for show? Pierce couldn't risk finding out, not until Iris was safe. He'd let her out of his sight for just a few moments earlier and come back to find her tucked away with her supersuspicious brother.

They burst onto the first floor. The Feds were just rushing through the entrance doors. Someone was slow.

Or was that deliberate?

Bryce's eyes widened when he caught sight of Pierce—Pierce carrying Iris.

Pierce didn't slow down. He barreled forward and Bryce—and his gaping partner Travis—had to scramble out of his way. As soon as they were outside, fresh air slammed into Pierce's face.

"This is ridiculous." Iris's voice shook with her fury. "Put me down, *now*."

He did. He lowered her until her feet touched the ground.

She shoved the hair back from her face. "Do you have any idea how uncomfortable that trip down the stairs was?"

He stepped closer to her. Toe-to-toe. "Do you have any idea how fucking scared I was when I realized some asshole was hiding in your apartment? He could've had a gun on you, could've had a knife at your back, could've—"

"That asshole was my brother," she gritted, voice carrying only to him. "The brother I haven't seen in years! And *you* scared him away!"

Oh, hell, no. "Wrong." A response that burst out before he had the good sense to stop it. "I didn't scare him away. He ran away. Again. He left—" Hell. His lips clamped together. Too late.

The damage was done. He could see it on her face. Her lower lip trembled as pain darkened her gaze.

"Iris—" His hand reached for her.

"Don't." She swallowed. Glanced toward her building. Toward the Feds who had followed them out and were watching her. Watching them.

Colt stood there, too. A whole freaking audience had eyes on them.

An audience that didn't include Remy. Probably because he was long gone. *I bet he set up the alarm to shriek. Dropped off a few smoke bombs. Disappeared through his tunnel.*

Iris wrapped her arms around her body.

Colt stepped forward. "We should get out of here." He pointed to the right. "Black Jeep. It's mine. Let's go."

Bryce marched closer to Iris. He curled his hand around her shoulder. "You need to come with me."

Iris looked at his hand, then back up at his face. Pierce knew she was thinking about what her brother had said.

"Baby..." Pierce began. She couldn't trust the Feds.

At his voice, Iris flinched.

"What happened upstairs?" Bryce asked her. "What's going on?"

Her lips pressed together. Pierce wished he could read her mind because he had no idea what Iris was going to do or say or...

"My brother is in the building. If you think he's some sort of super criminal, I would suggest that you and your partner get busy searching for him. I don't think there really is a fire inside. I learned...Franco told me once that on some of the heists my father worked, he would practice the grand art of deception." Her voice remained low. Almost sad. "To get access to his targets, he would need to clear out museums or auction houses. A few well-placed smoke bombs would trigger the alarms. While everyone else was running away, my dad would run inside. I-I think Remy might be picking up my father's old tricks."

Bryce immediately yanked out his phone and demanded backup.

Travis Clark raced into the building.

"Don't you leave," Bryce barked at Iris as he, too, turned for the doors. "I have questions for you, Iris! Don't go anywhere!"

Pierce watched both Feds vanish. They were intent on finding Remy.

"We're not staying here, right?" Colt asked. "Just to be clear."

"Not a chance," Pierce replied.

Iris still had her arms wrapped around her stomach. "Going to carry me away? Because, you know, that's what the guys in the park tried, too."

He winced as he took that direct hit. "Iris..."

Her gaze met his. So much pain. It knifed right through him. "I don't know who to trust."

He offered his hand to her. Held it open between them. "Me."

A tear slid down her cheek.

"You can trust me, I swear it."

She still didn't take his hand.

Colt coughed. "This is an emotional moment and all—totally get that—but we're in the open, the Feds called for backup, and if we don't haul ass soon, we will be missing our escape moment."

He didn't want to force her to leave with him. Even though every instinct Pierce possessed screamed...*She's in danger. Get her out of here! Her own brother said she couldn't trust the Feds. They are using her. Everyone is using her.*

Her chin lifted. Tears clung to the tips of her lashes, but her gaze was steady. "Take me to Wilde."

"Great choice," Colt praised. "Top notch security. An army of agents. Wonderful place to regroup. Of course, it's also the first location the Feds will search, but we can handle them."

"I'll take you anywhere," Pierce promised her. He still kept his hand outstretched to her.

And slowly, she lifted her right hand. Put her hand on his.

Yes.

They hustled into the back of the Jeep while Colt jumped in front. And—

"What in the hell is this?" Colt demanded.

Pierce jerked forward and saw the big, black duffel bag in the front seat. His first thought...*bomb.* "Out of the vehicle, *now.*" He turned back toward Iris.

Saw the terror on her face.

"Run," he told her. *"Run!"*

They leapt out of the Jeep and hauled ass.

***

"You've certainly had an eventful day."

Pierce glanced up at Eric's Wilde voice. "Do not start with me."

His boss—and friend—tossed him a slow smile. "Feeling pissy, are we?"

"I thought it was a fucking bomb." And he'd thought that Iris would die. That he wouldn't be able to get her to safety fast enough.

"It wasn't a bomb. It was twenty grand."

Twenty grand from the mystery bastard who wanted to hire Iris. The cash had been deliberately placed inside Colt's vehicle because the SOB had wanted them to know he was aware of all the players spinning in his web.

Pierce leaned back in his office chair. They were in the Wilde building. Iris had stepped into the connecting bathroom moments before. She'd been too pale. Too tense. And all he'd wanted to do was take her into his arms.

"The Feds are downstairs," Eric said.

"How long can we stall them?"

"They don't have an arrest warrant for your lovely client. Or for you. So I think my lawyers can keep them busy for quite some time."

Pierce rubbed the back of his neck. "Thank you."

Eric crossed to stand near the desk. "Are you in over your head?"

He dropped his hand. "Nah. Not even close."

"No? Because it seems like this case has become more...complicated."

That was a good word. "Things are definitely complicated."

"Is it the client?"

Pierce glanced up at Eric.

Eric stared back at him with an inscrutable gaze.

Pierce shrugged his shoulders. *What the hell? Why not have a face-off with him?* Pierce rose. "I don't like being in the dark."

"Who does?"

Pierce slid from behind the desk. Closed in on Eric. "Something you want to tell me, *boss?*"

Eric's eyes narrowed. "What would that be?"

"Oh, you know...maybe it would be a bit about Iris's brother, Rembrandt. Because I'd wager a month's salary that you know the man."

The bathroom door opened.

"You don't want to have this conversation now," Eric murmured.

"Yes, I do." He was at his limit. "You're the one who told me about the apartment being available in that building. *Her* building."

"Pierce?" Iris inched forward. "What's the problem?"

Oh, there were lots of problems. Lots and lots of them. He slanted her a glance. "Eric is the one who told me about the available apartment in your building."

She kept inching closer.

Eric glanced at her. "Hello, Iris."

"Hi, Eric."

Pierce did a double-take. There was a whole lot of familiarity in their tones. A familiarity he hadn't expected. "The two of you know each other?"

Iris waved one hand toward Eric. "His wife Piper and I are friends."

And it clicked. Eric's wife owned a gallery. *Of course.*

"She sells some of my work," Iris explained. "And I met Eric a few times through her."

Pierce's gaze zeroed back in on Eric. "That's how you found the building. Because you knew Iris was there." Now he felt like an idiot. For a moment, he'd believed that Eric and Remy had a connection. That Eric had deliberately sent him to the building because—

"I do know Remy." Eric's tone was guarded. "You aren't wrong. Guess you don't lose a month's salary."

What. The. Hell?

"Our paths have crossed before. He has...interesting connections."

Iris's mouth hung open. She snapped it closed. "You and my brother—are you friends?"

"Oh, no." A fast shake of his head. "Remy doesn't have many friends. He's too dangerous for friendship." His eyes cut to Pierce.

A definite warning.

"More," Pierce demanded. He wouldn't be in the dark any longer.

"He did a few favors for me in the past. So when he asked for me to make sure that someone trustworthy be put into the empty apartment next to Iris, I figured it was an easy enough repayment for the debt I owed him."

Well, damn.

"Pierce *is* trustworthy," Eric added as he inclined his head toward Iris. "He's not the kind of man who will sell you out for anything. I don't know what Remy is involved with—there is never a way to understand all his secrets—but I believed him when he said that he wanted you to have someone close by who could be a safe haven for you." He grimaced. "I should add that I never knew his name *was* Remy, not until very, very recently. During our interactions, he had other names."

Names. Plural. More red flags were flying high.

"I didn't even realize he was your brother, not until I saw your eyes for the first time."

"Uh, my eyes are brown. Lots of people have brown eyes. I think I read an article once that said like half to seventy-five percent of people in the population have brown eyes. Hardly anything special—"

"They're brown but with flecks of gold deep inside. An amber hue that comes out and catches the light," Pierce said. He thought her eyes were damn special. "They get darker with your emotions, and the amber heats up."

She shook her head. "I...okay."

"The eye shape is similar, too. Though your eyes are a little wider than his." He probably sounded like an idiot as he went on about her eyes. Pierce lifted his chin and waved a hand toward Eric. *Let's get back on track.* "Any other secrets you want to spill?" he demanded.

"When I had dealings with Remy, it never involved anything illegal. So in regard to the apartment, as far as I knew, I was just offering one of my friends a nice place to live."

"Uh, huh. This is me. I know you would have run a check on Iris. Every instinct you have would have been on alert."

Eric's gaze cut to Iris. "I did enough checking to realize she could use a friend that she could count on when things got intense."

Friend. That word again. She could count on him, but he wasn't just her friend. He was the lover who would walk through hell any day of the week for her.

"I feel like you two might want to talk alone. How about I go give those Feds some trouble downstairs, hmm?" Eric swung for the door.

Sure. Just drop a bombshell and leave. No problem. "Remy told Iris not to trust those Feds.

So we need Wilde to dig hard and deep on them to see if they are dirty."

Eric glanced back at him. "I'll see what we can find."

"And while that's happening, we need a safe house. Apparently, Remy has just been running back and forth in our building, and I want Iris in a place that is completely secure." No more surprise visits from her dear, old brother.

"I'll make several properties available to you. You can pick what you want." Once more, he made for the door.

"What's he like?" Iris asked.

Eric stilled.

"Remy. Or…or whatever you called him when you knew him. What's he like?"

Eric turned toward her. "Intense. Focused. Secretive as hell."

She swallowed. "Is he dangerous?"

"Yes." An immediate reply.

Her shoulders slumped.

"He's not someone you want to cross," Eric added, seeming to choose his words carefully. "An enemy you don't want."

Iris's gaze fell to the floor. "I know that Wilde has a great many connections. Is it possible—can you find out if he is wanted for any particular crimes? Other than, of course," a bitter twist of her lips, "forgery."

Pierce edged closer to her, pulled helplessly. "I've got a Wilde buddy who is former FBI. We can get him to reach out to some people he trusts." He knew that Elijah Cross would be able to get them some information that they could use.

Eric met his gaze. Nodded. Obviously, they were on the same page.

"Thank you." Her voice had gone softer.

Once more, Eric turned for the door.

"What was he called...when you knew him? I mean, in your interactions or—or whatever they were."

His fingers curled around the doorknob. "Different places meant different names. Michael. Paul. Henri. Even went by Sal once..."

A mocking laugh escaped her. "All artists he loved. Michelangelo, Paul Cézanne, Henri Matisse, and Salvador Dali."

Pierce absorbed every bit of info. He picked up what Eric said and what he didn't. Yes, Eric claimed her brother was dangerous—Pierce could absolutely buy that bit. But Eric didn't make a habit of working with monsters. Eric had his own strict code that he lived by, and he wouldn't partner up—no matter the circumstances—with someone that he thought was a cold-blooded criminal.

Remy had been the one to call himself a monster. Remy had been the one to tell Pierce to take Iris far away. And Remy was the one with a ton of aliases that Eric knew.

"Where did you see him?" Iris asked. "When your paths crossed, that is."

"Paris, mostly. Once in England. Once here." He didn't look back. "Some people do bad things, but they do them for the right reasons."

What the hell was that supposed to mean? But the twist in Pierce's gut told him the answer.

Eric glanced back once more. Met Pierce's stare. Inclined his head.

Well, sonofabitch...

"You have proof?" Pierce demanded. Because if so...

A shake of Eric's head. "Suspicions. And that says a lot that with my reach, I wasn't able to get more."

It did.

"What are you talking about?" Iris's tone broke with impatience. "I don't like riddles. And I am sick to death of secrets."

Yes, understandable.

"I'll get working on that safe house," Eric murmured. He slipped away. The door closed behind him with a soft click.

Iris rounded on Pierce. Her hands went to her hips. Fisted. "Why did I just feel like two completely separate conversations were happening? And I only got the gist of *one?*"

Because two had been occurring. Pierce didn't want to say the wrong thing. He didn't want to get her hopes up only to have them plummet back to earth. He needed more intel. "I'm calling my friend Elijah. He's former FBI." He turned away. Headed to the desk. Picked up his phone and had Elijah on the line in moments.

"I need a favor." Blunt, straight to the point. Pierce could feel Iris's eyes on him.

"Don't you always?" Elijah drawled back. "Do you know that you are interrupting while I am attempting to sun myself on a most lovely beach?"

"Aren't you the lucky SOB?"

"Indeed I am." Waves crashed in the background. "It's important?"

Iris still watched him. "The most important case I've ever worked." He could hear the tension in his own voice.

"What's wrong?" Obviously, Elijah did, too.

"Wilde's tech teams are digging, but I need your more personal touch to get me some info from the FBI."

A low whistle. "You know I'm not the most popular guy with them...seeing as how I *left* the Bureau and burned all the bridges I had there."

He didn't think all those bridges had burned. "You're also the *former* agent who brought down serial killers like it was child's play, so I'm figuring you still have some people there who are loyal to you."

A sniff. "Not child's play, for the record."

No, he doubted it had been. He'd seen the darkness that lingered in Elijah's eyes. But his friend had recently found love, with the last victim he'd saved while working at the Bureau. "I've got two agents dodging my steps, and I want to know if they're clean."

"Names."

Pierce rattled off their names. "And..." His gaze lifted. Locked on Iris. There were deep shadows under her eyes, and she appeared far too pale to him.

"You're keeping me in suspense," Elijah noted. "What's up with that?"

He just hated to say this in front of her. "I need you to see if anything shakes loose on a guy with the first name of Rembrandt, Remy for short.

He goes by a ton of aliases, always using names that tie back to great artists. He's a skilled painter. Been known to do some forgery work."

"Okay, you've got me interested." Elijah sounded it. "Anything else to go by?"

"His father was murdered, and his sister was placed in witness protection when she was seventeen."

Iris never looked away from him.

"She is currently using the name Iris Stuart, so I'm betting her files will mention him."

She flinched.

"Iris is the client. An important VIP. When you reach out, be sure it's to people you trust. Her handler was recently found dead."

"Damn." A hard exhale. "Sounds like one hell of a case."

"It is."

"You got good backup?"

"Colt's on my six."

"Want me front and center, too?"

That was Elijah. Always willing to go the extra mile for a friend. "No, stay with your lady." Because they were enjoying time in Florida together. "If you can get me the intel, you'll be helping me more than you can imagine."

"On it."

A few moments later, he put down the phone. He needed to say something to Iris, something to reassure her, something to take away the pain he could feel beating at her...

"It was a setup."

His hands flattened on the desk. "What do you mean?"

She motioned between them. "You. Me. Our chance meeting. There was nothing chance about it at all. Everything was arranged. Planned."

The way I feel about you sure as hell wasn't planned.

"Why?" She shook her head. "Why did Remy want you in my building?"

"To protect you." That answer was obvious, and it also showed that Iris was a weakness for her brother. He'd been keeping tabs on her for all these years. Did she get that?

"From what threat? The mystery art creep? The Feds? What is going on? Everything is so out of control!" Her head tipped back, and her hair slid over her shoulders. "Franco is dead. I liked him."

Franco might have been selling her out. Pierce didn't mention that just yet because he could feel the fragile edge of her control fraying.

"You got dragged into my nightmare." Her eyes closed. "You didn't have a choice."

"Sure I did."

Her eyes opened. Her head snapped up so that she faced him. Her steps were fast as she rushed toward the desk. She put her hands down, not touching his, but close. So close. "How? You were manipulated from the very first moment."

Is that how you feel, sweetheart? Like you've been manipulated? "I didn't have to move in. Could have said no." A shrug. "I like the building."

She leaned a little closer. Her eyes blazed with a dark fire. "You are in *danger*. The last man who had a job of looking out for me is dead."

"I'm not planning on dying."

"I'm sure Franco wasn't, either!" A huff. Some color had *finally* come back to her cheeks. "Being involved with me is dangerous. I knew that getting close to anyone was a bad mistake. It's why I tried to—"

"Friend-zone me?" he finished.

A jerky nod.

"We are far, far past that point," he told her. *You're mine, baby. No going back.*

"Walk away from me," she said.

He laughed.

She didn't. "You need to leave me. Tear up the contract. Get a new place to live. You don't need me and my danger. You *don't* need me in your life."

He leaned closer, too. So close that their mouths were only a few inches apart. "That's where you are dead wrong."

Her eyes widened. "Pierce?"

"*You* are the one person that I do need in this world, and I will never, ever walk away."

***

"I'm afraid we have a problem," Constantine said into the phone.

"I pay you to make problems vanish."

Constantine winced. "Yes, true, but in this case, it's not gonna be that easy. No waving my hand and saying 'abracadabra' this time." He stared up at the building across the street. What a shit-show the day had turned out to be.

"You left the money?"

"Oh, absolutely. Sure did. They got the money. Or, actually, I think the Feds have it now."

A colorful burst of swear words exploded in his ear.

"Not my fault," Constantine defended. "Apparently, Remy has decided now is the perfect time for him to waltz back into Iris's life. I picked up that he was in her place, and the Feds were searching for him. They were there during my money drop, so I had to get a little creative with placement. I'd hoped Iris would just take the money and we'd merrily move on to the next stage but..." But that hadn't happened.

"Where is she?" A growl.

"Currently in the Wilde office building. I'd imagine she's bundled up tight behind lots of security."

"And the Feds?"

He squinted as cars rushed past him. "They got stalled in the lobby."

"They're trying to get her."

True enough. "I don't think Team Wilde is in any hurry to turn her over. I'd lay odds that in order to get her, the Feds will have to pry her out of Pierce's cold, dead hands."

"That can be arranged."

Not the response he'd wanted to hear. But one he'd feared. "What are you saying?"

"I'm saying keep your position. I'll be sending Iris to you very soon."

"Uh, how are you going to do—"

The line went dead.

"I hate that sonofabitch," Constantine muttered. "Too bad he pays so well."

CHAPTER SIXTEEN

Shock. Hope. Both exploded inside of Iris at the same time. She wanted to surge forward, to jump across that desk and wrap her arms around Pierce and hold on tight. Never let go.

He's been used. Manipulated.

She pushed away from the desk. Took a half-step back. "Don't say things you don't mean."

He also leaned back, a much slower movement. Pierce crossed his powerful arms across his chest. "You think I'm feeding you lines?"

"I don't know what to think." A trembling hand shoved back her hair. "Everything around me is crazy and confusing. Nothing makes sense."

"We do."

Her hand fell to her side.

"We make sense, baby. When I'm balls deep in you and you're screaming my name, everything is right. Perfect. There is no doubt or fear. There's pleasure and clarity. An absolute sense of knowing..."

Her breath had frozen in her lungs. "Knowing what?"

"That you were made for me."

She shivered at the hot, possessive look in his eyes.

"And I was made just for you," he added roughly.

She wanted that to be true. She *wanted* him so much. So much that it scared her. In a world where everything was already coming apart around her, the consuming need that she felt for him was just another thing that terrified her. "I shouldn't want you so much."

"Who the hell told you that?" His hands fell. He stalked from behind the desk. Came toward her.

Iris started to back—

"No. Don't. You don't need to be scared. Not of me. Not ever of me. Because I might have a dark past, I might have that bad side I warned you about, but I would never, ever do anything to hurt you. I pretty much just want to destroy anyone who so much as makes you shed a single fucking tear." He stopped in front of her. Didn't touch her. Just stared down at her with a hunger clear to see on his handsome face. "Do you know how much I love it when you smile?"

He was talking about her smile? *Now?*

"The dimple on the left shows first. Then the one on the right peeks out. Sounds stupid to say, but...it's kinda like watching the sun come out from behind a cloud."

Her lips parted.

"I don't say poetic shit often, so that probably didn't come out right."

She'd thought it had. She'd thought it might be the sweetest thing anyone had ever said to her.

"So let me tell you things in my *real* way." A ragged exhale. His shoulders squared. "Might be harsh but...*This* is how I feel when I'm with you. I feel like I want to own you and possess you and make you mine. I want the whole world to know you belong to me. I feel like I can't touch you enough."

But he wasn't touching her. She wanted him to touch her. Wanted him to pull her close and make all the cold she felt disappear. The cold that wanted to drag her under.

"I can't get close enough. I want to taste you. Every inch of you."

He had. He'd done things to her—with her—that no one else ever had. Then everything had come crashing down on them. Her heart beat a little faster.

"When you're in danger, it drives me crazy."

Not that Iris was exactly thrilled about danger, either...

"I want to hunt down those who are after you." His voice roughened. The blue of his eyes sharpened. "I want to destroy any threat to you."

A shiver skirted down her spine. "Why?" Too husky.

"Haven't you figured that out yet?"

She thought of her brother's sudden appearance in her life. All the secrets. "There's a lot that I seemed to have missed."

"Then let me explain things to you." His hands reached out. Curled around her waist. Pulled her slowly closer. Closer. "This isn't about a case."

Iris could not look away from him.

"This isn't about being a friend or a good freaking neighbor."

If it had just been about being a good neighbor, she'd say he had gone above and beyond—

His head lowered toward hers. "This is about me needing you, wanting you, more than I have ever wanted anyone else."

"I feel the same way," she admitted. It was true. She did.

"What are you gonna do about it?" Pierce asked. Dared.

She shot onto her toes. Her emotions were one hundred percent out of control. Iris knew it. She also knew that she didn't care.

Her hands curled around his neck, and she dragged him down to her. Their mouths met in a maelstrom of need and raw desire. Their lips parted, their tongues stroked, and everything else fell away.

The pain from her past.

The fear. The shock. The dread.

He kissed her. She kissed him. Need built. Desire spread. She gave in. The way he made her feel—it could wipe everything else away. She wanted the pain gone.

He lifted her up. Her legs immediately curled around his waist. Her body rubbed eagerly against him. She wanted to be even closer, but their clothing was in the way. Iris needed it gone. She needed to be with him.

Always, with him.

The thought caused a faint flutter of alarm inside of her. She was feeling too much. Too fast. Her head lifted.

Their gazes met. A consuming lust stared back at her.

"We shouldn't," she managed. Not there. Not with Feds waiting downstairs, and Wilde agents running around the building. This was not the right place. There were people beyond the door. She'd *never* acted this way.

"We should," he returned in a voice gone savage. "We will."

He took her mouth again. Kissed her deeply and ravenously even as he carried her across the room. She rocked her hips against him. Heat and need pooled in her core. There were a thousand reasons to stop.

And one reason to say to hell with it and take him.

Because I want him.

He lowered her down, and she realized he'd put her on the couch that waited near the big windows in his office. Sleek. Leather. He lowered her onto it and stared at her with a gaze that seemed to eat her alive. "I'm locking the door. Then I'm fucking you."

That was quite a nice to-do list.

He stalked away. She heard the flip of the lock, and when she levered up, she saw that his strong hands were going to the front of his jeans.

There was no missing the straining erection that pushed toward her.

She should strip. Kick off her clothes. Do something more than just stare at him. She should—

Iris knew exactly what she wanted to do.

"Baby, the clothes have got to go." He stopped near the edge of the couch. She shifted position. Realized that the couch didn't put her at the right angle. So Iris slid to the floor. Her knees touched the lush carpeting.

"No." His hands went to her shoulders. "If you do what I'm thinking, I will not last. I will not—"

"Yes, you will. I have faith in you." She also had her own to-do list. She'd go down on him. Then they'd make love.

I want more than fucking. With him, she wanted so much more. Maybe she always had, and that was the reason she'd tried to keep him at a distance. Maybe she'd realized just how dangerous he was to her.

Because he was a man who made her want to imagine a different life.

"Remember how I told you I'd never done this before?" Her hand lifted. Touched the heavy cock that sprang toward her. He wasn't wearing underwear. From what she'd gathered, he never did. When he'd unzipped his jeans, his thick dick had surged forward. "I think I want to cross this one off my list."

"Iris..." A hiss of her name that turned into a growl because she'd taken the head of his erection into her mouth.

She might not have any practical experience, but Iris had always considered herself a fast learner. And it didn't take her long to realize exactly what he liked. Yes, she might be a little awkward, but Pierce didn't seem to care. His hands curled around her shoulders in a tight grip.

Her lips opened more. Her tongue slid out to taste him.

"Baby, you are wrecking me."

She hoped not. She had plans for him. Plans that went far beyond this moment.

She took him in deeper. Sucked and let her cheeks hollow. He rocked toward her, and she took in a little more. Licked him, took, and—

"Can't." He pulled away, chest heaving. In a flash, he lifted her up, spun them around, and he was sitting on the couch, with her straddling him. "Fuck, your clothes—they have got to *go*. I want in. I need in, *now*."

She wanted him in. She pushed up. Managed to get to her feet. Her breasts ached, her sex felt hot with need, and she knew her panties were wet. Iris toed out of her shoes. Shoved down her jeans—took her underwear with them. She didn't bother to remove her shirt and bra. There just wasn't time. Eagerly, she slid back onto him.

But—

"Protection," Iris said. Her nails dug into his arms. "Tell me you have protection." Maybe in his desk?

No, he'd better not have condoms stashed in his desk because that would mean he did this too often with other women.

Jealousy flashed through her.

"Your nails are digging deep. Hot as hell, trust me, it is, but you don't have to worry, I have protection. I will *always* protect you."

Her eyes narrowed.

"Got a condom in my wallet. Been there a while, but I am damn glad it was saved for you."

Been there a while. Okay, that was good. That meant—

He kissed her. She stopped thinking and went back to feeling.

His fingers slid between her thighs as she straddled him. He stroked her with that wicked skill of his and had her shuddering.

They both grabbed for the condom moments later, but she was the one to roll it onto him. She'd barely gotten it in place when he lodged at the entrance to her body.

"Take me," he told her. "All the way."

She lowered onto him. Not fast. She couldn't take him fast because he was so big. Slowly. Inch by careful inch.

"You are killing me," he growled. His voice was low. Had been, the whole time. Just as hers had been.

She took a little more. He stretched her. Filled her. Her sex quivered around him, and her head tipped back. So good.

"All of me," he urged her. His hands were on her waist again. "I need...*all.*"

She pushed down at the same time that he surged up. Iris gasped as he lodged fully inside of her. Filling her so completely that it was almost a mix of pleasure and pain. His fingers left her right hip. Moved to her clit. Rubbed. Petted. Stroked.

Pleasure. That was what she felt. She lifted and fell, riding him with growing speed as the driving need thundered through her. Iris could feel her climax bearing down on her. It was getting closer and closer.

He kissed her just as the pleasure exploded through her body. He drank in her soft cries and moans, and his powerful thrusts had her nearly flying off him.

But both of his hands clamped around her hips again as he ground her against him.

Pleasure. So much pleasure...

She could taste the pleasure as she kissed him.

A tremor shook his body as he climaxed, but his fierce hold never eased. She kept kissing him and savoring the aftershocks of release as they quivered through her core.

Slowly, ever so slowly, the quivers eased. After one more kiss, her head lifted.

He stared at her with eyes still bright with need. "And you think I'd ever let *you* go? No way in hell."

He was still in her. She didn't know a graceful way to get up and off him. She also didn't want to move. "Because the sex is good?" A low question.

"The sex isn't good. It's fantastic, but, no, that's not it."

What is it? "Then why?"

"Oh, sweetheart..." He gave her a slow grin. No dimples flashed with his grins. If anything, his smiles somehow made him look even more dangerous. He picked up her right hand—the hand that had been gripping his shoulder so fiercely. He moved it to rest over his madly racing heart. "Don't you know?"

Iris shook her head. "No...I—I..."

"Then let me be clear. I am completely—"

"*Pierce!*" A bellow. A masculine cry from *outside* the office.

His eyes squeezed shut. "That is not Colt shouting my name."

Her head turned toward the door. "I think it is." She also thought that she had to get off him, *now*. She snatched her hand back from him. Rose to her feet. Steadied herself by curling her fingers around his arm—

"Why is the damn door locked?" Colt wanted to know. "And why aren't you answering your freaking phone?"

The phone had rung? Iris hadn't heard it. But then, she'd been rather involved with other matters.

Iris scooped up her discarded clothes and double-timed it to the connecting bathroom. She felt the flush in her cheeks. *What was I thinking?*

She hadn't been, though. She'd been feeling. The way only Pierce could make her feel.

He followed her and ditched the condom in the connecting restroom. Straightened his clothes. So did she. She also stared at her reflection in the mirror and tried to make sense of the madness consuming her.

We just had sex in his office. "This is not me."

He appeared beside her in the mirror. "No? Then who is it?"

"I mean—" Iris turned away from their reflections. "I don't do stuff like this. Don't just drop everything to have sex."

His grin came again. The one with the dangerous edge that sent little shivers darting over her. "You're saying it's a reaction reserved just for me?"

Actually... "Yes."

His hand curled under her chin. "Good." He pressed a soft kiss to her lips. "Because I only go insane for you."

She felt a little flutter in the pit of her stomach. "Are we good for each other?" Her gaze searched his. "Or bad?"

"*Pierce!*" If possible, Colt was even louder.

Her cheeks burned.

"I think you already know the answer to that. But if it helps..." He didn't seem in any hurry to respond to Colt. Pierce kept gazing tenderly at her. "I'm bad with everyone else but you." Then he eased back. "Let's see what emergency we're facing now."

I'd rather not. She'd much prefer just sinking into oblivion with him again. *Oblivion*. That was exactly what he'd given her. A rush of pleasure so intense that it had destroyed everything else, if only for a little while.

Iris smoothed back her hair and lifted her chin as she followed him back into the office. His steps were strong and purposeful as he strode for the door. He flipped the lock and swung open the door. "You wanted to see me?" His tone was as mild as possible. "Sorry, Iris and I were in the middle of an important discussion."

"Oh, I'm sure," Colt muttered. He shoved past Pierce. "We have a major problem on our hands."

Pierce shrugged. "That seems to be the normal status."

"No." Colt stopped. Pointed at Iris. "They are going to take you."

She shook her head even as dread pooled in her belly. "Excuse me?"

"The Feds. Eric is with them now, but there has been a big damn development that we can't control."

Her worried gaze flew to Pierce.

Immediately, he stepped closer to her. "It's okay."

"No," Colt returned. "I'm sorry, but it's not. Even our team of lawyers won't be able to stop them. They say that they found forgeries she made. Forgeries that tie her to crimes that have been committed."

Forgeries. The canvases—she'd left them in Pierce's bedroom.

"They have an agent bringing over an arrest warrant for her now. And they say if you don't give her up, they'll arrest you, too, Pierce."

This couldn't be happening.

Colt's lips curled down into a frown. "When the warrant arrives, they will be taking her."

"The hell they will." Pierce's instant denial. "No one will take Iris from me. *No one.*"

CHAPTER SEVENTEEN

Possibilities and escape scenarios spun through his head. "We can be long gone before they get up here with the warrant." Pierce nodded. He'd spirit her away and leave the Feds in his dust. He reached for Iris's hand. "There's a private elevator that only staff members can use. We'll go down to the garage and get in one of the company cars—"

"They have Feds staked out in the garage." Colt drove his fingers through his hair. "They started an all-out swarm situation while you and Iris were, uh, having that deep discussion of yours."

"Then we go to the roof." If they couldn't go down, they'd go up. "Eric's chopper is up there, and I know how to fly—"

"Grounded," Colt bit out. "And, dammit, don't you see that if you run with her, you'll be a wanted man? They will shove your picture onto every media outlet they can find. The Feds want her, and they are determined to take her. There is nothing we can do."

There was plenty Pierce could do. No way was he just going to give her up.

"It's okay." Iris tugged against his hold.

His attention whipped toward her. "There is nothing fucking *okay* about this situation."

Her lips lifted into a weak smile. Putting on a brave front that he could see right through. Her dimples winked at him, and his chest ached because the smile never made it to her dark eyes. "They aren't going to hurt me."

How the hell did she know that? Her brother had said some of the Feds were on the take.

"They want to use me. They probably think that if they take me into custody, they'll lure out Remy."

Yes, he got that. But... "Your brother has been in the wind for years. They could have used you at any time to pull him out—or to try pulling him out—but they didn't. Something has changed." He knew exactly what that something was.

A dead U.S. Marshal.

"They want me to finish the case for them," Iris said. Her hand gave his a little squeeze before she pulled away. "We got the twenty grand. They want me to finish the job."

"That doesn't make any sense." Colt stalked closer to them. "Eyes had to be on your building. Any secrecy was blown to hell and back. The Feds must have been spotted with you." But his brows lifted as he seemed to consider that possibility. "Maybe that's why they're going all-in with the arrest? To make it look as if Iris wasn't cooperating with them? To build an even stronger story to show that she's an art forger for their real target?"

That could be it. It could be—

The door to his office swung open. Eric stood on the threshold, his expression grim and his gaze glaring. "They have the warrant."

That was insanely freaking fast. So fast that he knew the warrant must have been on the back burner for a very long time. Another strategy that the Feds had just waited to employ.

FBI Agent Bryce Robertson and his partner Travis Clark crowded behind Eric. The two Feds seemed to be on the verge of shoving their way inside Pierce's office.

"Iris..." Eric exhaled. "They are going to take you into custody." He moved to the side. He also inclined his head toward a watchful Colt.

Bryce bolted toward Iris.

Pierce moved to intercept the bastard. "You're not taking her."

"Got a warrant that says otherwise." Bryce's stare met his. "You gonna do this the hard way?"

Pierce pretended to think about it. "*Is* there another way?"

"Sure, it's the way where you don't play hero. You don't interfere in an FBI investigation. You stand back and be a *good* citizen, and you let us take a forger into custody."

Pierce shook his head. "No, thanks. That way sounds boring. I'll stick with my original plan to—"

"I'll come with you," Iris announced.

What the actual hell? Pierce spun toward her.

He was distantly aware of Colt slipping from the office.

She offered him a weak smile once more. He didn't want her fake smiles. He wanted the real deal. The smiles that lit up the room and made everything seem a little bit better in his world.

"It's going to be all right. I haven't done anything wrong."

It doesn't matter, sweetheart. They don't care.

"We found several forgeries in *your* apartment, Iris," Bryce continued.

Her brows pulled low. She gave a half-shake of her head. "Mine? But—"

"I know your work," he continued briskly. "They are *yours*. The evidence is clear that you have been continuing the forgery efforts that your father began so long ago."

Her gaze held Pierce's. He could see her thoughts.

All the paintings were slashed. They hadn't been used in any forgery efforts. And they weren't in *her* apartment. They were in his. Stashed in his bedroom. What in the hell was happening?

But he knew. *The Feds are just making up this story. They are lying so they can take her away from me.*

"I don't want to lead you out in cuffs," Bryce said, voice gruff. "But if you make things difficult, I won't have a choice."

"I would like to see you try that move," Pierce snarled back because this was a setup. This guy was the enemy. He was *not* going to take her—

Iris's hand pressed to his chest. Right over his heart. The same position it had been in just before Colt interrupted. "There's something important you need to know," she said.

The room grew quiet. One of those weird moments that people talked about when they said you could be able to hear a pin drop.

"I've been keeping a secret from you," Iris added. She blew out a breath. Her hand didn't leave his chest. "And I don't want to do that anymore."

A fast check showed the Feds had satisfied expressions on their faces. All smug and knowing. Like this was the moment when Iris would reveal that she was a criminal. That she'd played him. Tried to play them all.

He ignored them and focused on her. "It's going to be okay." He would move heaven and fight hell to fix things for her.

"I love you," she said.

Fucking fuck. His body stiffened.

"I think I might have fallen in love with you when we were sitting on your couch and watching that cheesy horror movie. I felt safe and happy and like I was just...normal. And you looked at me, and I could feel butterflies in my stomach every time you smiled at me."

His hand moved to the curve of her cheek.

She turned her face into his touch. "When the movie ended, you did two things. You offered to be a nude model for me." Her lips twisted.

"What the hell?" A disgusted exclamation from Agent Clark. "We need to go, *now*."

"That prick Bentley made me jealous," Pierce confessed. Agent Clark could be as disgusted as he wanted. Pierce didn't care. Iris was what mattered. "Figured it was time for me to step up my game."

"Bentley had nothing on you, I promise. Never a competition." She pressed a kiss to his palm. Stepped back. Her hand fell from his chest.

"Then you asked if I was afraid of you. You didn't want me to be afraid."

"You should never fear me." Now, though, he did let his gaze move back to the Feds. He marked them with his stare, letting them know unequivocally...*Be very afraid*. He would be coming after them.

"I wasn't afraid. Not then. Not now. Because I love you."

The second time she'd said it. And the words made his head want to spin as his stare flew to her face.

"That's another one of my never-done-before items." Both of her dimples came for him. Her eyes gleamed. "It was good to check that off my list."

He grabbed her. Wrapped her tightly in his embrace. "Baby, you aren't going anywhere." She loved him? Hell, yes. Part of him was so euphoric that he felt like roaring. But for another part of him—the dark, savage part—her love was even more reason for him to keep her close. To fight the bastards who wanted to take her. To never, ever let—

"I have to go." Soft. Sad. "But I know I'll be seeing you again."

No, no, she didn't have to go anywhere—

"I've been alone a long time."

"You're not alone any longer." She'd never be alone again if he had his way.

"This is touching and all that shit," Bryce growled. "But we have to go *now*."

Pierce's head whipped up. "You can go and screw your—"

"Goodbye, Pierce." She pulled away.

"No."

But she headed for the Feds.

Sympathy flashed—for just a moment—on Bryce's face.

"No." This wasn't happening. Pierce shot forward.

Eric wrapped a hand around his upper arm. "You can't stop them. They're taking her."

He looked down at the hand, then back up at Eric. "You don't want to get between me and Iris." No one would be between them.

"Colt should be back any moment."

What the hell did Colt have to do with anything?

But then Colt burst through the door, slightly out of breath. His wide-eyed gaze took in the scene in an instant before he barreled toward Iris, seemingly ignoring the Feds. "Gonna miss you like hell." He wrapped her into a giant bear hug, lifting her off her feet, and holding her tightly.

Pierce thought the guy had lost his mind.

Then Colt pulled back. Swiped a hand under his eye. *As if he was crying?* "We'll clear this up. You're no criminal. We'll prove it," Colt said.

"That's a Wilde guarantee," Eric vowed.

Screw Wilde guarantees. Pierce went to—

Both Eric and Colt grabbed him. Held him tight. And these guys were supposed to be his *friends?* "Get your damn hands *off* me!"

"Go!" Eric ordered the Feds at the same instant.

Pierce fought harder against their hold.

"That's it," Colt whispered. "Make it look real. You got this."

It *was* freaking real. Iris was leaving. She glanced back once, and then the Feds pushed her through the doorway.

His whole world seemed to explode in a haze of red. He threw off Colt. Elbowed Eric and lunged after her. There was no way this was happening. He was not going to lose—

Colt tackled him. They slammed into the floor. Pierce twisted and came up swinging. A hard blow to Colt's jaw.

"Damn. Forgot you're a boxer on the weekends." Colt slumped to the side.

Pierce sprang to his feet. Only to find Eric in his way. "I don't want to hurt you," Pierce warned. *But if you don't move...*

"Think you can?" Eric's smile held a challenge.

I know it.

"Maybe you should try having a little faith in us," Eric directed with a lift of his brows. "I do know how to come up with spur-of-the-moment plans, you know."

"What in the hell are you talking about?" He had to be stalling. Giving the Feds time to get away...

"I tagged her," Colt said. He rubbed his jaw as he rose. "When I hugged her and did my ever-so-dramatic goodbye scene, I slipped a tracker on her. The Feds won't find it. We'll be able to follow them wherever they go."

Hope burned through Pierce as he spun toward Colt. "You're sure they won't find it?"

"They won't even look. Not like they think she was just wandering around with a tracker on her the whole time. We've got this." His hand fell. "Relax. Take a breath. We'll wait for them to clear out their crew. Then we will go downstairs, get one of the extra cars, and be on their tale. We won't lose her."

He wasn't relaxing. Not until this mess was over.

The phone on his desk started ringing. Ignoring it for the moment, Pierce pointed at Colt. "I'm assuming it's standard Wilde tech? I can track her with our software?" A sweet little in-house setup that had been made just for such instances. *Not exactly an instance like this. Never planned for the Feds to spirit away my lady.* The phone kept ringing.

"Absolutely," Colt assured him. He sniffed. "Aren't you going to remark on my incredible acting talent? I did some community theater back in the day, and I've always thought that I could have been phenomenal—

Pierce yanked up the ringing phone. "What?" he nearly roared.

"Hello to you, too, sunshine," Elijah Cross fired back. "Here I am, pulling in every favor I've got owed to me at the Bureau and you're just—"

"Iris was just taken." He'd mentioned Iris before. "I was protecting her. They came with a warrant. They took her from me."

A swift inhale. "Who took her?"

"Two Feds. The ones I told you about before. They have an arrest warrant." A BS warrant. "And—"

"*Not* Bryce Robertson or Travis Clark."

He nearly shattered the phone. "*Yes.*" A hiss.

"Get her. Now. My intel suggests that either one or both of them are on the take. If they get her out of the building, you might never see her again. And as for her brother, he's serious trouble, you don't want to—"

Pierce dropped the phone and raced for the door.

"What are you doing?" Colt shouted after him. "I told you, *we have this.* We can track her. We can—"

"Tracking won't do a damn bit of good," he bellowed back, "not if she's dead!"

CHAPTER EIGHTEEN

"I haven't done anything illegal," Iris said as the elevator descended to the bottom floor. "Any paintings that I made—any reproductions," she amended carefully, "I destroyed them. Slashed them, as I am sure you saw."

Travis kept gazing at the buttons as they descended.

But Bryce's stare darted to her, and she saw the guilt in his eyes.

"You didn't see any paintings, did you?" she whispered.

His jaw hardened. "We have orders. This case has to end. You need to do the job he wants. After it's done, we can focus on getting you resettled some place safe. You won't go to jail, I can promise—"

"Don't make her promises you can't keep," Travis interrupted. His expression had locked into hard, angry lines. "We don't know how this thing will end."

Icy dread weighted her heart. "You still won't even tell me the target's name."

"The boyfriend had to be taken out of the picture." Again, from Travis. "He was going to screw things up. We could either have locked him away or pulled you into our custody."

"I thought you would rather have gone with this option," Bryce mumbled. "Knew you'd be pissed if we put him in a cell."

She turned her head to look fully at him. Did he think she was buying this story? "Federal agents don't operate this way. They don't arrest innocent people. They don't threaten to lock up good men."

"Told you before," Bryce shook his head, "that boyfriend of yours isn't what I'd call good. He's dangerous, by his own admission. I warned you, but you didn't listen."

The doors opened. "He's not dangerous to me," she returned.

Bryce urged her forward.

No cuffs, but it sure seemed exactly like a perp walk to her. Iris felt the eyes on them as they headed outside the elevator and into the atrium on the building's entrance level. But no one rushed forward. No one said this was a horrible mistake. No one stopped the Feds.

She'd gone willingly with them because she'd wanted to protect Pierce. If he'd wound up in cuffs with her, how would that have helped anything? And she couldn't have him arrested on trumped-up charges because of her.

Because I do love him. When you loved someone, you wanted to protect that person, no matter what.

The sun had set outside. She walked out to darkness. The busy street seemed deserted. Cold. Atlanta wasn't normally cold. Humid and heavy—that was the city's nature, but this night, everything felt cold.

"The SUV is this way," Bryce said as he curled his fingers around her elbow and turned her to the left.

As she turned, Iris caught sight of a figure moving across the road. A man who darted beneath a streetlamp. A man who seemed familiar to her.

She stopped, ignoring Bryce's urgings, and peered at the figure.

The light from the streetlamp showed the man's blond hair. The stylish, high-priced suit that fit his broad shoulders. A tie flapped as he hurried forward. "Iris!" he called as he waved his left hand in the air.

"Who the hell is that joker?" Bryce demanded.

She squinted at the approaching man. *What were the odds?* "I...it's a model I almost hired. Bentley Prestang."

"I'll get rid of him," Travis said. "You get her to the car." He moved a few feet away, heading toward Bentley.

"I need to talk with you!" Bentley called out.

Bryce kept his grip on Iris. "Not happening, buddy. Move along!"

Bentley halted in the middle of the road. "It's happening."

Had he just said that? Or had she imagined—

Bentley's right hand flew up. He'd had it tucked inside his suit coat. When that hand flew up—

Gun! It took her a moment to realize she'd actually screamed the word. A moment in which she saw things happen so very, very quickly.

Travis dove for the pavement. Bryce shoved her forward, sending her sprawling, and Bentley—the freaking model who'd come to her apartment days ago—fired his weapon.

The blast seemed to echo around her. It was like thunder that just rumbled and rumbled, and her head turned because something had fallen near her.

Not something. Someone. Bryce was on the ground, on his side. His hand reached out toward her.

Iris lurched to her knees and grabbed for him. "Bryce!"

She could see blood coating his chest. It was a big, shadowy spot in the darkness.

"G-gun," he gasped out. "G-get my gun—"

Her hands pressed to his chest. Tried to stop the blood. That was what you were supposed to do, wasn't it? Stop the blood flow. People always did it on TV shows.

The blood pumped so fast.

Hands grabbed her from behind. Yanked her up. And away from Bryce as he struggled to speak.

"Stop!" Iris screamed. She fought the hold. Her head slammed back and rammed into someone's chin. "He needs help!" She kicked back. Landed a hard hit.

"Grab her fucking feet!"

And her feet were grabbed. Just like before. In the park. The two men had charged at her. One had grabbed her feet. One had grabbed her upper body.

They'd tried to take her away. But Pierce had rushed to the rescue. He'd come hurtling in like some kind of avenging god, and he'd kicked their asses. *"Pierce!"* A desperate scream for him.

"G-gun..." Bryce gasped out. He sagged back as his body went limp.

Pierce wasn't there. Bryce was hurt, possibly dying, and the two bastards holding her weren't letting her go. She screamed again and twisted, but they didn't ease their hold. Beyond Bryce, she could see the Wilde building. People were rushing toward the glass doors.

They aren't going to get here soon enough.

"Throw her in the back!"

And she was thrown into the back of a vehicle. Not the SUV that Bryce had indicated to her before. A car. Sleek. Expensive. Smelled of leather.

"What in the hell—" A sharp cry of surprise from the front seat.

Iris shoved back her hair—it had fallen over her face when she'd been tossed into the back seat. Frantic, she looked toward the direction of that surprised voice, thinking she might could get help.

In the front seat, Constantine had just turned around to gape at her. His eyes were huge as the vehicle's interior light glared down on him. *"Iris?"* he choked out in shock.

He won't help me. She grabbed for the door on her side. Tried to shove it open.

A gun jabbed into her hip. "Don't make me shoot you."

A car door slammed.

Her head turned. The man beside her—the man holding the gun—it was Bryce's partner.

Travis glared at her. "I'm not going to kill you," he said, "but I can sure make you hurt."

"What the fuck—" Constantine exclaimed.

"*Drive.*" An order from the man who'd just slammed the front passenger door. A man who also had a gun. One he aimed at Constantine. "Earn the money I've been paying you," Bentley ordered him. "Get us the hell out of here before those fools from Wilde reach us."

"Constantine, *no,*" Iris pleaded.

"Constantine, *yes,*" Bentley fired back. "Now, or I will put a bullet in your head and drive myself."

Constantine floored the vehicle. The tires squealed as they flew away from the scene.

***

Chaos.

That was what Pierce saw when he burst out of the doors at Wilde. Other agents were swarming outside, and he saw a fallen figure near the edge of the sidewalk.

Someone shouted, "Get an ambulance!"

He pushed people out of his way, rushed forward, and saw Bryce's prone form.

One Wilde agent had his hands on Bryce's chest. Another had the light from a phone illuminating the scene. The scene—the blood.

"Shot," a terse explanation from the agent trying to stem the flow of blood. "Bullet is still in him, and from the location, I think it has to be real close to his heart. He needs a hospital, and he needs it *now.*"

Pierce fell to his knees beside Bryce. "Who did this?"

Bryce's eyes were closed. He barely seemed to breathe.

"*Bryce,*" he snapped. "Who the fuck did this?"

"He is way past the point of talking," the agent said. "Guy is lucky to still be breathing."

Wilde had security cameras all around the building. They would have caught everything that happened on the street. Pierce leapt back to his feet. His frantic gaze flew around the scene.

No Iris.

Rage built. Twisted. Nearly gutted him with its power. Bryce had been taken out. And Iris had been *taken.* "Where is the other FBI agent?"

There were murmurs. No answers. Nothing until—

"I couldn't get out fast enough," a woman said.

Pierce swung toward her. Recognized her as one of the staff members who worked the welcome desk on the first floor.

"I'm so sorry, Agent Jennings. I saw them take her. She was fighting, and I—I think she screamed your name."

She screamed your name.

He closed in on the woman. Kayton? Kadie? In that moment, he couldn't be sure. Hell, in that moment, he wasn't sure of many things.

I saw them take her.

"Who?" he bit out.

"The other FBI agent. He and...and some guy who was waiting across the street. They were working together. Must have been." Her shoulders straightened. "The guy who fired had blond hair. Wore a nice suit. I caught a glimpse of him when he ran under the streetlight. They got into a Benz, and they squealed away."

He remembered something about the woman before him. She had told him the other day that she wanted to be a Wilde agent. That she wanted to work her way up the ranks. That she'd been studying and practicing her observational skills because she knew how important it was to always study a scene.

"I couldn't get to her in time," she continued as her head dipped. "But I got the license plate."

She had the license, and he had a tracker on Iris. A tracker that Colt had made sure was hidden.

"I'm getting her back." The only option. And when he found her, when he got his hands on those SOBs who had taken Iris...

They are dead.

***

"So...I do recognize the voice from all of our phone conversations," Constantine said as he drove fast through the city, running lights and getting honks left and right. "Nice to finally meet you in person, boss."

"Shut the hell up." Bentley glanced frantically to the left and right.

Bentley was the boss? The guy who'd come to be her model was the one in charge of this madness?

"Will do, but, first, I have a bit of advice to offer." Constantine cleared his throat. "The FBI agent in the back—yep, I recognize you, Agent Clark, saw you hanging out at Iris's place a few times—he'll probably want to take her phone and toss it out of the window. That way she can't be tracked. Oh, and make sure she's not wearing a smart watch. Those things are always trouble."

Agent Clark—Travis—jammed the gun harder into her hip. Iris knew she'd have a bruise, but that seemed like an exceedingly minor issue considering the shit-show that she faced.

"Give me your phone," Travis rasped.

"Thanks a lot, Constantine." Her voice didn't come out strong and fierce, like she'd hoped. It was more cracking and scared. Iris dug out her phone.

Travis snatched it from her fingers. He lowered the window and tossed it into the street.

"That's littering," Iris informed him. "You'll get a ticket for that." She slanted him a furious glance. "And you're kidnapping me. You'll go to prison for that crime. I've h-heard that former law enforcement types aren't treated so well there."

"I'm not going to prison. I'm going to get a massive payout once you paint the picture that we need. Then I'll retire to some lush island and never look back."

So she'd been taken for her skills. That had been the plan all along, hadn't it? "What happens to me after I paint?" She tilted her head as she tried to look into the front seat. "Am I gonna g-get a massive payout so I can go to some lush island?"

"Sure," Bentley answered easily.

She knew the answer was a lie. But she pretended she didn't. "Maybe you should get your goon back here to lower the gun, then? Would sure, ah, make the whole trip less stressful."

He didn't give the order for Travis to lower the weapon.

"Another thing," Constantine said into the silence that followed.

"You talk too freaking much," Bentley growled at him.

"I was just going to point out that I'm sure someone got the license plate for this car. The Wilde agents were surging toward us as fast as they could. And we've passed about half a dozen street cams already. The cops—you know, those not on the take like Travis back there—will be swarming. We probably want to switch vehicles soon. But, hey, just my two cents. This is clearly your ball game. You're the man in charge. You do what you want to—"

"Turn here." A sharp order from Bentley.

"Here?" Constantine parroted. "But there is nothing here. This is just an old, abandoned restaurant. Oh, wait, is that a little alley next to it? I don't know about leaving the Benz in this part of—"

"*Here.*"

Constantine whipped the Benz into the alley.

Iris sucked in a sharp breath because she was afraid that Travis would squeeze the trigger during that crazy turn. That a bullet would burn through her, and this would be the end.

At least I told Pierce that I loved him.

At least she'd gotten the chance to *be* in love. A few precious days that had finally made her feel as if she belonged somewhere. And that somewhere? It was with Pierce.

The car shuddered to a stop. "Now what?" Constantine wanted to know.

"Get out. Everyone *out*."

Travis locked his hand around Iris's wrist and hauled her out. He made sure to keep his gun at her side.

Bentley rushed down the alley. Constantine strolled behind him as if he didn't have a care in the world. "Where are we going?" he called out. "Oh, hey, do you have another car stashed behind this restaurant? Looks like it used to be an Italian place called—"

Bentley whirled and fired his gun.

Iris screamed.

Constantine fell. He spun as he fell, and he slammed down onto his stomach as he crashed on the broken cement in that alley.

"Did you think I didn't realize the truth, you bastard?" Bentley took a halting step toward Constantine's form. "Travis got the intel for me yesterday. Your cover was good, but not that good. You gave yourself away too much." Bentley pointed his gun at Constantine's prone figure.

Constantine didn't move.

"You and your stupid conscience," Bentley raged. "You smelled like a plant. But you weren't going to take me down. No one will."

"*Move*," Travis gritted in Iris's ear.

She surged toward Constantine.

Travis yanked her back. "No, dammit, I meant move and get to the car that's waiting down the alley. Constantine's fool-ass can bleed out."

"He needs help!" Constantine was...he was a good guy? He'd been working to bring down Bentley?

Who the hell was Bentley, really?

"He's not going to get help," Bentley said. "He's going to die here, alone, in a stinking alley. And it's really what he deserves. Maybe Remy will eventually find him. Then he'll know that I realized what he was doing all along." He spun away from Constantine. "*Let's go.* The bastard was right on one point—we have to switch vehicles, *now.*"

Constantine wasn't groaning. Wasn't moving even a little bit. When Bryce had been shot, he'd tried to speak. Tried to reach for her.

Is Constantine already dead? A sob tore from her. "He needs help!" She wasn't going to leave a man to die alone in an alley. She twisted her wrist. Used her other hand to claw into Travis's cheek and he—he let her go. He—

Drove his fist into her face.

CHAPTER NINETEEN

"Here!" Colt shouted as he grabbed the dash. "The signal is coming from the alley right next to this restaurant. Turn, dammit, turn now!"

Pierce yanked the wheel hard, the tires squealed, and he zoomed toward the alley. He also nearly rear-ended the Benz parked inside the darkness of the alley. He slammed on the brakes, and the SUV he was driving lurched to a stop.

"She's back there!" Colt jerked off his seatbelt. "She's here, we've got her! I told you this would—*wait!*"

No damn way. Pierce jumped out of the SUV and ran for the Benz. The...empty Benz. He slammed his fist into the driver's side window and whirled as his gaze searched that darkened alley. Where the hell was she? He and Colt had followed the signal from her tracker. They should have been able to find her, no problem.

Except...Problem. Big fucking problem.

He ran forward, bringing up his phone so he could use the light to search the darkness. The alley snaked back, turned to the right, and sure enough, there was another way out back there. The freaking thing didn't dead end. It would have been the perfect location to—

Crunch. He'd stepped on something. Not a rock. More like plastic that had just snapped beneath his shoe. He lifted his phone, shined his light in that spot.

"Oh, no." Colt's voice. Coming from right beside him. "That's her tracker. That's why the signal came here."

He yanked the light up. Blasted it into Colt's face. "Where. Is. She?"

"Look, I-I don't know how they found the tracker on her! She didn't even know it was there! And I told you—I *told* you that Constantine is working undercover. He has to be! That scanner you had me look at was pure bullshit. It didn't do anything. He was just trying to fool his boss, to make him think he was on the guy's side, but Constantine—"

"Constantine is out of the picture." A low voice that came from the darkness, up ahead, from where the dirty alley snaked behind the restaurant.

Pierce instantly brought up his gun and took aim.

"If you shoot me, that will just hurt her."

Beside Pierce, Colt swore as he raised his flashlight. Not a phone, but a real flashlight. He gripped it over his gun as both he and Pierce leveled their weapons at the man walking from the darkness.

Remy.

Remy had his hands up and appeared unarmed. Pierce knew appearances could be deceiving.

"Where is Iris?" Pierce's voice emerged as a snarl. Barely human. Too thick with animal rage.

"An old enemy has her."

"What kind of answer is that?" Colt demanded. "How about you just give us a name, asshole?"

"Names are meaningless in my world. People change names as easily as they change clothes. It's what you do that matters. And this man...he's a killer. He killed my father. He tried to kill me. If we don't stop him, I think he'll kill my sister, too."

"Not happening," Pierce vowed even as his blood turned to ice.

"Yes, well, hero, it's easy to say, but unless we can find Iris—*fast*—he won't have use for her much longer. He'll make her paint, and when he's done with her, he will eliminate her."

Pierce bounded toward him. "You're in on this whole mess!"

"Not the way you probably think."

"How did you get here? How did you know that Iris's tracker would lead to this alley?" His grip was too tight around the gun. His heart drummed too fast. And fear boiled too hard and heavily within him.

He will eliminate her.

Not possible. Not happening. Pierce couldn't imagine a world without Iris.

"I didn't follow her tracker." Remy's head tilted. "That what you've been doing? Tracking her? For how long? Did she know or did she truly think you cared for her so she—"

Pierce grabbed the bastard. Shoved him up against the wall with one arm while his gun went to—

"*Pierce.*" Colt's voice was sharp. "Take a breath."

"I *do* care for her," he bit out.

Remy didn't fight him. Under Colt's light, he glared back at Pierce. "I thought I could trust Eric. Thought he would send in a guy who would watch over my sister."

I am that damn guy.

"Instead," Remy didn't seem the least bit worried about the gun near him, "you just wanted to fuck her. Fuck her and then sell her out to the Feds. I heard about the money you demanded—twenty grand, huh? Was that the cost of selling out my sister—"

"You don't know what the hell you are talking about. Everything you know is twisted to hell and back." He let him go. Sucked in that breath Colt had urged him to take. It didn't do a bit to cool his rage. "I wouldn't sell Iris out for twenty grand. I wouldn't sell her out for *anything*. Iris is mine, and if I have to rip apart this town to find her, I will do it."

"I'm supposed to believe that?" Remy didn't move from the dirty wall. "One day, Iris is safe. Her life is normal, then the next thing I know, you explode into her world. You were supposed to just keep watch! Instead, everything went to hell."

"Her life wasn't normal. She was alone. She was worried about you. She wasn't letting anyone close. She'd walled herself off from everyone else, but I broke through those damn walls!" *Do not attack her brother. Do not.* "She loves me," he snapped. "She loves—"

Remy lunged for him.

But Colt dragged them apart. "You two are idiots! Stop! *Stop!*" He shoved at Remy's chest.

"The mission is Iris. Beat each other up later, got it?" He turned on Remy. Put the flashlight directly in Remy's face. "How did you get to this alley?"

Remy didn't speak.

"You were working with Constantine," Pierce charged, because to him, it was the only explanation that made sense. "He was your old friend. He's *always* been your friend, am I right? So you sent him in because you wanted to find out the identity of the man who'd killed your father."

"The killer is a shadow," Remy rasped. "Pulling his strings. Taking what he wants. Leaving destruction and death in his wake. With more money than God, he thinks that justice won't ever come for him. And he wanted *Iris*. He wanted my sister!"

"A sister that you tried to get out of the business," Colt said. He didn't lower his light.

"I made a deal with Bryce. I agreed to let the Feds use my skills in certain situations if they protected my sister, but the deal went to shit with my father's death. I knew that someone working with the Feds had sold me out. *I* should have died that night, too. I didn't because my dad saved my ass. He was a sorry piece of shit most days, but he died for me." A ragged breath. "And I left Iris because she deserved better than to be trapped with me and my enemies forever."

"But your enemies still came for her. This bastard *has* her," Pierce thundered.

Colt cleared his throat. "Focus, gentleman."

They both glared at him.

"How'd you get to this alley, Remy?" Colt asked him again.

"Constantine has always been working with me. He was wired. I was listening to everything as I tried to get close enough to help." His voice changed. Grief roughened the words. "But I wasn't fast enough. When I got here, it was too late."

"Too late?" Pierce felt his heart stop.

"She's alive," Remy said quickly. "They—I think they knocked her out."

They hurt her.

"But Constantine...shit..." He ran a hand through his hair. "He was just helping me. When we first met, he was a junior agent with the Feds, did you know that? They sent him in undercover and I made him on day one, but I wanted a change, and I thought..." His words trailed off. "He's gone. They're both...gone."

"I want to hear the recording." An order from Pierce. If there had been an audio transmission, there should have been a recording. "*Tell* me you were recording—"

"I-I was. But it's not going to help. I *don't* know where they went. They had another car waiting."

At that, Colt moved back and pulled out his phone. "On it," he said with a nod. "I'll get the Wilde techs to start accessing street cams near this location. We'll see what cars came up—they couldn't be far ahead of us. We'll track them."

"Wait—you can access street cams that quickly? Your techs can do that—" Remy tried to follow Colt.

Pierce got in his path. "We can do just about anything."

"Even the things that aren't legal? That how you play? Hard and dirty?" A new respect seemed to have entered Remy's voice.

"I'm not playing." Not with Iris. Never. "I want to hear the damn audio. *Now*."

***

A groan slipped from Iris as she cracked open her eyes. "Ass...hole...you hit me."

She expected to see Travis looming over.

Instead, she found Bentley. And...*we're not in the alley*.

She bolted upright. They were in the back of what looked like a limousine. Soft, muted lighting filled the interior as classical music drifted in the air. A warm leather seat cushioned her. Bentley lifted a glass of dark liquid in a salute. "We're going to make a great team."

Her hand flew to her aching jaw. "He knocked me out."

"Um. You have a bump on the back of your head from where you hit the pavement. I was vaguely worried you might have a concussion."

Her careful fingers found the bump when she searched her scalp. Iris winced. "Your concern is overwhelming."

"I don't want to hurt you, Iris..."

A little late for that.

"I offered you a deal in the beginning. You should have just taken it. Things would have been easier."

She shook her head. Immediately felt a wave of nausea fill her. "I don't...think so. I think things would have ended the same way, no matter what."

"With us together in a limo, heading off to paint a masterpiece?"

No. More like... "With you taking what you wanted and leaving death behind."

Bentley swallowed the last of the liquid before slamming his glass onto the small bar near him. "Maybe. I do like to take whatever I want." He smiled at her. "Is that a crime?"

"Yes," she told him, very serious. "It is. So is murder. You *shot* an FBI agent. Then I saw you shoot Constantine."

He shrugged. "I don't exist, Iris. You can't charge a man if he isn't real."

She had no idea what he was going on about. Obviously, he was real. He was right in front of her. If she wanted, she could have reached out and touched him.

She didn't, though. Touching him was the last thing she wanted to do.

"I have more identities than you can count. I have homes all over the world. I have enough money to buy and sell a sitting senator any day of the week." A mocking laugh. "I don't usually come out and get my hands dirty with work. But you made me change my normal rules."

"Why am I so lucky?" She had been lucky, once...when Pierce had moved into her building. She'd been sure her luck had changed.

Apparently, it hadn't. She still had shitty luck. Iris looked down at her hands. And realized that blood stained her fingers. Blood—from when she'd tried to help Bryce.

He'd been gunned down in the street. Right in front of one of the biggest security firms in the nation. "They will have you on video. They must have seen you."

"I won't worry too much about that. I'm sure I can make any footage vanish. Not like I haven't done that before." He didn't even seem mildly concerned as he studied her with a faintly wistful air. "You have a gift, Iris. I've admired your work for a very long time."

Can't say I admire you. Can say you terrify me.

"Actually," his tone turned musing, "you should have been in my employ years ago. I thought you were coming to me when you were seventeen. But then your brother demanded that your father grow a conscience. Such a useless accessory, by the way. I warned Constantine about that very fact. He should have listened to me."

"You...you killed Constantine." She could still see his body in her mind.

"Travis is currently dumping his body. I thought about just leaving Constantine there, in that dark alley, but then I realized it would make things much more interesting if we had him be discovered in your lover's apartment. Nothing like a little murder charge to keep a man *out* of my business."

He was planning to frame Pierce? "*No.*"

"I don't remember asking for your opinion on the body dump site." He leaned forward and his hands dangled between his knees.

"Leave Pierce alone! If you don't, I-I won't paint anything for you!"

He laughed.

"I'm not joking. I won't do it. I—"

"If you don't paint exactly what I want, I will call Travis and I will have him put a bullet in your boyfriend's head."

She sucked in a breath.

"Ah. I see you understand me very well now." His head inclined. "Have we made a deal then? Reached an agreement that satisfies us both?"

No, they had not.

"Excellent. Let's discuss the painting."

Just like that...he seemed to think the plan was in motion. That she wouldn't give him any more trouble. That she'd just be a good girl and shut the hell up.

I was never the good girl. And she wasn't just going to meekly do what he wanted.

His voice drifted to her as he continued, "The original will be in town for a limited tour in the near future, so I need you to get to work and create me a true masterpiece. I have a very skilled thief who says the best time to make the exchange will be *before* the display ever opens to the public. We will get it the moment it is unloaded at the museum..."

***

"Where are we going?" Constantine's voice. It seemed overly loud on the recording. *"Oh, hey, do you have another car stashed behind this restaurant? Looks like it used to be an Italian place called—"*

Bam.

The gunshot cut through his words.

A woman screamed. *Iris* screamed.

"He was trying to tell me his location. He was talking the whole time, telling me what was going on. What was happening. Our goal was to get the bastard confessing to all the crimes he'd committed." Remy ran a hand over his face. "Or, fuck, just confessing some of them. He's been making the world a nightmare for years."

"Did you think I didn't realize the truth?"

"That's him talking," Remy explained. "Got a name for him. Earlier, Iris called him Bentley."

The name rocked through Pierce. "You have got to be shitting me—"

"Travis got the intel for me yesterday," Bentley continued to say on the recording. It played from an app on Remy's phone. *"Your cover was good, but not that good. You gave yourself away too much."*

"Hold up, you know the guy?" Remy's tone held shock.

"Met him once. Sonofabitch was at Iris's place."

Remy swore.

Now Pierce understood that the SOB hadn't been at Iris's to model. He'd been there to scout her out, to see if she was the woman he'd searched for—the woman he'd sought for so long. He'd even gone in her place, gotten access *from* Iris. Bentley had probably checked the whole building. Collected intel, then he'd sent in Constantine.

And from the sound of things, he later turned on Constantine.

"You and your stupid conscience," Bentley was saying. *"You smelled like a plant. But you weren't going to take me down. No one is."*

There was a brief cut, as if the transmission had temporarily been lost, and then—

"No, dammit, get to the car that's waiting. His fool-ass can bleed out."

Pierce knew that voice. "The Fed," he said. "Travis Clark."

"I thought Bryce was the one on the take." Remy's lips curled down. "He was the senior agent. Back when my dad died, Travis was some fresh-faced wannabe, barely older than me. Didn't realize it was him..."

"He needs help!"

Pierce flinched when he heard Iris's voice.

"He's not going to get help." The bastard. Bentley. *"He's going to die here, alone, in a stinking alley. And it's really what he deserves. Maybe Remy will eventually find him. Then he'll know that I realized what he was doing all along."*

Remy swallowed. "Didn't think he knew the truth. I went to ground. I stayed hidden, made so many different aliases. And Constantine swore he was good. Told me he was two steps ahead of the guy. That he just needed a little more time, and he'd be able to finally see him face to face."

Constantine hadn't gotten that time. Pierce exchanged a grim look with a watchful Colt.

"*Let's go.*" Bentley again. "*The bastard was right on one point—we have to switch vehicles, now.*"

Colt nodded. "So he did have another ride waiting here."

Their little group stood near the mouth of the alley. It had only taken moments to get the recorded audio rolling again—

"*He needs help!*" Iris. Her voice rolled through Pierce. She was alive. She was trying to help Constantine. She was—

He heard a thud. Pierce tensed. He knew the sound of a fist connecting with flesh. "Dead man."

"*You hit her too hard!*" Bentley seemed worried. "*She's not moving. Shit!*"

"*How was I supposed to know she had a glass jaw?*"

"*You're freaking twice her size, idiot! Dammit, get away from her!*"

Travis Clark *had* hit her. The Fed. Pierce's hands clenched and released.

"*I'll carry her. Don't you touch her. You've done enough.*" Then, softer, "*Iris...?*"

"*We just gonna leave the body here?*" Travis asked. "*How long will it take Remy to—*"

"*Better plan,*" Bentley cut in to say. "*I'll take Iris. You dump him at the boyfriend's place. Then give the cops a tip. Tell them where to find the body.*"

"*I'm not going with you?*" Travis seemed uncertain. Nervous.

"You have a separate car. It's behind the bushes on the other side of the restaurant. You think I didn't plan ahead? I always do. Always. Now go. We'll meet back up at the mansion once I have her settled."

A door slammed.

"And that's the end." Remy's voice held a grim edge. "He drove away with my sister. When I arrived, Constantine's body was gone. They're taking her to some damn mansion, and I have no idea where it is. I guess we could bang on every door in—"

Pierce turned away from him. Marched to the other side of the old restaurant. Studied the trees. The bushes. There was one hell of a lot of overgrown bushes near the place.

His eyes narrowed as he stalked forward.

"Uh, Pierce?" Colt called. "Where are you going?"

To thoroughly search the full scene. "There could be tire tracks that we can use. Or maybe Travis dropped something on his way out."

"The techs are working on the street cams," Colt reminded him. A reminder he didn't need. "We're gonna have a hit soon. I swear it." He rushed after him. Caught his arm. Jerked Pierce to face him. "I know you think this is my fault."

Pierce stared back.

"I screwed up. I *thought* the tracker would lead us straight to her. I thought—"

Behind the nearby bushes, something moved. The faintest rustle of sound.

Colt heard the rustle, too. He stopped talking and snapped to attention.

Pierce motioned with his hand. They separated, and then they closed in. Moving fast and silently, Pierce went to the left. Colt took the right.

And...

They burst through those overgrown trees and bushes.

A white Mercedes SUV sat perched beyond the covering. Colt's light revealed a man's body as he lay spread-eagle in front of the SUV. His head was turned toward the driver's side, his arm outstretched as if he'd been opening the door.

The rustle came again. The sound was like...fabric sliding.

Colt shone his light toward the rustle.

"Yeah," a masculine voice croaked, rough and broken. "He thought I was dead, so he never saw me coming." Constantine sagged against the side of the vehicle. The rustle had been the sound of his shirt sliding against the door. "Choked his ass out from behind. He's still alive..." He winced. Touched his chest. "Lucky bastard."

Remy erupted from the bushes. He saw Constantine. Staggered to a stop. Did a double-take. "Con? I thought you were dead!"

"Getting that..." A wince. "A lot." He reached into his open shirt. Tapped the... "Bullet-proof vest. Great in, ah, theory, but in reality, I think I broke a rib. Maybe two." His breath heaved out. "Lost my...transmitter when I tried to g-get the vest..." His legs gave way. "Shit."

Remy bounded forward. "Dammit, man, I thought I had gotten you killed!"

Travis groaned.

Pierce looked down at his prey...and smiled.

Colt clapped a hand on his shoulder. "He has to tell us where he's meeting that Bentley bastard."

Pierce tucked the gun into the back of his jeans. His hands balled into powerful fists. "Don't worry. He will."

Travis rolled over. Reached up and touched his throat. Colt had his flashlight on the fellow once more. Travis winced and raised a hand to cover his eyes... "Move that shit..."

Then he realized exactly *who* was closing in on him.

He tried to lunge up—

And when he did, his face slammed into Pierce's fist.

"You should never have hurt her."

CHAPTER TWENTY

"We don't have to be enemies."

Iris glanced up from the blank canvas before her. Another mansion, another nightmare. One thing about Bentley—as if she believed for a second that was his real name—he sure liked to live in style. Her father had been that way, too. He'd always liked to have the best things in life.

Even if he had to steal and lie in order to get them.

Bentley lounged on a couch near her. Not a couch, a settee, and no doubt, it was an antique. Probably worth several grand. His limo had taken them far from the city, far past the busy roads of Atlanta, and seemingly into another world.

Not Buckhead, not this time. Instead, they'd driven until she was sure they were just going to kill her and dump her in the endless expanse of woods. Until she was sure he didn't need her to paint, that it was a lie, and she would be dying that night...

Then the car had turned down a long, private lane and taken them to what looked like a fortress. Big, foreboding, surrounded by armed guards—and dogs. Dobermans who had watched her with a steady gaze as she was led up the marble steps and through the double doors.

She'd barely glanced at the opulence around her. Instead, she'd kept her eyes straight ahead as he guided her up a massive staircase and to the third floor. On that floor, a studio waited for her. One filled with everything that an artist's heart could possibly desire.

"Monet's *Meules* sold for over one hundred and ten million dollars," Bentley said as he casually swung one foot. "Did you know that?"

"Yes." She picked up a brush. Smeared colors together on her palette. "I make a point of keeping up with the sales of all his major works." She slanted her captor a glance. Tried to sound cool as she added, "*Meules* or his *Haystacks* painting was sold by Sotheby's just a few years ago." *How do I get away?* She had to make him think she was going along with his plans. That she was no threat. For the moment, anyway. "That was twice its estimated value." Iris tried to sound awed as she added, "It was the first time that art from an Impressionist passed the one hundred million mark."

"I was at the auction."

She mixed more colors. "How lovely for you." Okay, she hadn't sounded awed then. So much for her acting talent. She'd sounded annoyed. Angry.

I am angry. I hate the bastard.

"I could have bid on the art but..."

"But where is the thrill in that?" she finished.

He laughed. "You understand me completely."

Hardly. "Technology is incredible these days. You can use programs and printers to re-create nearly any work of art." *So why are you forcing me to do this?*

His laughter died away. "A computer can never match your skill. Your father used to tell me that even your brush strokes would match Monet's perfectly. You knew how to mimic him in a precise way that no one—and no machine—could duplicate."

For a moment, she thought her hold would shatter the paint brush. "So you and my father talked a great deal."

"Um."

What sort of answer was that? She struggled to keep him talking because she knew this was important. "You know, my work only tricks when you look on the surface. Anyone going for a serious appraisal will learn the truth. They can age the painting, they can analyze—"

"I am well aware of all that can be done. And I'm not concerned. Your work will be a visual match that more than satisfies any critic. They will have no need for any immediate appraisal. By the time anyone does get around to that, I will be long gone with my prize."

Yes, she'd suspected as much. And where would she be? Though Iris suspected she knew that answer, too.

Dead.

"I gave you all the right tools. Not like you're working with some cheap brushes that will leave bristles in the art to give us away. I spared no expense with the supplies before you. I never do."

She glanced around the well-stocked studio. "I can see that."

"I told your father I would take care of you. All he had to do was send you to me."

Don't break the brush. Don't. "When I was seventeen."

"Yes. I had an opportunity back then, and I intended to seize it. Sadly, plans altered. I was denied what I wanted." A beat of time. "Then."

Her gaze swept over him. "You're awfully young to have amassed so much power." With an effort, her voice came out calm.

He preened. "My father built the empire I now possess. I took it over when he died."

A shiver slid over her. "You had something to do with his death, I take it?"

He rose from the settee. Came toward her with slow, careful steps. She wanted to run, but where would she go? If she made it outside, the dogs would stop her, even if the guards didn't.

Bentley positioned himself right before her. His hand lifted, and his fingers trailed over her shoulder.

She shivered again, from sheer terror and disgust.

"He was in the way." A tender smile. "Just as yours was."

The brush snapped. "You killed my father."

"You're welcome."

Iris shook her head.

He smiled at her. "Come now, don't tell me you didn't hate him? You must have. He used you. Gave you no power."

Part of the broken brush fell and hit the floor.

His gaze slid to the jagged piece. "Luckily, we have more." He took the other broken piece from her hand. Stared down at it thoughtfully. "Do you know the story of Rumpelstiltskin?"

"Why is everyone telling me fairytales?" Did it look as if she wanted to hear a freaking story?

"He could spin straw into gold." He looked up at her. "Spin me some gold."

I'd rather send you to hell.

"Take that canvas and turn it into a treasure for me." He tossed down the broken half of the brush. It rolled on the floor. "And then that will be the start for us. You and I—we can have a very beneficial relationship."

He wasn't going to let her go. Not ever. She saw her future in his gaze. She'd either stay with him, do what he wanted, or she would die.

"And perhaps, you'll even come to enjoy your time with me." His hand lifted to her cheek.

She eased back so that he didn't touch her face. "I can't paint with you watching me." Iris cleared her throat. "I'm sure you watched the test video. You saw that Pierce left so I could have privacy. I need you to do the same. Give me time to make the art."

His hand fisted. "Very well." But his stare lingered on her.

Her chin lifted.

"I will be back to check on your progress, though." Slowly, he turned around. Strolled for the door. All confidence and swagger.

"Little Red Riding Hood," she whispered.

He paused. Glanced back. "Excuse me?"

"That's the story I like the best."

His lashes flickered. "Do you think I'm the big, bad wolf?"

"No." *I think the big, bad wolf is going to come and kick your ass.* She also thought that Little Red hadn't been quite as defenseless as the world wanted to think.

"I can be," he said as his greedy gaze seemed to drink her in. "I can be as bad and evil as I need to be in order to get what I want."

He'd killed her father, kidnapped her, shot a federal agent, and then he'd taken aim at Constantine. Oh, she certainly got that he could be evil.

"Give me my masterpiece," he told her.

A few moments later, the door closed softly behind him.

Iris glanced around the room. Bentley thought he held all the power. He thought she was helpless. She rushed to the window. Stared out into the night.

No phone.

No mode of transportation.

No ally anywhere in sight.

All she had was a room full of paint.

He's not going to let me go. He thinks he has all the power.

Her steps were slow as she padded back toward the paint supplies. Her hand drifted over them. Lingered over another brush.

He wanted her to paint Monet's *The Flowered Garden*. An oil on canvas work. Her breath shuddered in and out. A true masterpiece.

She could paint it for him. She could give him exactly what he wanted. And if she did...

Is Pierce being arrested? Did they find Constantine at his place?

If she gave Bentley what he wanted, he still wouldn't let her go.

What choice did she have? What could she do?

Pierce's image flashed in her mind. This wasn't the park. He wasn't going to barrel in and save her.

Her shoulders straightened. She grabbed a brush.

She would do what needed to be done. Iris went to work painting, and the hours slipped away.

***

Pierce lowered the night vision binoculars. "Two more on the right perimeter." The house was surrounded by a mini-damn-army. In the middle of nowhere, Bentley had just set up his own kingdom.

But that kingdom was about to fall.

Pierce looked back over his shoulder. He had his own team. Wilde agents had already scattered. They were connected via comm links that allowed them to speak freely. But it wasn't just the trained Wilde team that waited for the attack.

Remy had insisted on coming, too. As had Constantine. They were quiet and grim in the dark.

Eric had taken charge of FBI Agent Travis Clark. The dirty Fed was in custody, and Eric was personally making sure he didn't get even a moment to somehow warn Bentley about the attack that was imminent.

They had the element of surprise on their side.

Iris, sweetheart, I am coming for you.

"How are you going to handle the dogs?" Remy whispered.

Pierce inclined his head. "Colt."

"On it." A fast and confident reply from his partner. "I'll have those sweet babies eating out of the palm of my hand."

Colt always had a way with the animals. As soon as he had them out of commission...

We take the house.

Remy clamped a hand on Pierce's shoulder. "I don't want my sister hurt."

Like he wanted that shit. "Her safety is my main priority." His head inclined toward Remy. "I will do whatever it takes to get her back."

Silence from Remy. Then... "Because she's a Wilde client?"

Hell, no. "Because she's mine." Too much time had already been wasted. They'd had to get the right gear, assemble the best people...

Hours had passed. No more. *We move, now.* He raised the night vision binoculars once more. "Colt, do your thing..." he ordered.

Time to attack.

***

The door to the studio opened with a squeak of its hinges. She didn't glance up from the painting before her. Iris had taken the liberty of moving the easel and canvas. They now stood between her and the door, and she was the only one who could see the beautiful work of art from this position.

To view it, Bentley would have to walk around the supply table. Turn and move to her side.

"How's it coming?" Bentley asked.

She smiled at the painting. "Perfect."

He took a few quick, startled steps toward her. "You're...you're already finished?"

"Um." Hadn't that been his response to her earlier?

"But that's too soon! You can't—"

Iris finally looked up at him. "I felt inspired."

The lights flickered. Went off for the briefest of moments, then turned back on.

Bentley frowned and glanced up at the ceiling. A lick of excitement filled her. Maybe it was just bad wiring...*In a stupid, expensive house.* Or maybe...

Maybe it was more.

"Don't you want to see the painting?" Iris asked. "It's a masterpiece that you won't soon forget. I can assure you of that." *You will never forget this work.*

He took another step toward her.

A shout came from below. She didn't turn her head toward the window. That shout had come from *outside*.

"Did you hear that?" Bentley's brows shoved together.

She stared straight into his eyes. "Hear what?" Iris shrugged. "Look, you don't have to view my work. Not like you kidnapped me at gunpoint or anything to make what I *thought* was something important." She backed away from the painting. "Can I take a break? I'd like to go downstairs. Maybe get something to eat. Give my fingers a chance to rest because they are starting to cramp."

His jaw tightened. "I want to see it!"

I know that you do.

Iris waved her hand in a come-and-see manner as she took a few more steps away from the painting. She put her brush on the table. She'd made sure to get paint thinner ready to help clean up...

He hurried around the supply table. His shoulder brushed against her as he closed in on the masterpiece—

"What the fuck is this?" Bentley shouted.

His shout *almost* masked the yell she heard from outside.

He hadn't noticed that other yell, though, because he was too busy glaring at the work she'd created.

His fingers jabbed angrily toward the painting. "Why the hell would you do *this?*"

Her hand closed around the cup of paint thinner. "Don't you remember?" *Stay cool. Stay calm.* "It's how we met. I was in the market for a nude model." A pause. "I didn't choose you, though. I decided to use Pierce as my muse."

He whirled toward her. "I don't want a picture of his damn naked—"

She threw the paint thinner at his face. He screamed, and his hands flew up to bat at his eyes and mouth. Iris shoved her whole body at his, going in toward his hips, and they hurtled to the floor. Paint rained down on them.

He screamed and spat thinner out of his mouth.

Her hands flew over his body. She'd planned to grab his phone and call for help—

"Iris!" A roar of her name. A familiar, beautiful roar.

Her plan *had* been to call for help, but it looked as if help might be there, already.

She snatched up the phone even as she rammed her knee as hard as she could into Bentley's groin. He howled, and she loved the sound. Iris jerked away from him, ignoring the paint that covered her arms and clothes. She turned to crawl to safety—

"No, you bitch, *no!*"

His hand clamped around her ankle, and he yanked her back. Her upper body slammed hard into the floor with that vicious yank. Her hands flew out in front of her, and she caught one of the broken pieces of her paint brush.

The door to the studio banged against the wall. *"Get your fucking hands off her!"*

Pierce's voice. His angry, bellowing, wonderful voice.

But Bentley didn't let her go. He yanked her harder, and this time, she went willingly. She let him pull her toward him, and as soon as she could…

Iris drove the broken paint brush handle into his thigh. It had been a wide, strong brush with a wooden handle. Using the sharp, jagged edge of that handle, she gouged it in deep and enjoyed his scream of agony because she definitely had a bad side, too. Pierce had been right about bad sides.

In the right circumstances, everyone's *bad* side would come out.

Using all her strength, Iris yanked the broken chunk of the brush's handle to the left as she tried to do the maximum amount of damage possible.

"I will *kill*—" Bentley yelled.

He didn't get to say anything else.

Suddenly, his hold on her was gone. She kicked back, slammed her foot into his chest for good measure, and scrambled away. Strong hands reached for her and hauled Iris to her feet.

"*Iris!*" Remy wrapped his arms around her. Held her so tightly that she almost couldn't breathe. A shudder rushed over the length of his body. "You're okay," he said. "You're okay."

She'd be okay when she saw Pierce. Iris pushed against Remy's chest. His hold eased, but he didn't let her go.

"You're okay," he repeated.

She wiggled in his grasp. "Pierce!"

"He's beating the hell out of the bastard who took you," Constantine replied. "Give him a minute."

Constantine? Her jaw nearly hit the floor. Her head turned just enough so that she could see him.

He winked at her. "Hey. Guess who is still alive?"

"*You never touch her again! You never threaten her! You—*" Pierce's blasting words seemed to shake the room.

She broke from Remy's hold. "Pierce!"

He looked up. One of his hands gripped the blood-and-paint-covered front of Bentley's shirt.

The other was drawn back into a powerful fist. A fist that was inches away from Bentley's face.

Bentley already appeared to be out cold.

"That had better be paint on you," Pierce said in a voice that probably would make the devil quake. *"Only paint."*

She looked down. Realized that a whole lot of red paint had fallen onto her clothes and body. "It's paint."

He let go of Bentley. The bastard fell back onto the floor with a thud as Pierce surged toward her.

"Yes, sure," Constantine drawled. "We'll take care of him. Don't mind us at all, you just focus on—"

Pierce hauled Iris against him, and his mouth plunged down on hers.

"That," she distantly heard Constantine finish.

Then she stopped caring about what he was saying because she was kissing Pierce back with a wild, desperate abandon as happiness exploded inside of her. He'd found her. They'd taken down Bentley. They were together.

She locked her hands around him and just held on as hard as she could. She could taste the need in his kiss. The stark desperation. The fierce desire that matched hers. But...

More.

She could feel *more*.

Pierce lifted his head. Stared down at her with turbulent baby blues. "I was afraid." A stark admission.

"Me, too," she whispered back. Afraid that she wouldn't see him again. Afraid that she'd never have the chance to hold the man who'd come to matter so much to her.

Pierce's hand lifted. Curled carefully around her jaw. "You have a bruise."

She didn't care. She had Pierce. Everything was going to be all right. "You can kiss it better."

"I am going to kiss every single inch of—"

"*Right* here," Remy announced. "Standing right the hell here, and I don't want to know where you are going to kiss my sister!"

They both turned to frown at him.

"But I do want to thank you," Remy added, voice going gruff. "For going above and beyond to find—"

"Keep your thanks." Pierce shook his head. "I've got what I need." His eyes came back to her.

The expression on his face...

She started to smile.

"Let me see the sun, baby."

And she couldn't stop the full grin that bloomed on her face.

"I love you so much," he breathed.

Her eyes widened. "What?"

"Love you, am obsessed with you, freaking worship the lucky ground beneath you—all that. Everything. *I. Love. You.*"

Her smile couldn't get bigger. At least, she didn't think it could. Iris knew she had to be smiling from ear to ear. "I love you, too."

His mouth took hers again. The kiss was different this time, though. Softer. Sweeter. Tears stung behind her closed eyelids.

"What is that thing?" A startled cry from Constantine.

Once more, Pierce pulled back. But slowly. His gaze caressed her face. "I'm taking you out of here."

Wonderful. Brilliant idea.

"We're getting a bed, and we're staying there for days," he added.

Sounded like a perfect plan.

"Would you look at this?" Constantine demanded. *"Why?* Just...*why?"*

Pierce shot a glare at him. "When you were dead, you were quiet."

"She painted *you.*" Constantine pointed to the canvas. "And you're naked!"

Pierce sidestepped. Looked at the canvas. And started laughing.

Remy peered at the canvas and then snapped his eyes shut. "I did not need that."

Iris felt red sting her cheeks. "It's a nude, it's not a naked picture. It's *art.*"

"The question remains," Constantine said as he still stood over an unconscious Bentley. *"Why?"*

Pierce twined his fingers with hers.

She gave him a squeeze. "It was part of my escape plan."

"Your escape plan involved a naked Pierce?" Constantine asked as his eyes widened. *"How?"*

"Bentley wanted me to paint him a masterpiece, so I did."

Remy squeezed the bridge of his nose. "You must love the bastard."

Her gaze slid over Pierce's face. "Yes, I do. Very much."

He brought her hand to his mouth. Kissed her knuckles.

"You said you wanted to be my model," Iris reminded Pierce.

He smiled at her. "That is so going on the wall at our place."

Our place. She sure liked the sound of that. "I used the painting to distract him. There was no way I could give him what he wanted. He wasn't going to control me." She was done with being controlled. It was time to live her life, her way. "When he saw the painting and freaked out, I used the distraction to make my move." The only move she'd had available to her. "I threw paint thinner at him. When he fought back, I attacked him with the wooden handle of my broken brush." A glance down showed that his thigh still pulsed blood. "I planned to swipe his phone and call you. Thought you could triangulate the signal and find me." She looked back up. "But you got here before I could."

He kissed her knuckles once more. "I was going insane worrying about you."

"I'm safe," she assured him, voice soft and tender. But her head tilted. "How did you find me?"

Bentley moaned.

Pierce didn't bother glancing his way. "I convinced Travis Clark to cooperate with my investigation."

Travis had cooperated? That seemed...odd. Then she noticed the faint bruising on his knuckles. "Pierce..."

He scooped her into his arms. "You ready to get the hell out of here?"

She was, very much, yes. She'd been ready for the longest time.

"Authorities will be swooping in," Remy said as Pierce carried her toward the door. "Lots of questions to answer."

Pierce didn't slow. "Something tells me you and Constantine can handle all of that."

She twined an arm around Pierce's neck. "Bentley killed my father."

"I know, baby."

He knew?

"And I'm sorry," Pierce added gruffly.

Iris swallowed. "Me, too."

He took her down the stairs. Murmured to some Wilde agents they passed, then they were outside. In the fresh, clean air. And Colt waited for them, standing beside two Dobermans.

His hand gave one a quick pat as his gaze scanned over her. "You good?"

Iris didn't know that "good" was the right word. She was terrified, shaken, twisted with grief, and so incredibly grateful to be alive. To be alive and to be with Pierce. "I will be." True enough. She *would be*. Her head turned. She stared into Pierce's eyes. "One day soon, I will be."

"Baby, you already are," he rasped back to her. "You're better than good. You're the best thing that has ever happened to me."

He could say the sweetest things.

"And if anyone *ever* comes after you again..." A darker, harder rumble. "I will rip the sonofabitch apart with my bare hands."

The sweetest things…

"I would do the same for you." She'd do anything for him. It was that way when you really found someone to love. You'd take any risk. Fight any battle.

"I love you," Pierce said. "Always."

She very much liked the sound of that…

EPILOGUE

Bentley Prestang had about fifteen aliases. He was also looking at over a hundred years in prison. The Feds in charge of his case—Feds who were very much *not* on the take—had assured Iris that Bentley would never be seeing the light of day again.

Bryce Robertson was healing nicely in a local hospital. He'd been furious with his partner, and he had sworn to do everything in his power to make sure that Travis Clark would be punished for his deception and long list of crimes.

Two men who were heading to prison and two men—Constantine and Remy—who were not. At least, according to the information that Pierce had given her. Constantine and Remy seemed to be walking away from the nightmare with no charges pending against them.

Everything was over. Iris didn't have to look over her shoulder any longer. She didn't have to worry about the past biting her in the ass, and she could finally focus on having a *normal* future.

A future with the man she loved. The smoking hot guy next door.

A knock sounded at Iris's door. She glanced down at her watch. Pierce was a few minutes early. They'd planned to meet for movie night at 7 p.m., and it only was a quarter to seven. Not that she minded his early appearance. Iris bounded to the door and started to swing it open with exuberance—

Check the peephole first.

Some instincts wouldn't fade. At least, not yet, they wouldn't.

She pressed her eye to the peephole. Pierce wasn't waiting on the other side of the door. Remy was. The brother who'd come back from the shadows and just dropped into her life. The brother she'd barely spoken with in the last two, tumultuous weeks.

After taking a deep breath, Iris opened the door. She didn't quite know how to greet him. They weren't in the throw-your-arms-around-each-other phase of their relationship. Things were still too awkward and tense. And Remy held far too many secrets.

Secrets that she could see in his eyes.

"I think we need to talk," Remy said.

She'd talked to plenty of people. Feds. Cops. Wilde agents. Talked until she was blue in the face, but Iris stepped back and motioned for Remy to come inside.

Squaring his shoulders, he did. He shut the door softly behind him. "I know you have questions for me."

Only a million or so.

"And I'm sure you've been able to, ah, piece together some things because of what's gone down recently."

Her head tilted to the right. "At first, I thought you might be an undercover agent. Working maybe for the Feds. You and Constantine."

"I'm *not* an FBI agent." He shuddered. "Have you seen those suits?"

She simply stared back at him.

"Right. Not the time for jokes." His hand shoved through his hair. "I was more... freelance. And the work I did—the work that Constantine and I both did—it wasn't limited to the FBI. It was more of a task force situation, one that involved both the FBI and the CIA and just a lot of secretive shit that I'm not supposed to talk about with anyone."

"Yet here you are." She swallowed down the lump that had risen in her throat. "Coming to *talk* with me."

His hand fell back to his side. "I didn't have a face for the man who killed our father. I had a name that wasn't real. I had a money trail that went cold. I had a man that I knew wanted to use my seventeen-year-old sister. I was desperate and scared, and I made decisions that I regret."

She didn't move. "Like the decision to leave me?" Just asking the question hurt.

"I had to get you someplace safe. That was the first demand I had before I agreed to do *any* jobs. And Franco Lopez swore that he would always look after you. He was a good man." A ragged exhale. "Bentley killed him. Bentley—the man was obsessed. I thought he'd move the hell on after dad died and you were taken away. I hoped he'd forget you and the work you could do. But through the years, he would come back to the idea of you. Over and over, I would catch bits of gossip, news that he was trying to close in on you..."

"And I would be moved." It made sense to her, now. The sudden relocations. At the time, it had hurt like hell. She'd thought that she was finally getting a home, and then the home had been ripped away. Over and over again.

"I just wanted you safe."

Her lashes lowered. "You never asked me what I wanted." She'd just been left to find their father. To hold him while he died.

Remy stepped closer to her. His hand lifted and curled around her shoulder. "What did you want, Iris?"

Her head rose. Her gaze met his. "I *wanted* my brother back. I wanted a family again. I wanted to know that I wasn't alone."

"I watched you," he confessed. "I came close when I could, just to check on you, but it was dangerous for me to be too near you. I had to take him out. Permanently. Either have him locked away forever—and Constantine was trying to help me get enough evidence for that—or I had to kill the bastard. And, yes, that was an option on the table for me." A muscle flexed along his jaw as he seemed to brace himself.

As if he expected her to be afraid of him because of his confession. As if he expected her to wilt or cry.

He didn't know her very well. But then again, it had been years since he'd truly been in her life. "Killing the bastard was an option on the table for me, too," she told him quietly. "Because I wasn't going to stay his prisoner. I was getting back to Pierce, one way or another."

"Pierce." A shake of his head. "The two of you—that is a development I did not expect. I just thought it would be good to have a person close by who could look out for you."

Pierce did look out for her.

"Do you really love him?" Remy asked her. A little line appeared between his eyebrows. "You know, he's kind of an asshole."

"No, he's not. He's strong and he's fierce and he's loyal." He was so much more than that. "He likes to watch really cheesy horror movies because he knows they make me happy." She exhaled. "He gets extra pepperonis on his pizza, but then he winds up giving most of those pepperonis to me. He's always extra careful when he touches me because he doesn't want to ever hurt me. He treats me like I am the most important person in his world, and when I was taken...I *knew* he wouldn't stop looking for me. Bentley was saying that Pierce would be locked up, charged with killing Constantine, but I kept thinking...*He'll get out.* He'll hunt for me. He won't stop. I had one-hundred-percent faith in Pierce...because I love him."

A knock rapped against her door.

"And that's him now," she murmured. "Another good thing about Pierce. He never makes me wait." She hurried around Remy.

"He would never leave you."

Her shoulders stiffened.

"That's what you think, isn't it?"

She looked through the peephole. Saw Pierce standing there—and holding sunflowers. "It's what I know." She opened the door. Smiled wide and hard.

In response to her smile, Iris saw Pierce's hard face soften. His arms opened for her, and she went straight into them. He lifted her up against him and kissed her. Sweet. Passionate.

Possessive.

I love this man.

He eased her down until her feet touched the floor. He pulled back, and his gaze darted over her shoulder. "I see the brother is here."

Yes. Iris heard Remy closing in with steady steps.

"Are we going to have a problem?" Remy asked quietly.

The two men measured each other.

"If you don't ever hurt Iris again, then no, we won't have a problem," Pierce assured him. "Because you're her family. If she wants you around, then so do I."

Remy cleared his throat. "Iris...do you...would you...is it okay if I'm around?"

Her stare drifted over him. The brother she'd missed for so long. There was plenty of pain between them, but there was also hope. A whole lot of hope. "I would like that very much, and not just because you own the building." She smiled slowly. Saw *his* face soften.

"I missed you," he whispered.

"I missed you, too, Remy."

He hauled her into his arms. She squeezed him just as tightly as he squeezed her. Some of the pain inside eased. Things were going to be better.

The future would be so different.

He slowly let her go.

"How about you come by for breakfast tomorrow?" Iris offered.

"I would like that very much." The same words she'd given to him. Remy swallowed. Cleared his throat. "I should go. Um...Thank you, Iris."

From the shadows, he'd protected her for years. She might hate his methods, but she still loved him. Always would. "Thank you, Remy."

He swiped a hand over his cheek as he strode into the hallway.

Pierce watched him with a hooded gaze. "Oh, one thing..."

Remy stilled.

"I know you've got all sorts of connections with the FBI. Lovely to have those." His voice was all mild and almost innocent. "So how about when the investigation is all wrapped up, you do me a favor?"

Remy glanced back at him.

"The painting," Pierce explained cheerfully. "Iris's latest masterpiece? Of yours truly? I'd like it back. I hear it's making the rounds in evidence, and it's a waste for that beauty to be locked away."

Remy gaped at him. "You are not serious right now."

"But I am. Completely. I plan to put that canvas over my couch."

"Over the couch?"

"Yep."

Remy's eyes squeezed closed. "I'll see what I can do."

"Thanks. I'll consider it an early wedding present."

Remy's eyes flew right back open. "Wedding? You're planning to marry my sister?"

"Of course. That was the plan all along. Day one." Pierce's gaze returned to her. "I want to marry Iris at the very first possible opportunity."

She wanted to tackle hug him.

"Don't worry," Pierce added. But he didn't look away from her. "We'll give you all the details soon." He kicked the door closed. Flipped the lock.

She backed up, half a step.

His gaze noted the movement. His eyes narrowed.

"You...don't really want that painting. I can do better, you know. It was rushed and—"

"I want you."

"I always want you," she told him, voice going husky.

"I also want to marry you. I wasn't lying about that. I *don't* lie when it comes to you. I'll play dirty with the rest of the world, but never, ever with you."

"I, ah, don't see a ring." She was kidding. Trying to lighten the thick tension that had swept into her apartment and wrapped around them both.

Then Pierce dropped onto one knee.

She started to back up—

His right hand caught her wrist, and he froze her retreat. His left hand pushed into his pocket, then came back up with a sparkling ring. "Iris..."

This was happening. It was *happening*.

"Will you please make me the luckiest man in the world and marry me?"

She looked at his face. Saw the flash of nerves. The unwavering love.

Then she looked back at the diamond. Absolutely dazzling. And she remembered what she'd thought the very first time she'd seen him...

"Iris?" Worry. A little fear.

"I am so going to lick you all over," she said.

His eyes widened. "Is that a...yes?"

She jumped on him. They fell back and hit the shut door. "Yes!" She kissed him. "Yes!" Kissed him even deeper, harder. Rougher. "*Yes!*"

And ten minutes later, when he was driving deep into her core, when her body was hurtling toward an orgasm as he stroked her just right, she screamed one more time for him...

"*Yes!*"

Because she just wanted to be completely sure that Pierce knew...

Oh, yes, she would be marrying him. She would be loving him.

Forever.

He was her protector. Her lover. The bodyguard who'd risk all for her...And he was her friend. A friend to hold tight and trust with her darkest secrets and wildest hopes. He was the soulmate that she had never expected to find.

Yes, she'd marry him.
Yes, she'd love him.
Yes, yes, *yes*.

THE END

A NOTE FROM THE AUTHOR

Thank you so much for taking the time to read THE BODYGUARD NEXT DOOR. I can't believe that this was book 15 in my Wilde Ways series! When I wrote the first book in the series (PROTECTING PIPER), I had no idea that so many fun stories would come out of the Wilde protection agency.

When I write a Wilde book, I always try to make sure there are lots of twists, some danger, extra hot romance, and, of course, a guaranteed happy ending. Life is so stressful, sometimes, you just need to let yourself be a little Wilde.

If you'd like to stay updated on my releases and sales, please join my newsletter list.

https://cynthiaeden.com/newsletter/

Again, thank you for reading THE BODYGUARD NEXT DOOR.

Best,
Cynthia Eden
cynthiaeden.com

ABOUT THE AUTHOR

Cynthia Eden is a *New York Times*, *USA Today*, *Digital Book World*, and *IndieReader* best-seller.

Cynthia writes sexy tales of contemporary romance, romantic suspense, and paranormal romance. Since she began writing full-time in 2005, Cynthia has written over one hundred novels and novellas.

Cynthia lives along the Alabama Gulf Coast. She loves romance novels, horror movies, and chocolate.

For More Information

- *cynthiaeden.com*
- *facebook.com/cynthiaedenfanpage*

HER OTHER WORKS

Ice Breaker Cold Case Romance
- Frozen In Ice (Book 1)
- Falling For The Ice Queen (Book 2)

Phoenix Fury
- Hot Enough To Burn (Book 1)
- Slow Burn (Book 2)
- Burn It Down (Book 3)

Trouble For Hire
- No Escape From War (Book 1)
- Don't Play With Odin (Book 2)
- Jinx, You're It (Book 3)
- Remember Ramsey (Book 4)

Death and Moonlight Mystery
- Step Into My Web (Book 1)
- Save Me From The Dark (Book 2)

Wilde Ways
- Protecting Piper (Book 1)
- Guarding Gwen (Book 2)
- Before Ben (Book 3)
- The Heart You Break (Book 4)
- Fighting For Her (Book 5)
- Ghost Of A Chance (Book 6)
- Crossing The Line (Book 7)
- Counting On Cole (Book 8)

- Chase After Me (Book 9)
- Say I Do (Book 10)
- Roman Will Fall (Book 11)
- The One Who Got Away (Book 12)
- Pretend You Want Me (Book 13)
- Cross My Heart (Book 14)
- The Bodyguard Next Door (Book 15)
- Ex Marks The Perfect Spot (Book 16)

Dark Sins

- Don't Trust A Killer (Book 1)
- Don't Love A Liar (Book 2)

Lazarus Rising

- Never Let Go (Book One)
- Keep Me Close (Book Two)
- Stay With Me (Book Three)
- Run To Me (Book Four)
- Lie Close To Me (Book Five)
- Hold On Tight (Book Six)

Dark Obsession Series

- Watch Me (Book 1)
- Want Me (Book 2)
- Need Me (Book 3)
- Beware Of Me (Book 4)
- Only For Me (Books 1 to 4)

Mine Series

- Mine To Take (Book 1)
- Mine To Keep (Book 2)
- Mine To Hold (Book 3)
- Mine To Crave (Book 4)
- Mine To Have (Book 5)

- Mine To Protect (Book 6)
- Mine Box Set Volume 1 (Books 1-3)
- Mine Box Set Volume 2 (Books 4-6)

Bad Things

- The Devil In Disguise (Book 1)
- On The Prowl (Book 2)
- Undead Or Alive (Book 3)
- Broken Angel (Book 4)
- Heart Of Stone (Book 5)
- Tempted By Fate (Book 6)
- Wicked And Wild (Book 7)
- Saint Or Sinner (Book 8)
- Bad Things Volume One (Books 1 to 3)
- Bad Things Volume Two (Books 4 to 6)
- Bad Things Deluxe Box Set (Books 1 to 6)

Bite Series

- Forbidden Bite (Bite Book 1)
- Mating Bite (Bite Book 2)

Blood and Moonlight Series

- Bite The Dust (Book 1)
- Better Off Undead (Book 2)
- Bitter Blood (Book 3)
- Blood and Moonlight (The Complete Series)

Purgatory Series

- The Wolf Within (Book 1)
- Marked By The Vampire (Book 2)
- Charming The Beast (Book 3)
- Deal with the Devil (Book 4)

- The Beasts Inside (Books 1 to 4)

Bound Series

- Bound By Blood (Book 1)
- Bound In Darkness (Book 2)
- Bound In Sin (Book 3)
- Bound By The Night (Book 4)
- Bound in Death (Book 5)
- Forever Bound (Books 1 to 4)

Stand-Alone Romantic Suspense

- It's A Wonderful Werewolf
- Never Cry Werewolf
- Immortal Danger
- Deck The Halls
- Come Back To Me
- Put A Spell On Me
- Never Gonna Happen
- One Hot Holiday
- Slay All Day
- Midnight Bite
- Secret Admirer
- Christmas With A Spy
- Femme Fatale
- Until Death
- Sinful Secrets
- First Taste of Darkness
- A Vampire's Christmas Carol

Printed in Poland
by Amazon Fulfillment
Poland Sp. z o.o., Wrocław